Aliens
in Delhi

AF527679

Aliens in Delhi

SAMI AHMAD KHAN

NIYOGI
BOOKS

Published by
NIYOGI BOOKS
D-78, Okhla Industrial Area, Phase-I
New Delhi-110 020, INDIA
Tel: 91-11-26816301, 49327000
Fax: 91-11-26810483, 26813830
email: niyogibooks@gmail.com
website: www.niyogibooksindia.com

Text © Sami Ahmad Khan

Editor: Saachi Khurana
Design: Shraboni Roy

ISBN: 978-93-85285-71-4
Publication: 2017

This is a work of fiction. The names, characters and incidents portrayed in it are the work of the author's imagination. Any resemblance to actual persons, living or dead, events or localities, is entirely coincidental.

All rights are reserved. No part of this publication may be reproduced or transmitted in any form or by any means, electronic or mechanical, including photocopying, recording or by any information storage and retrieval system without prior written permission and consent of the Publisher.

Printed at: Niyogi Offset Pvt. Ltd., New Delhi, India

This is dedicated to
the Indian Space Research Organisation (ISRO)—
your untiring, exemplary endeavours give
wings to countless dreams.

Key Players

Bipolab Roy—Prime Minister of India

Dr Ajay P. Mishra—Cabinet Secretary to the Government of India

Manish Ranjan—National Security Advisor, India

Bishwanath Barua—Squadron Leader, 125 Squadron (HU), Indian Air Force

Prof. Kavita Aggarwal—Nuclear Scientist, India

Yasser Basheer—Colonel (retired), Pakistan Army

Parvez Chaand Mahmood—Intelligence Officer, Pakistan

A.C. Wilson—President of the United States of America

Sean Miller—Director, Central Intelligence Agency, USA

Jason E. Cartman—Director General, Combined Intelligence Corps, USA

Sonya Loewe—Senior Correspondent, Deutsche-Welle, Germany

Imran Bhatt—Press Photographer, India

Red—Chief of the Conglomerate High Council

S'aulk—Commander, Qa'haQ Space Cruiser *D'bHin M'aGh*

Prologue

Two possibilities exist: either we are alone in the Universe or we are not. Both are equally terrifying.

Arthur C. Clarke

Earth Report 1: On board Qa'haQ Shuttle *D'bHin*, Punjabi Bagh, New Delhi, India

Today; zero hour

The skies groaned softly.

A gentle ripple ran through the polluted air above Delhi's Ring Road as the Qa'haQ planetary landing vehicle uncloaked for a split second and shimmered into existence. Some pieces of junk—which human cars kicked into the atmosphere with an alarming nonchalance—had collided with the invisibility shields. The organic circuitry of the ship chattered to compensate for this tactile assault.

Ensnared in a gridlock, a bewildered Madhav Khanna stared at the apparition through the tinted glass of his teak-brown Audi Q7. Before he could finish gawking and raise an alarm, the spaceship disappeared again, leaving Khanna cursing his eyesight. Was he seeing things?

Oblivious to the blaring of car horns outside, the resident AI aboard the dark, dank bridge of the alien craft was playing a soothing meditation song. The Qa'haQ mother ship in orbit was but an exploratory science vessel with a complement of fifteen, and two officers were assigned to take a cloaked shuttle down to the earth's surface for a reconnaissance run.

Commander S'aulk, leader of this small surface party, was in his chair, humming a melody under his breath. Sub-Commander Dac'ish, pilot and executive officer of the shuttle, sat in front of the faintly glowing Operations Console as she navigated the narrow, SUV-infested by-lanes of Punjabi Bagh—attentive, efficient, and observant.

An instrument beeped thrice. Dac'ish slid a slender reptilian claw across an octagonal panel. A screen sprang to life. Her eyes focused on a pulsating blip and blinked, processing the new information with the help of neural implants. She assimilated the data and tensed ever so slightly.

'Commander S'aulk,' Sub-Commander Dac'ish reported, a note of concern creeping into her voice, 'we have a development.'

'Report,' S'aulk shrilled absentmindedly.

'We've received a priority message from the Qa'haQam—it is being relayed to us via the mother ship.'

The oval bridge suddenly fell quiet as the song automatically muted itself. The soothing forest noises of the Qa'haQ home world faded into nothingness as a beeping of instruments took their place.

'What is it?' Commander S'aulk dropped the precious Orcheum flower he was sucking, his yellow eyes widening to perfect circles.

Dac'ish's short tail quivered for exactly two seconds to denote certainty. Her claws became a blur. After a few moments, she slowly turned around and hissed, fighting to keep her voice even. 'It is confirmed, Commander. We have been ordered to activate the Genetic Transmutor.'

'What? Are you sure?'

Dac'ish waved her claws across a few lighted panels. 'Order has been authenticated by the Qa'haQ Central Command.'

S'aulk muttered to himself, 'But we were only supposed to observe and report back.'

He was so lost in thought that he did not realise that Dac'ish was impatiently drumming her claws on the console. Her eyes were a shade of brown by now and her skin had changed colour to match that of the bridge—basic Qa'haQ defence mechanisms, even if involuntary, had kicked in. Her senses were heightened in anticipation of danger and a piece of hard, green cartilage slid over her neck from inside her exoskeleton, protecting the soft reddish flesh of her throat from any immediate physical attack.

Dac'ish had already taken up a battle posture by inserting a claw into the computing input device to provide the ship with immediate instructions. After all, such fragile situations demanded split-second decisions or new commanders who could issue them.

She cut in coldly, 'We have our orders, sir. Should I contact the CentCom for a direct, verbal command?'

At that precise moment, a monstrously filthy DTC bus swung so close—with a passenger leaning out to retch explosively—that the navigational computer of the *D'bHin* had to engage in an emergency course correction. Inertial dampeners groaned to protect the occupants of the ship from unwanted jolts.

'No, no need for that,' S'aulk hastily countered her, mindful of the implications of doubting orders from the home world, and unmindful of the crazy traffic outside. 'Do it!'

Sub-Commander Dac'ish nodded and input the information into the genetic warhead. 'Powering up and activating Genetic Transmutor. Priming the radiation amplifying devices. Rewriting their software now.'

'Good.'

'Target, sir?'

S'aulk was not sure where exactly he wanted the genetic incursion to begin. He spun a holographic globe and randomly pointed a claw at one location. 'Here.'

As the globe stopped spinning, the first officer nodded and acknowledged the order.

Dac'ish withdrew her claw from the input machine and looked squarely at S'aulk, who just stared back at her.

'What else do you want me to do, sir?'

The bridge had suddenly warmed up. S'aulk grinned in response, knowing that Earth Sector JVHN-20, or New Delhi, the location where they had initiated the genetic assault, was going to get much, much hotter.

Part I: Dial 'M' for Mutation

I have never listened to anyone who criticized my taste in
space travel, sideshows or gorillas.
When this occurs, I pack up my dinosaurs and leave the room.

Ray Bradbury

Uri, Jammu and Kashmir, India

Two hours into the invasion

She was startled by a loud knock.

Sonya Loewe instinctively tossed her head back with a feline grace, reached for a towel, and nimbly stepped out of the fogged-up bathroom. She darted towards the four-poster bed and lunged for her wardrobe.

The visitor persisted. There were two soft, slow knocks.

'Just a moment!' Sonya struggled to get into a pink top and a pair of frayed blue jeans, rushed to the mirror for a quick, appreciative glance, and was at the door in five long strides.

'Hey, come in.'

'Evening to you too, Sonya,' Imran greeted as he sauntered in. 'How're you doing?'

Her eyes flicked over Imran's toned, athletic frame. He had donned a black leather jacket over beige trousers. His wavy, black hair was tied in a ponytail and his dazed brown eyes were hidden behind thick-lensed glasses.

'I just thought I'd come and check on you.'

Sonya almost guffawed. His boyish charm and dreamy eyes, she thought, were accentuated by the shit-eating grin permanently plastered on his face.

Imran moved towards a cushy sofa, subconsciously caressed the armrest, and settled down. The room around him was somewhat familiar. A chestnut-wood bed lay in a corner, right next to an old dressing table. Bang opposite the bed sat another maroon sofa, alongside a television trolley, and a disconnected telephone. A disused fireplace, which clearly had seen better days, adorned the far side of the room.

Seeing Sonya again had sent Imran's brain into overdrive. He fondly recalled how he had met Sonya almost a month ago. As a freelance photographer, it was his job to socialise. It was a get-together at a friend's house and he'd reached early, as had another person.

Sonya was a tall, skinny girl whose finely chiselled face had a do-not-mess-with-me look. She stood in a corner, nursing her drink, acutely unaware of the pining glances she had unwittingly garnered the moment she walked in. Without thinking, Imran had made his way towards her.

'I wish I were the Planning Commission and you were a proposed five-year plan,' he declared even before she'd had a chance to see him coming, 'so I could have thoroughly vetted you.'

Imran had then fervently hoped the juvenile non sequitur had worked—it usually didn't.

Sonya turned around and looked him squarely in the face with an arrogant confidence that had done little for Imran's faith in his mojo. 'I majored in Economics, too,' she replied in a level voice.

A tongue-tied Imran sputtered on his drink, and the glass almost slipped out of his hands.

'Ah! That was just my invisible hand. It sometimes jokes with me purely in enlightened self-interest,' he'd rambled.

A flicker of interest played in Sonya's eyes. 'Adam Smith, *ja?*' She walked to a chair, and sat down with a patrician grace. She beckoned him to follow with a wave of her hands.

Imran played with his drink for a few seconds and then burst out with his carefully practised pièce de résistance. 'I feel terribly macroeconomic. You want to meet later and create some surplus value?'

She grinned mischievously. 'I'm more of a Friedman girl. I'd rather you do some verbal labour first. But tell me, are you always this ridiculous?'

'Only when I am in the company of GDPs,' Imran shrugged and gave a mock bow.

Sonya raised an eyebrow. 'GDPs?'

He leaned forward and mumbled in Sonya's right ear, 'Gross desi products.'

'And you think *I* am the one who is gross,' she shoved him back.

'I wouldn't be talking to you if I thought you were,' he started laughing.

Sonya looked deep into his eyes, unblinking, and whispered, 'Then what's stopping you?'

Imran had kept silent for some time, and then muttered a single phrase that had hooked her: 'RBI.'

She had laughed uncontrollably and agreed to meet later for dinner. The day had gotten even better when...

Crack!

Imran heard a noise in the distance that dragged him back to the present. He realised it was Sonya clapping to get his attention.

'Houston to Imran; do we have a problem?' she asked him.

'Oh! Sorry,' Imran hastily apologised, rubbing his eyes. 'I was—ah, never mind. What were you saying?'

'I was just thinking about the story we should do next…Life under the AFSPA? The recent protests have made the valley even more fragile than it was.'

'Whatever you say, boss.' Imran smiled. 'God, it's been such a long day. I hope you don't mind if I smoke. I can always roll a joint if you have more refined taste. We should support our Afghan friends with their exports, right?'

She wagged her right index finger to convey a no-no.

'Oh, by the way,' he said nonchalantly, bringing her focus back to their conversation, 'you've forgotten to wear something today.'

Sonya's smile vanished in an instant, and she cringed in horror. Had she in the zealous hurry to open the door forgotten... Her left hand instinctively slapped her jeans. Yes, she was wearing them. Her hand crept up—she was wearing her top, too. She swung back to look at him questioningly. '*What*?' she barked, her eyes on fire.

'Hey!' Imran said defensively. 'I meant you aren't wearing your glasses today. Contacts?'

Sonya sprang up from the bed and snatched her glasses from the dressing table. She put them on and focused on her reflection in the mirror, just in case. Sonya suddenly realised that there was something about this man she couldn't quite put her finger on. A colleague from Bonn had recommended Imran when she had told him that she would be going to India to do a story on Kashmir. Imran, as she was told, was a local, talented photographer, and could prove to be a valuable asset to a foreign investigative journalist.

The nicotine finally hit Imran's system. 'So,' he asked in all seriousness, not even looking at her, 'you never told me what Deutsche-Welle was doing in these dangerous parts?'

Sonya considered telling him the truth, but then decided against it. As a journalist, she prized her sources' anonymity, especially because this one was particularly good, and had led her to many juicy stories. Still, she chose to tell Imran a bit of the truth. After all, she *did* feel a certain sense of comfort with him by now.

'I majored in Economics at Frankfurt and then moved to cover fashion in Berlin. But then I realised I wanted something more from my life than just writing about clothes, so I opted for war journalism. Before I took the leap, I thought I'd take a sabbatical and travel to Kashmir on a personal visit, but then the Indo-Pak war broke out, and my Bureau chief told me to do some war reporting. I couldn't say no to such first-hand experience, of course.' She then hastily added as an afterthought, 'It's a pity that it comes with such a loss of life.'

Imran had flinched when she had said 'Bureau' but had relaxed when she had mentioned journalism. Luckily, she had not noticed. 'Personal visit?' he asked.

'Well, my father was a pandit from Uri. He shifted base to Germany a long time ago, searching for greener pastures,' Sonya smiled. 'Apart from getting a job he also met my mom.'

'So you came here to meet your dad's family?' Imran continued inquisitively.

The room suddenly felt silent. He thought he could feel a heaviness come over her but dismissed it as his imagination.

'Yes,' she replied curtly.

'Good! How are they?' he asked.

She did not reply.

Imran persisted. 'Well, do I get to meet them?'

'You can't,' Sonya replied.

'Why not?' Imran said in a mock-hurt voice.

'Because they're *dead*!' she snapped.

Imran floundered for words. 'What? How?'

'Militants...' she murmured. 'Evidently, some did not feel that my family should be allowed to live in an *azaad* Kashmir because of the gods they prayed to.'

Imran was dumbstruck. 'I am so sorry!' He staggered towards Sonya and sat down right next to her. He placed a supportive hand on her shoulder, for he knew how loss felt, how it broke something deep inside. 'What happened? Let it out. It helps, trust me.'

Sonya turned around, and saw the concern, the understanding in his eyes. 'One day my family was well and alive, the next they were just gone. I didn't know them well but that doesn't mean I don't mourn them.'

'I am so sorry.' He squeezed her hand '...This house...' Imran's voice trailed off.

'The neighbours kept this house for me, hoping I'd return one day. I did—but only temporarily. I'm here now only as a tourist.'

'But you are not a...'

Sonya didn't let him finish. 'What was Kashmiri in me died with my family—all that's left now is German. I even took my mother's name as my own...I am a Loewe now, nothing more, nothing less.'

Imran had not expected the carefree girl, whom he thought he was beginning to know, to be struggling with this kind of pain. 'I just want you to know that we're trying to end this circle of violence. Kashmir wants a new life. We are working towards that future.'

'Will it bring back the departed?' She spat the words out with such ferocity that Imran was taken aback. Stung, he stood up and withdrew to his sofa.

Sonya looked up after a few moments, her eyes still cold, and mumbled, 'I'm sorry.'

'It's okay,' he said, 'I *empathise*. You're not the only one who has lost loved ones. One fine day a long time ago, I came back from school only to find my house, my street, my family, simply gone. I was told later that my entire family had become unwilling martyrs due to cross-border shelling. Not the first innocent civilian casualties in Kashmir...and certainly not the last.'

Sonya stopped sniffling and her brown eyes widened in sympathy.

'It just makes you wonder how short life is. Perhaps that's what taught me to enjoy every second of it.'

'I am so...' Sonya opened her mouth but Imran cut her short.

'Don't say anything. Please.'

Sonya shut up instantly. The realisation that he was as broken inside as she was, maybe even more, drove her to make amends.

Imran, on the other hand, had been stung by his own admission. Even his closest friends did not know much about his family. His failure to protect his loved ones at a time of need was why he had made the career choices that presently defined him.

He sighed, leaned back and closed his eyes, trying hard to repress bitter memories. Imran knew he had to put aside his personal shit and wrap up this assignment soon. Islamabad would soon be expecting a report from the Inter-Services Intelligence's (ISI) point man in Kashmir.

From him.

Imran hadn't lied to Sonya—at least, not much. His family *had* been killed in cross-border shelling. Except that the mortars that had got them had not been Pakistani—they had been Indian.

Imran Bhatt was from *across* the Line of Control.

Washington Metropolitan Area, United States of America (USA)
Four hours into the invasion

Two nicotine-stained fingers deftly flicked a cigarette, sending glowing specks of ash floating into nothingness. A faint smile played on Yasser Basheer's chapped lips as he stroked his greying beard.

Basheer's features were a delicate balance between his two heritages. With an Afghan mother who had died during childbirth and a white father who'd deserted Basheer's mother even before he was born, Basheer had learnt to distrust both the cultures that had spawned him—he now despised the Afghans and the Americans with equal measure. It did not help that Basheer was raised by a maternal relative in Pakistan's Federally Administered Tribal Areas, and in due course had opted to join one of the most anti-Afghan, anti-American institutions he could have come across—the Pakistani Army.

The unpleasantness of the situation hit him, but he controlled himself. This was no time for self-pity; it never was. Out of habit, he sniffed. Like a wolf on a hunt, his nose tried to catch what the air was trying to tell him—an old habit. Basheer's furry eyebrows—which almost met in the middle—contorted as he took another drag. The past few days had been more than unforgettable: they had been *brutal*.

After meeting with Jason E. Cartman, the Director General of the Combined Intelligence Corps (CIC), Basheer was told to report to Quantico for debriefing. He was led to a waiting GMT900 Chevrolet Tahoe and driven away.

His chauffeur had opted for the shortest route to Quantico from DC. He took the I-395 S towards Virginia, and then the Interstate Connector 95 S, passing through Springfield and Lorton. The hush-hush nature of it all made Basheer wonder if he was leaving as an agent or a prisoner of the CIC. To test his hypothesis, just before they reached the Triangle/Quantico intersection, Basheer had asked his chauffer to take a right towards the Prince William Forest Park, instead of the left that went straight to Quantico. However, his fears had been unfounded. The driver had complied without a word and taken the exit towards the Park. Unsurprisingly, when Basheer asked to stop at the Park, citing mundane reasons ('I always need a smoke before heading off to deal with the bureaucrats, don't you?'), the driver had merely smiled and acquiesced.

His stomach rumbled. A stab of fire in his abdomen dragged him back to the present, though the pain passed almost as soon as it had struck. He leaned back against a tree and took another drag, his mind frantically whirring. He was going to the FBI, at least ostensibly, but something did not add up. True, Cartman had been extremely secretive about this entire operation from day one—not sharing details even with the Central Intelligence Agency (CIA) or the National Security Agency (NSA)—but Basheer could not deduce why Cartman chose not to publicise Operation Ragnarök once it was successful, inter-agency rivalry notwithstanding. After all, it had unearthed the *truth*.

Moreover, it was not the FBI headquarters that was his final destination (which should have been the standard operating procedure), but a residence near the FBI Academy in Quantico. Basheer sensed that he was not being directed to the FBI, but to someone within the Bureau—someone who was with Cartman in this entire operation and did not want the FBI, the CIA or even the Department of Defense to know about Yasser Basheer.

The more he thought about it, the more it confirmed his fears. He knew that his orders in the past hadn't come from the White House, but now it was beginning to look as if they weren't coming from the CIC either. He reached for the can of ginger ale stuffed in his jacket pocket, opened it, and took a sip. He grimaced as the cold, fizzy liquid burnt his throat.

Basheer's eyes hardened. The past few years had killed a part of him. He had infiltrated a fundamentalist cell and made a name in jihadi circles. He had then colluded with some disgruntled South Asian Maoists, roped in a friend from the Pakistani Army, and led an Indian missile base to be compromised. The ramifications had been horrifying: old rivalries had surfaced, tempers had flared and lives had been lost. But the mission objective, the capturing of Osama bin Laden (so he might be used to blackmail the incumbent president to allow some business lobbies free reign) had been achieved. The fringe benefit of having select multinational corporations bagging tenders worth billions of dollars to develop the war-shattered economies of India and Pakistan was the icing on the cake.

Cartman could not have envisaged this on his own, Basheer thought. He knew Cartman would never have gotten official approval for capturing the real deal because of its ghastly political ramifications. The death of OBL was a major reason why the current president was still in power. Basheer had a gut feeling that he was being manipulated, and so was Cartman. The question was by whom. Who would have the balls to envision an operation of this magnitude, he wondered. Who wanted the current quasi-socialist American president replaced by a more conservative, hawkish president, one who could incite hatred and anger amongst the masses—someone who saw the world both as a stage and, even more importantly, a market to be exploited, and was capable of envisioning such a lethal, convoluted outcome?

The answer hit Basheer like a brick.

It was *them*.

With this sudden epiphany, crease lines appeared on Basheer's forehead and a sinking feeling assaulted him. Even the mere name caused him to wince, for the International Military-Industrial Conglomeration (IMIC) did not just kill, they *decimated* their enemies. Basheer knew that those who dared raise their heads against the IMIC didn't just die a painful death—they were never born.

The IMIC was a dreaded organisation—and its lethality was enhanced by the fact that not many even knew about its existence. If knowledge was power, then to be unknowable was to be invincible. Basheer had had to pay in blood for whatever scraps of information he had on the IMIC—an ultra-secret think tank that brought together the world's biggest, richest and mightiest financiers, hotshot politicians, media barons, corporate honchos, defence companies, drug cartels and moneyed aristocracy. The IMIC was all-pervasive, yet hidden from view, for it knew that real power, in order to operate, had to remain hidden. Though that did not mean it was not supremely influential. The IMIC, for example, controlled the global flow of capital, and decided which country would become the next big investment destination. Once that cycle was completed, the IMIC engineered wars, bureaucratic hassles, diseases, or economic meltdowns for the investors to move on to the next region depending on *where* the IMIC had made its own future investments. The IMIC worked on the principles of perfect inception. Through its covert sub-chapters deployed all over the world, the IMIC dictated policies of corporations and countries alike. Force was never used to that effect: it was all done so subtly that no one even suspected that they were being led towards a particular decision—the decision that the IMIC *wanted* them to take.

Basheer had regarded it all as a paranoid conspiracy theory till he had come face to face with the IMIC. He had come to regard it as the Matrix, just like in the film—only this one was built, operated and controlled by a few *real* people. It was the ultimate coterie of all-powerful architects. Those who stumbled upon the IMIC's existence faced a simple choice: either join the IMIC, for it rewarded talent and understood that it took effort and skill to have uncovered its existence, or simply disappear from the face of the earth. The choice was not that hard, was it?

He felt another jolt. He could swear something had moved inside his stomach again. However, before he could be alarmed, the strange nausea was gone. Basheer got up and started moving towards his parked car. Within moments he was inside, and the car was headed to Quantico.

Basheer closed his eyes and squirmed in his seat as he recalled the day when *he* had been drafted by the IMIC, or the Conglomerate, as it was referred to within its own circles.

If it was the Conglomerate that had made Cartman go rogue and fight against the interests of his own country, then why had Basheer not been told about the existence of this operation? Deep down he already knew the answer: Basheer belonged to the lower echelons of a shadowy organisation where information was only released on a need-to-know basis—sometimes not even then. It was said that even those high up in the Conglomerate did not fully know what the High Council, the apex decision-making body, was planning. Still, IMIC members followed their orders, and were rewarded with absolute power and everything money could buy. Sometimes even with things money could not buy—life, for example. This was why *he* had joined the Conglomerate. He was still alive, though the pestilence ravaging his body should have killed him a long time ago. But it didn't, thanks to the Conglomerate.

Before he could mope any further, he felt a sudden restlessness again. A feeling of tremendous discomfort struck the pit of his stomach. Without thinking he leaned forward and tapped the glass partition.

The driver looked at him in the rear-view mirror. Basheer gestured with his right hand. 'Please take the next exit and pull into a motel. I am not feeling well.'

The driver nodded, though hesitatingly—he suddenly seemed aware of the fact that they were getting late.

Basheer did not care. He needed space at the moment; he could feel something alive inside him, something painfully gnawing at his innards.

Literally.

Vasant Vihar, New Delhi, India
Six hours into the invasion

Bajra rained from the blue skies, and scattered the flock of hungry pigeons. Madhav Khanna threw the last fistful of grains into the air, muttered, '*Jai mata di*,' again, and paternally clucked at the cooing birds.

Khanna's A-Block house comprised, among other areas, an artfully decorated veranda and a sprawling garden. His portly frame ambled to a cane chair and settled down. He reached forward to pick up a glass of his favourite, though slightly peculiar, evening drink—iced vodka with Rooh Afza and a dash of lime—from a table nearby. He pressed the cold glass to his lips and his eyes closed automatically as he savoured every droplet of the intoxicating nectar.

Khanna could feel the house slowly coming back to life. His wife was about to return from a kitty-party being held in the nearby Basant Lok Complex, while his two sons were gearing up for an outing to the Delhi Gymkhana Club. Khanna stretched his legs on the settee in front of him, opened the day's *Economic Times* and started reading, his half-moon spectacles perched on his bulbous nose.

His slightly pockmarked face diverted one's attention from the larger-than-average ears and the few white hairs emerging from his flaring nostrils. Khanna downed the remainder of his drink, asked the petite maid for a refill, and tried to get rid of the apparition he had encountered that day at Punjabi Bagh.

He chuckled inwardly, and blamed the unknown flying object on his overwrought nerves—business was not as good as it should have been, and it was taking a toll on him. The rains were plentiful—and it sucked. He prayed that the heat would be particularly nasty and that the monsoons would stop as soon as possible. After all, there was so much money to be made distributing air conditioners.

Khanna had subconsciously started drumming his potbelly with ring-studded hands. The *pukhraj* he wore on his right index finger—given to him by Jyotikund Baba himself—reflected the rays of the setting sun, giving the ring a golden brilliance of its own. His body swayed with a gentle rhythm as he put the paper down and stared at the old neem tree in his garden.

He stood up with considerable effort, folded his hands in a gesture of deference and bowed to the tree. Khanna thanked the gods for giving him *janam* at the right place and time. Being born even 10 years earlier or later than when he was would have ensured he missed *the* chance, when the planets were all aligned, for his business to boom. The small window of 25 years appeared when a rapidly developing India was being heavily invested in by global corporations. This was also when a consumerist, rising middle class was forced by soaring mercury to perceive air conditioning as a necessity, not a luxury. Khanna, foreseeing this demand, had led his firm into a new era of providing centralised air conditioning using domestically produced hardware that had cut down manufacturing costs drastically, and had led to higher margins. Fate, coupled with his business acumen, had ensured he would become one of the India's biggest AC dealers.

The golden future of air conditioning wasn't the only thing the visionary in Khanna foresaw—he had also portended the rise of mobile telephony. He had negotiated with foreign players and domestic companies alike, greased the palms of officials to expedite his tenders, and had been one of the pioneers who ushered India into a true telecommunications age. Not only was he the proud owner of the first cell phone in north India, but his house was also the first location in which a cell phone company had installed a cell tower, the Base Station Site, in Delhi.

He stared at the tower with a visible pride he usually reserved for his younger son, a graduate of Wharton business school. Khanna's garden was covered with exotic plants and fruit-laden trees, but right there in the middle, alongside the 10-foot neem his grandfather had planted, was a structure that had become an integral part of the house. The Base Station Site was an elevated structure, around 60 metres in height. It supported antennas, as well as a GPS receiver, electrical power sources, one set each of transceivers, digital signal processors, and control-electronics—the pulsating heart of cellular telephony in the city.

Khanna kicked off his slippers and gingerly stepped into the garden. The moist blades of grass felt cool and refreshing under his feet—a smile automatically formed on his face as he smelt petrichor. He loved the heady scent of fresh water sprayed on parched Earth. It reminded him of his childhood antics in Lyallpur. The naturally perfumed *mitti* of West Punjab, he often used to say, somehow did not smell the same as the East's. Lost in bittersweet memories, Khanna walked up to the neem, lovingly caressed its bark, and then sat down near the cell tower to meditate.

Khanna had half closed his eyes when he thought he saw a bolt of lightning shoot out of the tower. His eyes snapped open in alarm.

However, there was nothing out of the ordinary—it had to be nothing more than his mind playing tricks again.

He shrugged and closed his eyes again. His back was now ramrod straight and his feet were crossed under him in a perfect yogic pose. Khanna tried to visualise and focus on a little dot—

moving like a red blip across his eyelids—and attempted to blot out the stray horn or shrill voice still audible despite the high walls of the compound.

Sometimes, when he was really able to tune in, Khanna could swear that he heard a distinct hum emanating from the tower, an energy that infused him with a new life. For the past 27 years, not a single day had passed when he hadn't meditated for an hour right at the base of the tower and the neem. It gave him the will to live and fight another day. He needed that will.

All members of the Conglomerate did.

Khanna controlled his breathing, and then slowly drifted into subconsciousness. He imagined himself detaching from this shell of a body, and floating away into karmic nothingness. His mind was being pulled towards a radiant ball of pulsating cosmic matter that promised to liberate him as pure energy.

Jai mata di, he kept chanting, mentally.

A tremor seemed to pass through his body as he felt a chakra activate itself. 'Is this what nirvana feels like?' Khanna was about to ask himself, but then stopped as he realised that he was supposed to be in a mental state where neither questions nor answers really mattered.

Breathe, he told himself. One. Two.

Flash!

He felt uneasy, as if overwhelmed by his recent experience. A stab of pain made him cry out loud.

Another flash. Khanna burst out screaming as he experienced a sharp, sizzling pang shoot through his chest. Before he could begin to wonder what had caused it, he shrieked again—the agony had returned, this time even more severe. The second cardiac arrest he had experienced a couple of years ago was nothing when compared to what was happening to him now, he felt. It was as if someone had thrust a scalding knife between his ribs and was twisting it.

Hard.

I must get up, his brain hollered. I must ask for help. Khanna's eyes snapped open, and he screamed till he ran out of breath and thought his vocal cords would rupture. He fell back on the moist Earth and writhed like a fish out of water. Raw, red-hot agony blinded him.

Khanna felt something thrash *within* his chest. He could swear there was an army of microscopic ants moving from his collarbone towards his heart.

Doctor. I need a doctor. He groaned and tried to block the pain, desperately trying to condition his mind to ignore it.

Khanna could feel his blood turn cold, frigid to the point that it felt like liquid ice flowed in his veins.

By then, his fervent pleas for help had caused the entire house to converge at his location. Khanna heard several pairs of feet rush to him. His younger son stood right next to him, gawking, and reached for a cell phone.

'*Ki hoya*, Papa?' his elder son shouted frantically and tried to make sense of the situation. 'Are you okay?'

Must fight pain, Khanna repeated in his head, must fight pain. He soundlessly worded something and frothed at the mouth. The younger son placed an immediate emergency call for an ambulance. The daughters-in-law, their mouths agape, rushed forward and sprinkled Khanna's face with water.

Khanna instinctively tore open his clothing and clutched at his chest. That was when it happened.

Either the pain was beginning to lessen on its own, or it was the pain-control technique Khanna was employing that had worked. In an instant, the pain stopped and his eyes started to water. His vision became blurred and the world went out of focus. Khanna could swear the cell tower was glowing, but then, there were other things vying for his attention.

His chest was heaving madly. No, it was not his breathing alone. His chest was *actually* moving. He could see tiny objects swarming around in it. As he looked at them, aghast, he saw globules of subcutaneous fat oozing out of holes that had appeared all over his body. He seemed to be getting smaller, lighter, and covered with a sticky substance. *Oh God,* he thought in sheer horror, *what is happening to me?*

Someone wailed—high-pitched, full of horror, and unpleasant to the ears. Maybe it was his granddaughter; he could not tell. His son, who had taken Khanna's head in his lap, jumped back in alarm. Not only was Khanna foaming at the mouth, but his bare-chested torso was no longer covered with his hairy, brown skin. The liquid he was covered with a moment ago had mysteriously evaporated in a swirl of blue-green vapour.

His skin had simply disappeared and was replaced with a yellow-green, leathery substitute. Khanna's body had sprouted something all over that looked like scales. His fingers were claws and his nose had shrunk. His eyes too had turned yellow, his tongue was forked, and his ears were slits.

He lay still, almost lifeless. Yet, he felt at peace with himself, as if he had just won a marathon. The pain had completely vanished by now. Khanna's cold blood, which had tormented him earlier, soothed him wherever it flowed. He could hear and smell better, though his eyesight had perceptibly weakened. He could hear the heartbeats of his family, their murmurs and smells. Khanna could, inexplicably, see mental images being formed within the heads of those present. He could sense the humidity pressing against his eardrums and feel the ground vibrate as his family members stomped their feet and beat their breasts in confusion and horror.

In the distance, he heard the shrill siren of an ambulance. The sound burrowed in his ears and made him quiver. Finally, he felt something stir inside him. A presence inside his head at such a primeval level it both scared and empowered him.

Khanna felt life returning to his limbs. With a low growl, his eyes shot open.

He realised he had grown a scaly tail, which he angrily swung at the cell tower, slicing through its steel legs like a hot knife through butter. He watched merrily as the tower swayed as if drunk and toppled over, destroying his garage and the Audi Q7 parked inside it in one swift, satisfying moment. He felt a powerful wave of pleasure engulf him as the destruction commenced, and hissed joyously.

Madhav Khanna was back in business.

Bahawalpur, Punjab, Pakistan

Eight hours into the invasion

'I can prove anyone guilty of *anything*, anywhere,' Parvez Chaand Mahmood groggily mumbled to himself, 'but I still can't prevent this *haraamkhor* from duping me.'

His six-foot, sleep-deprived body lurched towards the main door. The sun was beginning to rise by then, and drowned the unkempt red-brick house in a pale yellow glow. Parvez ran a hand through his crew-cut hair, yawned lazily and unlocked the door.

A sturdy, buck-toothed lad from a nearby *pind* stood fidgeting at the door. He smiled at Parvez, muttered, '*Salam*, sahib—*doodh*!' and pointed at a rusty can strapped to an old Yamaha bike.

'*Salam ke bacche*,' Parvez spat out, his drowsiness infuriating him even further. 'I'm no longer buying milk from you. You call this milk? Then what does water look like?'

'Sir ji!' the *doodhwallah* pleaded as the happiness vanished from his face. 'I swear on my kids. This is the purest milk you can get in all Bahawalpur. Not one single drop of water here, *kasam Khuda*...'

Parvez raised his eyebrows questioningly. As General Zia-ul-Haq had made Pakistan realise Khuda may have been many, only Allah was one. Thus, the correct form of address to divinity, especially for *true* Muslims—incidentally the only people who mattered in Pakistan—was Allah.

'Er...*Allah kasam*,' the milkman bit his tongue and instinctively corrected himself. He wasn't sure what this customer did exactly, but he knew he had links to the army. That was more than enough to make him behave with Parvez. 'Believe me, sir, my own children drink this!'

The words tumbled out in such a rapid fire succession that Parvez wondered if they weren't memorised and often practised daily. *All the world's a stage*, after all.

Parvez didn't only know that; he lived it.

He gave the milkman a murderous stare and reached for an aluminium utensil he carried in his left hand, hidden from view, so that the milkman took his earlier threats seriously. Parvez extended the bowl, positioned a sieve over it and nodded at the milkman. The milkman picked up the container with a heave, tilted it gently and grunted as the sweet white liquid started to flow.

They weren't even finished when Parvez heard a honk. An unmarked white Honda Civic rolled up to his gate, raising a plume of dust in its wake.

The car came to a halt, the doors swung open and a uniformed officer stepped out. Major Faisal was a short, barrel-chested man with curly hair and a haughty arrogance in his stride. He waved and moved towards Parvez with a marked familiarity.

'Morning, PCM!' Faisal boomed as he strode towards the open door, and upon seeing the gallons of milk being poured into a utensil, taunted in a tone laced with sarcasm, 'Now I know the secret to your health!'

'Major Faisal.' Parvez acknowledged Faisal with a curt nod and a raised eyebrow.

Parvez motioned the milkman to hurry and spoke again, 'Since when have you started appearing in uniform?'

The major simply grunted, and slipped past Parvez into the drawing room.

Major Faisal looked at the messy duplex and inwardly sighed in distaste. Clothes, magazines and newspapers were strewn all around. A huge bookshelf covered an entire wall. A folding bed with a few stripes missing, a wooden chair, a small portable TV, and three laptops on an old study table were the only other things in the room. Nothing out of the ordinary, he thought, but he expected better organisation from Parvez.

Faisal was about to sit down when a concealed object in the bookshelf opposite him caught his eye. It was tucked away in such a surreptitious manner that it was visible only from where he was standing. Anyone would have missed it from any other angle. Honed by instinct, Faisal crept closer to investigate the 32mm Colt revolver hidden in the shelf, just behind copies of some dog-eared history books. He turned around to say something but Parvez was back before he opened his mouth.

'Don't give me that look,' Parvez said, pre-empting Faisal's objections. 'Yes, I am planning to get something more modern than the Colt from the quartermaster. But as they say, a true soldier never needs to fire a weapon. He only has to use his mind.'

Parvez put the milk can on the kitchen slab and tapped his right temple with his index finger.

Faisal looked at him incredulously. 'Who said that?'

'Someone,' Parvez replied cryptically, and a sly smile spread across his tanned face.

Faisal gave Parvez an intense look and muttered something under his breath. He walked across the littered room, switched on the television and plopped down right next to it on a filthy *dari*. He surfed through channels till he reached *QTV*, increased the volume, and motioned Parvez to come sit near him.

Parvez was not surprised. Faisal was operating under standard ISI directives. The noise from the television would distort their voices so any attempts to record their conversation from a hidden spy camera or monitor it from a surveillance van parked nearby would prove futile. However, the precautions irked him.

'This is my house!' Irritation was clear in Parvez's voice. 'It's not bugged.'

'These days you don't know what is,' Faisal retorted dismissively. 'Anyway, it doesn't matter. Get ready. We've to go.'

'Arre.' Parvez's arms shot up. He had barely sat down when he was being asked to get up again. 'It is so early in the morning!'

'Early?' screeched Faisal, unable to believe his ears. 'What the hell is wrong with you? You've been out of uniform for too long, mate. No wonder the Americans and the Indians screw us with such impunity!' A menacing tone crept in Faisal's voice, and he paused for a few seconds before adding, 'By the way...I was talking to Bilal the other day and we realised that you never told us about your days before joining the ISI. Which PMA Long Course did you attend?'

Alarms went off in Parvez's subconscious, and he was taken aback by the sudden outburst. Faisal was usually a calm, composed man, who hardly had to use his temper to get his way. Yet Parvez was also not one to take kindly to such a tone being used against him. He was a brother officer, after all.

Parvez snorted and returned the barb, 'You *know* why I have been out of uniform. You don't want uniformed army officers who could be directly linked to the ISI roaming the streets, do you? Where would your plausible deniability be then? And it doesn't matter when I graduated from the PMA as long as I can kick some Indian-Zionist ass. My record in Tel Aviv speaks louder than the year in which I graduated from Kakul Academy.'

A reconciliatory smile spread over Faisal's face as he shrugged in agreement. He had realised that he had come dangerously close to insulting a decorated intelligence operative. Both Parvez and Faisal were ISI officers belonging to the feared Special Services (SS) Directorate, responsible for monitoring terrorist group activities in Pakistan. Based on the Special Activities Division of the CIA, ISI's SS Directorate was tasked with covert political action and paramilitary special operations.

'Listen,' Faisal muttered, aggression ebbing away from his demeanour, perhaps due to Parvez's uncomfortable stare, 'we're in deep shit.'

'What happened?' Parvez was still miffed. The two of them held the same rank. Faisal had no right to talk to him that way.

'I just received word from a trusted source in JIX. GHQ Pindi is totally cheesed. Those backstabbing *penchos* want...' Faisal rasped urgently.

Parvez cut him. 'The JIX?'

Faisal nodded vehemently. Joint Intelligence X was the ISI department that coordinated with all the other wings in the ISI, a sort of a secretariat. Intelligence gathered by all ISI sections was sent to JIX, which processed the information and took further policy action. Hence, any news from JIX was bound to be important.

'We need to go take care of our safe houses. They could be raided.'

Ignoring the other man's tense body language, Parvez's body started shaking with laughter. 'Since when is the ISI afraid of raids? Don't we conduct them?'

'Times are changing. Lieutenant General Arif Chowdhury, awaiting a trial, is presently under house arrest for supplying arms to the group that attacked the Indian missile base. Guess who he had asked to arrange the weapons?'

Realisation dawned on Parvez. He opened his mouth to say something but then thought the better of it and closed it.

'I've been told to lie low. But before that, we need to erase our footprints.'

'What's the plan of action?' asked Parvez.

'I'll go sort out the safe house in Sadiq Colony. You go handle our Indian guest.'

There was a marked pause before Parvez spoke again. 'Handle?'

Faisal's tone became even more sombre. 'The ISI can no longer support him. He will have to fend for himself. You have to ensure he crosses over into Afghanistan. If the Indians find out he's here, we're both history.'

'What is wrong with you, Major? Since when are you so afraid of the Indians?'

'Since the early morning call I got!' Faisal looked positively freaked out by now, his skin pale. 'The president, prime minister, army chief, the whole bloody lot of them, are planning to blame everything on certain rogue elements in the ISI.'

'Rogue elements?' Parvez asked cautiously.

Faisal dropped the bombshell with a quiet resignation. 'Us! They will save their dirty, corrupt necks by showcasing us as the true face of what's wrong with Pakistan. We've been set up, Parvez-bhai.'

'But you were simply following orders! From the top!' Parvez, who had by now taken his position on the mattress, sprang up, horrified.

'Try telling *them* that,' said Faisal bitterly. 'This time *we* have become the scapegoats. You know how the system works.'

A shadow passed over Parvez's face. The next time he spoke up, there was steel—and acceptance of what had happened—in his voice. 'What do you want me to do?'

'Go to our safe house in the Plantation Reserve Forest. Kick the damn Maoist out. Tell him he's no longer our responsibility. Erase all evidence that we ever helped him. Got it?'

'Wilco. But how will he escape?' asked Parvez.

'Let him find his own way. I know he's still in touch with some Baloch insurgent groups, but we can no longer use him to infiltrate them. That *khota* is too volatile now. The cons outweigh the pros. This bloody headache better be over soon. My blood sugar and BP levels are already dangerously high.'

Parvez nodded. Faisal wasn't one to loose cool so easily. *Things must really be shitty*, Parvez thought.

Faisal stood up and moved towards the door. 'I'm off now. Call me when you're done.'

'Roger.'

Faisal slapped Parvez's shoulder once and then hurried to his car without looking back. There was a sudden sense of urgency and fear in his gait that Parvez had never seen before. Faisal's Civic started and screeched away.

Parvez couldn't believe what was happening. The ISI, afraid in its own country! What had this world come to? He wondered what would come next. An Ahmadiyya PM of Pakistan?

His chain of thought was broken by his cell phone's alarm. He switched it off, put the cell on charging, and rushed to get ready. Parvez ran to the bathroom, brushed, and got ready for a bath. He removed the plank from the bucket hanging on a nail above his head so that water could fall through the holes made at the bottom. Parvez scrubbed himself clean of the sweat and grime which last night's interrogation had so graciously bestowed upon him.

He came out, reached for a crumpled white kurta hanging on a nail, and a pair of faded brown trousers. He hopped to the small, rickety table, poured himself two glasses of milk and downed them in six measured sips. He wiped his lips with the sleeve of his kurta. Maybe this was why he liked wearing white, he mused, trying to make sense of what Faisal had told him.

His mind was processing the new facts that had come to light. The developments were fast, and provided him a golden opportunity to do what he had been planning to do for some time now. Deep inside, Parvez's heart was soaring. It was then that he took a decision that would forever change his life.

Parvez went to the bookshelf and took his Colt, checked its safety, and inserted it in his trousers. He took out a few documents from the bookshelf, neatly folded them into little square pieces, and stashed them in his pockets. Then, he went out of his house, double padlocked the door, and lunged for his scooter.

But before Parvez could kick-start his old scooter, something struck him. It took him less than a microsecond to determine his future course of action. That's precisely what was taught to people like him in specific academies around the world: think long-term, keep all the extraneous factors in mind, take split-second decisions, and then live with—and by—those judgement calls.

He immediately climbed off his two-wheeled vehicle, ran back to the house, and went straight to his kitchen. He rummaged through the contents of his ancient, whirring refrigerator. Parvez then, quite carefully, took out the milk, meat and eggs present in the house, and deposited them in separate earthen pots kept outside his main gate. Let his canine pals party and drink to his health, he thought and smiled.

Once finished, Parvez locked the door again, mounted the scooter, and started for his destination. He mentally drew a map of his intended journey. His house was in Medical Colony—he hoped not to be slowed down by traffic jams on his way. There were things greater than his career resting on the success of his mission.

Parvez came out of his residential area and took the Circular Road towards his quarry. He kept driving, honking less than he usually did to remain unobtrusive. He lurched past the cramped, dusty lanes of Bahawalpur that were beginning to get crowded as the residents of the city woke up to another warm morning. He passed a cart laden with vegetables and cursed as the vendor advertised his goods in a harsh but catchy sing-song voice.

Damn him, he'll cause an accident, Parvez thought angrily, and swerved as an autorickshaw passed within centimetres of him. Within a few minutes, at Ahmadpur Road he took a left that ran straight to the forest. Parvez had to drive for another 15 minutes before the traffic started to clear. He had left the city centre behind.

Parvez suddenly veered away from a bullock cart, slowed down, and parked his scooter at a roadside eatery. He wrapped a turban around his head, put on his black aviators, and walked towards the shop. Once there, Parvez shouted to the shopkeeper to give him a lassi, making sure to speak in heavily accented, almost unintelligible, Balochi. The surprised shopkeeper told him to repeat himself in Punjabi. Parvez motioned with his fingers at the earthen pots filled with curd, and then snapped his fingers twice. The message was instantly conveyed—a drink and it'd better be quick. The shopkeeper merely grumbled at this uncommunicative, arrogant Baloch, and got to work.

The actual reason why Parvez had stopped here was not his desire to get an industrial quantity of sugar into his system, but to make a phone call. He knew his own cell phone was tapped, and he had to find other ways to communicate.

Parvez quietly stepped inside a deserted public call booth right next to the lassi shop, and firmly closed the door behind him. He picked up the receiver, inserted a coin in the slot, and dialled a number he had been made to memorise.

The phone rang only twice before it was answered by a gruff voice. It was his source in the BBC Urdu Service.

'Yes?'

'The celebrity has been spotted,' Parvez whispered into the receiver.

'Where?' the other voice asked with evident curiosity.

'Government Guest House, Reserve Forest,' Parvez responded. 'Don't you want to interview him?'

'When?'

'30 minutes.'

The line immediately went dead.

Parvez came out of the booth, casually walked to the stall, and reached for the glass of frothing lassi. He gulped it down in one go, paid the shopkeeper, and left unhurriedly.

After travelling for another two minutes, he stopped his scooter again. Without getting off, Parvez removed his shades, turban and kurta, and thrust them in the luggage compartment. He now sported a dark blue tee shirt that he had donned under the kurta. The sun was beginning to unleash its potential by then. His exposed arms and feet felt like they were on fire. However, he had bigger concerns at the moment than sunburn.

Parvez knew that it would take the Signal Intelligence Department of the ISI five minutes to trace the call—he had ensured this public call booth was located between the blind spots of two ISI monitoring stations covering the area. He had to be gone by then. And when they did trace the call, they would start looking for a Baloch wearing a white kurta, not him. Parvez smiled and wore the helmet he had kept in his scooter's dickey.

It was good to be careful, Parvez told himself again.

Perhaps that was why he—who grew up in a congested, coastal city far, far away from Bahawalpur—was somehow still alive in this hostile, foreign land.

Uri, Jammu and Kashmir, India
8 hours into the invasion

Major Imran Bhatt recalled the sombre, terrified silence in his street when he had returned home from school that fateful day. Bile rose in his throat as bittersweet memories of waving bye to his mother for one last time on that bright, spring morning—a long time ago—slashed across his mind.

That day, when Imran had come back in the afternoon, his house no longer existed. His neighbourhood was no more. His mother, father and two sisters had been decimated in the shelling.

Imran's childhood ended that day.

Much to his dismay, the district administration had packed him off to a government-run boarding school for the underprivileged, which, as he found out later, also doubled as a feeder institute for the local jihadi training camp. He—an upper-class, English-speaking, spoilt brat—was an outsider there all his teenage years until he left Muzaffarabad to attend the Long Course at Pakistan Military Academy, Kakul. Imran had been unable to find rest, comfort or happiness till he came across a place where he felt at ease with what he was—the Army. Soon, he decided to apply to the ISI for deputation. He was accepted.

The road had been nothing if not rocky but the enemy *had* to pay.

Right now, Imran could sense himself being pulled in two directions. His duty and his heart were telling him opposite things. A competent officer like him, top of his batch, one who had never even earned a simple reprimand, had suddenly started slipping up—and it scared him. Imran couldn't forget the recent conversation with Sonya, who now sat in front of him, fiddling with her white MacBook Pro.

It was a few days ago, when Imran was accompanying Sonya to write a story on how cross-border shelling forced schools to stay closed and thus deleteriously impacted the primary education in the border districts of India and Pakistan. As Sonya had gotten busy talking with the local kids, Imran had sneaked away to an isolated corner to talk to his superiors about a routine touching-base task.

Imran had been talking to his counterpart in PoK and was in the process of issuing safe routes for another wave of infiltrators when Sonya had caught him with his pants down.

'Imran! You just said the word "ISI" on the phone?' Sonya had narrowed her eyes and whispered disbelievingly. 'What the hell?'

Imran had felt the ground slipping beneath his feet—how could he have been so careless? Not only did he not notice Sonya coming towards him, but he also used the name of the organisation he worked for. Imran almost kicked himself—Sonya was doing things to his mental guard, things which could expose him, or worse, get him killed.

He was about to drop it all and make a dash for it before Sonya went and alerted Indian authorities, when he was struck by sudden inspiration.

'Yes, the ISI,' he had blinked innocently, 'what's wrong?'

Sonya had stared at him with her mouth open, too surprised to react. '*Who* are you talking to?'

'I'm just talking to a few friends from the Indian Statistical Institute in Kolkata. I needed some data about education statistics in Kashmir,' Imran announced casually. He gave her a hurt look and then returned to his call, muttering, 'Can't a man ask for some information so he could counsel you better on this story?'

Sonya wasn't really convinced. A part of her, which had been telling her there was more to Imran than met the eye, was battling her perception that she was with a man so pure of heart that he actually thought the ISI meant 'Indian Statistical Institute' in a cell phone conversation being held 18 kilometres from the Line of Control.

She had apologised, though reluctantly, and left him alone—a fault for which she would soon pay.

Unforgettable images of Imran's family's lifeless bodies brought him back to the present. He shook off the memories with an aggressive shrug.

At that point, he heard a faint, rhythmic clicking in the distance, which made him feel drowsy. Sonya had begun to type out an email to the South Asia bureau chief, Deutsche Welle, Berlin, Germany—a casual update.

Subject: Re: Uri attack in Jammu and Kashmir

Dear Madam,

Responding to your mail, this is the information I have gathered so far from Uri, Jammu and Kashmir, India.

Uri has suffered severe bombardment at the hands of the PAF during the recently concluded Indo-Pak war. Twenty casualties have been reported by the administration and there has been significant infrastructural damage. Luckily, the dust has finally begun to settle in South Asia. The two nuclear neighbours are no longer at each other's throats—an uneasy truce prevails.

Coming after a possible nuclear meltdown, the ceasefire is being grabbed by the two sides with both hands. After a tumultuous month of utter madness, normalcy is returning and the state is limping towards a fragile peace. Offices have reopened, schools have started functioning, and markets have begun to finally bustle. The war effort, which had earlier sapped the life from this quaint hamlet, is now directed towards reconstruction.

It all started with the terrorist takeover of an Indian missile base in Andaman. Sukumar Saxena, spokesperson for the Indian Ministry of Home Affairs, told a media gathering in New Delhi that the perpetrators belonged to a joint team of Pakistani jihadis and Indian Maoists who were trained by a rogue officer of the Chinese PLA. A missile was fired at Pakistan, forcing it to go to war with India. After a mutually called ceasefire, fighting has stopped, but tensions still prevail.

Saxena said terrorists responsible for the attack were neutralised by decisive action jointly authorised by the Governments of India and Pakistan. However, sources say that the Maoist leader responsible for this missile attack has been airlifted to an ISI safe house. Moreover, the unnamed Chinese officer accused in this conspiracy is facing disciplinary action in China, though the People's Republic has declined to extradite him. Voices have also been raised towards curbing jihadi elements within the ISI who allegedly continue their anti-US, pro-Jihad rhetoric. An anonymous source within the Pakistani establishment has leaked a vital piece of information that implicates ISI safe houses in Pakistan as still harbouring Taliban jihadi fighters who have escaped ISAF's bombs and Indian artillery.

Hamza Siddiqui, Pakistan's National Security Advisor, has assured India that strict action will be taken against any ISI personnel found to have collaborated with religious fundamentalists in the past. Sukumar Saxena responded by saying that India would welcome any step taken towards peace. There have also been unsubstantiated reports of the involvement of an American intelligence officer in the affair, though no official source till now has confirmed or denied this fact.

Amidst this fresh conflict, people have almost forgotten India's first coup d'état. General Rohit Malhotra had earlier seized power and imposed Martial Law in India for a few days. He was not met by any robust resistance. This could be attributed to the short duration of his rule, the Indo-Pak war, and the numbness and disillusionment of the Indian public with the state of their contemporary political leadership. General Malhotra had already stepped down by the time those who were against him—for reasons political or personal—rallied their troops. The opening up of hostilities with Pakistan has kept the matter of India's coup out of the limelight it deserves, though it is expected that General Malhotra will have to face the music soon. However, the Government of India has initiated no legal proceedings against Malhotra till now, and he still retains his pre-coup rank and title.

In another development, local media assets speculate that minute quantities of a new element have been discovered near Uri. This element is believed by some locals to have 'magical powers', and is viewed by some clean energy R&D think tanks as possibly being the Uranium of the next generation.

I will file a report by Friday.

Regards
Sonya Loewe, Senior Correspondent

Sonya shut her laptop and turned to look at Imran. He had already fallen asleep on the couch, and was happily snoring. She did not wake him up. She knew they were supposed to go trekking the next day, and they could both use some rest before it.

Sonya rubbed her tired eyes, and prepared her mind for the trek. She wanted to make the most of this opportunity.

She *had* to.

Champ de Mars, Paris, France

10 hours into the invasion

The custom-made blue Citroën Metropolis slowed down as it approached the heavy *Gendarmerie Nationale* cordon spread around the Eiffel Tower. The car was only 10 feet from the checkpoint but displayed no intentions of stopping.

The gendarme on sentry duty eyed it uncomfortably, adjusted his assault rifle, and motioned the car to come to a halt.

Jean-Pierre Bazin, Assistant Manager of *Le Jules Verne*, a high-profile restaurant on the second floor of the Eiffel Tower, stood near the sentry to allow certain designated vehicles to enter. He moved to intercept, his walkie-talkie coming to life in the process, and stared at the windshield of the approaching car. He nodded in relief when he saw an oddly shaped sticker on the left side of the windscreen.

'Let it through,' Bazin told the gendarme, who shrugged and unhooked the chain.

As the car glided past, the chain was secured back in place. A few passers-by muttered amongst themselves unhappily, clicked pictures and resumed their frustrated strolls. Bazin directed the car towards the south leg of the tower, jogging alongside it in the process. His suit was beginning to get just a bit warm.

The Eiffel Tower complex was usually swarming with tourists this time of the year, but today it was eerily empty. The area had been cordoned off; the tower was closed to the public as both the lifts had suffered sudden hydraulic failure. The disgruntled crowds at the base of the tower had to be dispelled by the gendarmerie to aid maintenance workers. The Eiffel Tower, effectively, was defunct today.

The car came to a slow halt. Bazin reached for the door and opened it with a deference he usually reserved for visiting dignitaries or loaded businessmen. After all, his party had booked the entire restaurant for an evening. Whoever they were, they were nothing if not stinking rich.

A shining boot emerged from the car, followed by another, and a lanky, tanned man climbed out. He had a long, sallow face, an aquiline nose and thick brown hair. Like all others he had escorted today, Bazin realised that this man wore shades too large for his eyes, a hat that hid most of his face, and a muffler wrapped around his neck. Bazin asked himself if it was just the weather or if this man, like the others before, intended not to be seen, or remembered.

'*Merci beaucoup*,' the man nodded briefly and acknowledged Bazin's gesture.

Bazin tried to take a good look at him but was warded off by a cold smile beamed right back at his inquisitive gaze.

The man turned away and instinctively looked up at the Eiffel Tower, as if seeing it for the first time. He finally tore his gaze away from the tower to see Jean-Pierre Bazin—as the man from *Le Jules Verne* had introduced himself—point towards the main entry to the restaurant. Bazin led him to the special VIP entry. *Le Jules Verne* was on the second floor of the Eiffel Tower and had its own lift. As the public lifts were not working, entry to the tower was only permitted to those who had a reservation at the restaurant.

After a thorough security check, the man found himself in a lift. A few buttons were pressed and it started to rise with a gentle whirr. The man looked around to see Parisian lights coming into view. He suddenly shuddered and felt giddy. Heights—he could never get used to them. He clutched the railing tightly, and waited for the lift to stop.

It halted soon enough. Bazin opened the door for him and the man stepped out gingerly. He was led to the arched gates of *Le Jules Verne*. Bazin requested the man to go in. This was the last of the seven he had to escort to the restaurant.

Bazin's task seemed to be over.

The man thanked Bazin again in flawless French, though Bazin could swear he detected a slight accent. Bazin bowed and was about to withdraw when he saw a speck of dirt marring the man's classic, pin-striped suit. Bazin pointed at it, reached forward helpfully, and dusted it in a few practiced strokes.

The man smiled pleasantly as Bazin started to walk back towards the lift. Before Bazin got in, he glanced back and saw the man adjust his tie, exhale, and don some sort of a mask over his face. Before a curious Bazin could gawk some more, the man was gone, swallowed by the doors of *Le Jules Verne*.

The man entered like a jungle cat. He was used to opulence, but the views from the large glass windows overlooking Paris made his heart skip a beat. The restaurant was empty, save for a couple of tables joined together, around which sat a group of masked men and women he wanted to see no more of. The staff had been given unambiguous instructions not to intrude upon the special gathering until they were explicitly summoned.

As he stepped forward, discussions at the table suddenly stopped. He opened his mouth to say something but a calm, commanding voice greeted him.

'Ah. Blue is finally here. Welcome!' Red cleared his throat to garner people's attention—he did not have to try too hard; people were already tuned in to the conversation quite interestedly. 'Please join us, Blue. I believe we can start the meeting now. We have some *major* issues to discuss.'

Red's voice was even and radiated authority, though Blue could sense he was trying hard to grapple with something big. Red himself knew he had a major part to play today, and he knew he'd better play it well.

The man last to enter—Blue, as he was known to the Conglomerate High Council—moved towards his pre-allocated seat and settled down. He mentally clicked a picture of the panoramic view and focused on his immediate surroundings. The group was a strange sight—a collection of seven people from various walks of life who belonged to different nationalities, professions, and backgrounds. They were united by just one thread—they were all members of the Conglomerate High Council and sworn never to investigate each other's identity. Owing to the positions they held, they did know a little bit about each other, but no specifics were ever to be supplied—or sought. Hiding their identities was no big task, simply because they controlled those who had the means to unearth them.

The seven masked enigmas were all extremely high-profile names—the leaders and pioneers in their respective fields, countries and industries. Yet, they chose to refer to each other not by their names, but by colours. To the world, they did not exist. To the Conglomerate, they existed only as Newton's seven colours: Red, Orange, Yellow, Green, Blue, Indigo and Violet.

The High Council was seated around a collection of tables the staff had set up. 'Whose idea was it to meet in a public place?' asked Violet. He was a soft-spoken aristocratic youngster from the Middle East, the second generation in the Council.

'Only a public space can provide the maximum privacy, Violet,' Red remarked casually.

Red was not only the undisputed leader of the pack, but also the shrewdest amongst the wolves. A tactical genius, Red had realised early in his career that to be powerful, one needed to remain hidden. Consequently, his two alternate personas, which operated in different worlds and capacities, donned two very different hats.

'Please tell how this is a public place when you've booked the entire restaurant? We're the only ones here!' Green jumped in to the conversation. She was the rhetorician of the Council, perhaps because of her background. Coming from a long line of European bankers stretching back to the Renaissance, she was the de facto shadow owner of *the* global news corporation, which in turn had a majority stake in almost every other media house that mattered.

'Don't you think at least *some* privacy had to be maintained? We couldn't have talked about our plans with Mr and Mrs Harrington of Surrey having their romantic dinner conversation on the table right next to us,' Orange decided to back Red up.

No wonder Orange supported Red, Blue thought. Orange, Red's protégé, was the son of an Angolan diamond merchant whose business had been about to fail when Red stepped in and bought the entire operation. It was rumoured that the CEO position of a Fortune-500 company Orange currently held owed much to Red's recommending him to the Harvard Business School a long time ago and then supervising his meteoric rise. Blue knew how Orange was the classic example of how anyone, given the required drive, skills and talent, could rise within the ranks of the Conglomerate.

'And whose idea was it to mess up the elevators of the Eiffel Tower?' cut in Blue, having made himself comfortable over a glass of 2006 Bourgogne Chardonnay. Blue, whose family was one of the first to administer Australia, was the scientific liaison for the group. A trained scientist, he headed the research and development division of the Conglomerate—which effectively meant he directed almost all R&D activities undertaken by most major corporations around the world.

'Well, we just ensured both the lifts suffered some minor malfunctions,' said Indigo as she smiled innocently. She was the scion to one of the largest underworld families of South-East Asia, and connected as much to the Politburo of a global superpower as she was to the Yakuza and the Triads.

'Why?' asked Yellow. Yellow was the thickest of the group. The second-in-command of a notorious drug cartel, his membership relied on his shrewd father's erstwhile position as a major military player in a Latin American nation.

'You know why,' muttered Red.

'It's all about exclusion, is it not? No one else should be allowed to scale these heights because we have been able to.' Green mocked.

'Precisely,' said Yellow.

'It keeps us where we are,' nodded Orange.

'More importantly, it keeps *them* where *they* are,' smiled Violet, and reached for a croissant.

Red, having found the right words to tell them what was bothering him, gently slapped the table with his right hand and said, 'I have an important announcement to make.'

Everyone immediately stopped talking and looked at Red, their curiosity piqued by the uneasy edge in his usually calm voice.

'Red, what happened?' Green asked.

'We have...' Red replied with an eerie calmness, 'we have a Genetic Incursion.'

Someone dropped a glass.

It hit the white table cloth with a dull thud. The glass did not break but the contents spilled over. A waiter peeked in from a corner but was shooed away by an arrogant hand gesture.

'What?'

'Yes. We have recorded a Genetic Incursion,' Red repeated in a voice he fought to keep even.

'Where?' asked Violet.

'India,' Red replied, stretching his legs, 'Delhi.'

Yellow was aghast—even he understood what was happening. 'What...when...how...' he asked warily before his voice lapsed into stunned silence.

Green muttered an obscenity, but then stopped mid-sentence. It hit her that she had to be more concerned with damage control, and even more importantly, how to use these occurrences to the best of her advantage. 'What will happen now?'

'Simple,' Red replied laconically, 'we become them.'

'This will be disastrous!'

'But it is not possible! No one can know what these genetic markers are. No one has that sort of technology!'

'No one,' remarked Red, '...except the Qa'haQ.'

It was silent enough to hear a pin drop.

'But they are a helpful, benevolent race, are they not?' spluttered Green.

'Then *why* are they doing this?' countered Indigo.

The sun was, by now, bathing the group in a surreal glow—though it was no longer soothing or comforting.

'I said they could never be trusted!' thundered Yellow. He had found out whom to blame. He didn't like being in a position where things went wrong and heads didn't roll. He slapped the table in front of him with a raw fury that made Green jump.

'We had no choice. The Qa'haQ were here to help us. They gave us the chip. They gave us information on future stocks. They told us where to invest. They even gave us literary works ahead of their times! Could we have said no to their offer?' Orange defended them meekly. One of *his* self-help books had just topped the charts.

'If they were here merely to assist us, then why are they are meddling with our DNA?' asked a baffled Green. She desperately tried to form a macro-picture in her mind before anyone else did. It was what gave her power over others.

Blue's head swam at Red's words. A part of him quietly withdrew into his shell as he mechanically monitored the conversation around him. It still could not sink in.

Time flew by as Blue just sat there with his shoulders hunched, thinking about what could be done, and participated half-heartedly, that too only when he was asked something directly. Within half an hour, shock had given way to revulsion amongst the group.

A rumbling noise in the distance brought Blue back to the present. The fugue state was slowly ebbing away by now. Had it begun?

It was nothing but the two lifts—they had started working again.

This seemed to break some sort of a spell. The seven High Council members downed their drinks and stood up, some muttering to each other and some just lost in their own thoughts. Most of them had already started thinking hard about how to use this scenario to further their individual agendas.

'One last word before we leave. We need to ask our ground units to report on this. We will meet again soon to formulate a strategy. Blue, I want you to work on this,' Red said. 'You need to come up with some viable options. We meet soon—this time through a web conference.'

Blue nodded, wished the group farewell, and walked out.

A thought occurred to him on his way down, and he reached into his pocket. He took out his Blackberry and quickly typed a message to a man he thought might be vital in the times ahead. If the Qa'haQ posed a threat, then maybe someone who had had earlier dealings with the Qa'haQ might be of help.

He clicked 'send' on the cryptic message and wobbled towards the lift. Options, my foot, he cursed himself. He needed to tell the Conglomerate how to repulse an invasion by a highly advanced alien race, he raged to himself, and felt a tinge of vertigo as the lift started to descend. Paris no longer looked as pretty to him as it had when he was climbing up the tower.

Far below, unknown to the group, Jean-Pierre Bazin stood with a smug smile on his face and a chocolate croissant in his hands. He hummed a French country tune as he stuffed the croissant in his mouth, gulped it down with lukewarm coffee, and then removed his headphones. He unhooked a smartphone from his belt, browsed till he reached a folder, and clicked on a button.

The phone had received verbal signals from the tiny device Bazin had planted on Blue's collar when he had dusted his jacket an hour earlier. The audio file was swiftly uploaded to a secure server located in the CIA headquarters at Langley.

Now Bazin was finally done.

Genomics and Integrative Biology Research Institute (GIBRI), Delhi, India

12 hours into the invasion

'Aiyaa!'

Dr Revathi Balakrishnan swore as the shining I-card, which also doubled as her lab entry pass, slipped from her hand and fell to the floor. An outsized pink bag was slung over her left shoulder. Her lunch was held in her right hand, and she had been fumbling to swipe the card with her left.

Muttering to herself, she gently placed her purse on the floor and bent down to swoop the card up. Her Wayfarer spectacles almost fell off in the process and Revathi scrunched up her tiny nose in an effort to hold them back. Her kohl-rimmed eyes, instead of looking at the card, balefully stared at the purse instead. Despite the sterile, disinfected environment, she half expected to see something crawl up to her purse and get inside. Perhaps it was her paranoid multitasking skills combined with her germ-phobic streak that had made her opt for biotechnology as a career in the first place. If there were any bacteria, viruses, or protozoans around her, she would rather know where *exactly* they were, what to expect, and how to fight them.

She stood up straight and swiped her I-card again, this time successfully—the metallic door to her small lab-cum-office whooshed open to welcome her. She muttered a short prayer, as she always did before entering her *karmabhoomi*, and stepped inside. The automatic lights had already been activated by motion sensors. Revathi looked around out of habit. One wall was covered with a shelf that was full of vials and equipment. The other housed the experiment she was studying. The third, the one in front of her as she entered, was a huge glass window, against which stood her desk with its stack of yellowing books. She placed her lunch bag next to the books and swiftly made her way to the experiment.

It took her four short strides to reach the irradiation room attached to her lab. Revathi swiped her I-card again at the chamber entrance. Despite the white lab coat she was wearing, she could feel her nape hairs stand up, maybe due to the sub-zero temperatures in the chamber, which was hardly larger than a shower stall.

The walls were a glaring white. The five-foot one-inch Revathi felt her sneakers slip over the smooth tiles of the floor. She adjusted her glasses and carefully studied the metallic cylinder in front of her: about a foot in length and diameter, it was connected to a couple of computers.

Revathi typed in some commands at the irradiation console, and the cylinder—which had been slowly rotating and emitting a soft red light—beeped and came to a gradual halt.

She marvelled at the wonders of modern technology. With a few keystrokes, she had deactivated the irradiation mechanism that currently housed the tissue she was studying. The red light indicated that the sample she had kept inside the cylinder was being subjected to a controlled dose of artificial radiation, the degree and kind of which she was able to preset. With the light now gone, the radiation had dissipated and the cylinder was safe to be opened for observation.

She squinted at the cylinder. With a slight hiss, it parted in the middle, revealing the test trays. White vapours slowly disappeared as the sealed environment within the cylinder came in contact with the sterilised air of the chamber. Revathi bent her neck to see the tray better. It was then that it hit her.

Wait, she thought, something was not right. Instinctively, she cried out and jumped away from the cylinder.

She placed a gloved hand over her mouth and stared at the test sample again. The tissue, which had been dead and unmoving last night when she had left it, had somehow managed to mutate into a small, black reptilian torso—one that was currently thrashing as if infused with a life of its own.

Revathi backpedalled away from the experiment, trying her best not to panic, and then typed in commands to seal the irradiation chamber. Once the cylinder had closed, Revathi rushed out of the lab.

She knew she was required to immediately report this to the chief investigator—before the mutation was fully complete.

Revathi almost gagged as she ran across the glistening, polished floors of the complex—and stopped for a second to catch her breath and to rethink what had just happened.

Life in swanky biotech laboratories across the globe had prepared her for many strange things—but an undead, dancing reptilian body part was certainly not one of them.

Bahawalpur, Punjab, Pakistan
12 hours into the invasion

Agyaat leaned forward and coughed uncontrollably, his tongue poking out of his open mouth. Asthma had been making life hell for him. His nose was runny, he had a splitting headache, and he was having trouble breathing.

He hated the desert and its dust, having spent all his life in a rainy, humid jungle. Agyaat moved closer to the barred window of his room, peeked outside, and fervently hoped the change of air would do him good.

It was quite still outside. The angry, scorching sun kissed the dry Earth with a ferocity that made him uncomfortable. He was in the middle of a green zone, a forest, and he could still feel waves of shimmering heat assaulting everything around him.

Agyaat went to his rickety cot, the only thing in the room, and sat down. A small yellow flake drifted from the roof and settled on his pillow. 'So much for the interior decoration of ISI safe houses,' he muttered under his breath, and reached for a glass of water.

It was lukewarm, not cold, as he would have liked. He gulped it down and closed his eyes. He leaned his wiry frame against the wall, unmindful of the *choona* that might ruin his brown shirt, and his sallow face paled further as memories of recent events flooded his mind.

His source had been unambiguous—Yasser Basheer was gone, killed in a raid. Agyaat realised how lucky he was to have escaped the Indian army team sent to neutralise him. He had left just in time, thanks to a well-organised extraction plan executed by the ISI.

ISI, he thought, and spat in distaste.

Still, he owed this reactionary, pro-capitalist-and-Islamist intelligence service his life. Moments before he would have been totally surrounded by the Indians, routed, and thus killed in the Red Corridor, a disgruntled Agyaat had been contacted by an ISI handler in Nepal who had provided him with a way out. Though Agyaat had, by then, no love lost for the Pakistanis, he had been out of options. He accepted their offer in return for insight into leftist rebels in Pakistan's troubled Balochistan.

He was taken to a private airstrip near the jungle and put on a Lhasa-bound Cessna. When he reached China, he was given a new set of papers and booked on a PIA flight to Lahore. Agyaat had become a Malaysian businessman of Pakistani origin returning to the city of his birth. Once there, he had been whisked away from the tarmac itself, even before he passed through Immigrations and Customs at Allama Iqbal International Airport, Lahore. He was led to a waiting military vehicle, driven to Bahawalpur and thrown in this guest house. Agyaat had been rotting in this cell located deep inside the forest reserve since then.

He was not a prisoner, but he could not leave, either. He had tried once. The lone sentry had just muttered something in guttural Saraiki, pushed him back and waved his gun. Agyaat, getting the message, had pointed at his stomach in his defence and backtracked. As he now realised, he had been let off with a mild warning. Next time might be another story.

The furious sun peeked through the barred window, casting beams on the walls. A part of him was disappointed—with himself, the world, and his struggle. Another was bitter and guilty for what he had done. Agyaat was transported back to the fateful college reunion a few months ago; it had changed everything, and catapulted him from a minor rebel commander to a Maoist ideologue to reckon with.

A few close friends from college had been meeting at a place near him after a long, long time. Agyaat, knowing it was the last chance he would ever get to meet old acquaintances, had made bold plans to attend despite advisories against it—and how glad he was for having attended. For this was when Agyaat had come across Dr A.A. Suryakant, an old batchmate. That day, liquor had not only sharpened old memories, but loosened tongues. Not really aware of what Agyaat had become, an inebriated Suryakant—an Indian defence scientist—had unwittingly let slip the whereabouts of a cutting-edge missile and revolutionary software he had designed. Agyaat was sloshed, no doubt, but not stupid. Once obtained, he had put the knowledge to good use.

The ramifications had been disastrous.

Agyaat sighed at the memories, cursed himself, and rubbed his temples. He felt sick to the marrow.

He heard a noise outside and ran to the window—a rickety scooter screeched to a halt near the building. A new face was a rare sight. Agyaat inserted his feet into dirty-brown sandals, and went downstairs, hopping two at a time.

The sentry was nowhere to be seen. Perhaps he, too, had gone out to investigate. At that point, Agyaat saw a jeep parked in the distance—another new sight which made him hopeful. Curious, he thought; he had not heard it coming. Must belong to the new guard on duty, he assumed.

He looked in the direction of the *kutcha* road and realised the man on the scooter was cheerfully waving at him. Agyaat lowered his guard a little. The newcomer did not have a *fauji* bearing about him—the ones who could have passed the orders of his release or execution. Most likely, he was a messenger from the ISI, or from a Baloch insurgent group.

Agyaat started to walk towards him.

'*Lal Salaam*, comrade,' Parvez shouted out loud. 'How are they treating you?'

Agyaat's face broke into an uneasy smile. He raised his right hand with his palm facing the messenger as if it to convey all was well. He had no desire to talk to a lowly messenger. He had been hoping to talk to some general in the ISI or a Baloch tribal leader, not a carrier pigeon.

'I have a message,' the newcomer, Parvez, said between strides, sensing the lukewarm reception he had provoked. 'Let's go inside and talk.'

Agyaat nodded indifferently and pointed towards the guesthouse. The duo started walking in silence.

They reached the veranda moments later, entered the house, and, without a word, started up the stairs. Agyaat knew the message would only be delivered in private, not in the open. After all, his room was bugged—the ISI wanted to hear everything he said, or was said to him.

Back in his room, Agyaat plonked down on the cot and waited for Parvez, who walked in but did not shut the door behind him.

'Are you ready for the message?' Parvez asked good-naturedly.

Agyaat immediately sensed something was wrong. A stranger had come into an ISI safe house and the sentry had not yet made his appearance. His presence had been a closely guarded secret and it was unlikely that the ISI had suddenly started caring about his privacy.

Agyaat saw something emerge from the waistline of the newcomer's jeans. He opened his mouth to say something as panic clutched at his heart. The newcomer just smiled. Agyaat's eyes grew wider. He looked around for a weapon, but there was none. He lunged for the brass glass, hoping to somehow use it to defend himself. It was futile.

Parvez had whipped out a Colt by then and was pointing it straight at Agyaat's chest.

'What! What is the meaning of this?' Agyaat croaked, his throat suddenly dry, his vision blurry.

Parvez didn't reply. He just looked around the room, scanning for any documents he could take.

'What do you want?' Agyaat licked his lips and slowly got the glass in a position from where he could have thrown it. He was halfway through the action of hurling the glass into Parvez's face when it happened.

'*Bipolab dirgho jibi ho*,' Parvez said through clenched teeth and pulled the trigger.

The .32 slug entered Agyaat's heart with ease and came out the other side, bloodied and compacted. It embedded itself in the wall, just above a discoloured patch of paint. Agyaat slumped backward, half of his body falling over the cot. Parvez bent down to feel his pulse and sighed in satisfaction.

Agyaat would not survive the gunshot wound.

It was over.

Parvez quickly ran down, stashing the gun away. For him, this was only the beginning.

He headed towards his scooter, opened its fuel tank, and inserted a burning rag in it. Parvez then rushed in the opposite direction till he found a military jeep parked behind a cluster of trees, barely a hundred metres from the building. Yes, he sighed in relief, his extraction plan had been put into motion, thanks to the phone call he had made minutes before. There would be no going back now.

As the rag burned down and his two-wheeler exploded in a fiery shower of sparks, Parvez jumped in the driver's seat of the jeep—an ignition key was already kept on the dashboard. He inserted it deftly, revved the engine and accelerated towards the main road. He knew that the sentry would appear in another 10 minutes and hide the body, as he had been instructed. The ISI was very paranoid about such operations. Such hits were never to be witnessed by staffers with a low clearance level. This operational vacuum ensured that ISI hitmen would remain protected from betrayal, blackmail, bribery or sudden churnings of a man's conscience.

But before the sentry could show up, another development occurred, thanks to Parvez's phone call. In another three minutes, an Outside-Broadcasting van of the BBC Urdu Service parked itself right outside the guest house. Cameras, recorders and microphones thrust their way across the compound and darted towards Agyaat's room on the first floor.

BBC was not the only one to swoop in for the kill. Major Faisal, too, had sensed that something was not right when Parvez had failed to report in after the hit. He had immediately swung into action and sent units to the guesthouse. Unfortunately, by the time they reached, Parvez was long gone, Agyaat was definitely dead, and international media was crawling all over the place.

Miles away in India, All India Radio and Doordarshan had started airing confirmed reports that Agyaat, the terrorist India was looking for, had been assassinated inside an ISI safe house in Pakistan. The development was shared over social media to such an extent that it went viral within an hour. It was Op. EKIA Abbottabad all over again—this time aided by Twitter and Facebook.

Meanwhile, Parvez drove straight to the Bahawalpur railway station. He switched off his cell phone, making triangulation impossible, parked the jeep outside, and entered the station. Parvez ensured the newly installed CCTV cameras captured him boarding the Lahore-bound Shalimar Express. Once that was done, he jumped out of the compartment onto another platform where he knew no surveillance cameras were in place, and jogged towards the exit, navigating through the system's blind spots.

Parvez came out of the railway station and met a chubby, calm local, around 25. The man unhurriedly ushered him into a waiting red Mazda Carol and drove him to the outskirts of the city. There, he was met by another local, a shepherd, who transferred Parvez into the cargo hold of a livestock-carrying truck bound for Peshawar.

He had to reach his destination by nightfall, PCM thought to himself. As the Pakistanis focused all their might looking for him in Lahore and near the Indo-Pak international border, he used the Durand Line to exfiltrate instead, right on the other extreme.

He smiled; it was almost over. Parvez Chaand Mahmood, or PCM, as he was fondly called by his peers, was not actually Parvez Chaand Mahmood. He was not really an ISI officer; nor did he belong to the Pakistani Army. To top it all, he was not even a Pakistani *citizen*.

PCM was, in fact, the highest-ranking Research and Analysis Service (RAS) officer to have infiltrated the ISI.

White House, Washington DC, USA

14 hours into the invasion

'Damn it, Jason! What exactly is going on?' President A.C. Wilson slammed the receiver down. His infuriated eyes glared dead ahead.

He saw the doors to the Oval Office open. He knew who it was even before the person stepped inside. Wilson had summoned Jason E. Cartman, Director General of the Combined Intelligence Corps (CIC), the premier black-ops agency of the globe, to his office.

The newcomer, just a bit jetlagged from a covert transatlantic flight on board a fast, experimental military aircraft, cringed the moment he entered the room: the president was radiating absolute fury. Cartman's rotund body shook guiltily and a bald patch on his head gleamed in the sunlight from the windows. He may have been in his early sixties, but age had been kind to him, despite the fact that he had lived a harsh life in the rugged mountains of Afghanistan as a young American intelligence officer, one tasked with training the mujahideen against the invading Soviets.

Cartman rushed towards the presidential desk, sat down and imploringly stared at the C-in-C of the American defence forces. 'Sir, I'm sorry,' he panted, exhaustion writ on his forehead, 'but something needs to be done! We need to leave.'

President Wilson met his gaze, and a calm before the storm seeped through his soft tone. 'Leave?'

'Yes, Mr President. We need to send someone to Delhi with some critical information. ASAP.'

Wilson could not fathom what was going on inside Cartman's hard-boiled head. Had the man finally lost it?

He took a deep breath to prevent himself from blowing up and said, 'Jason, what is this? What in the blazes are you talking about? And what is this insane business in South Asia that you're involved with? The CIA just told me something so unbelievable I immediately wanted to see you.'

Cartman heard warning bells go off in his head the moment he heard the president mention the CIA. He gulped and immediately raised his guard. So engrossed had Cartman been in his own affairs that he had totally neglected to find out whether he was alone in the office with the president or not—a move that often ended careers. His worst fears were confirmed when he turned his head back and saw a man sitting in the shadows.

From the other end of room, Sean Miller, Director of the CIA, looked back at him. Miller sprang up from his seat, and headed towards Cartman. His wolfish smile did not augur well for the CIC, Cartman realised. He knew Miller would be relishing every single moment of this. The interservice rivalry between the CIA and the CIC was legendary. The CIC held the CIA responsible for forwarding its dirtiest and toughest cases to the CIC, and CIA perceived the CIC as a rogue, megalomaniacal, and ultra-secretive organisation that answered not to the American people but to unknown higher powers.

With a greying beard, Sean Miller looked like a hungry dire wolf; his cold blue eyes made him all the more menacing. He gently sat down next to Cartman and spoke slowly, as if chewing his own words. 'Jason! What a surprise. Good to see you, old friend. But tell me, is it hard for you to stand in this room and look at the very man who you tried to take down with your gimmick in South Asia—a man who incidentally happens to be the democratically elected leader of the free world?'

'What...How do you...but then it was...' Cartman stammered incoherently, his brain struggling to find ways out of this mess. A part of him forced his demeanour to be utterly confused. He knew he had to flawlessly execute the plan he had earlier formulated. There was zero margin for error.

President Wilson muttered through clenched teeth, 'Is this true?'

'The American people absolutely must know the truth!' Cartman spluttered.

Miller butted in. 'We have *irrefutable* proof that the one we killed in Abbottabad was the real deal!'

Cartman went silent, wincing as the words hit home.

'You goddamn fool,' the president spat out bitterly.

Cartman's shoulders drooped; all the fight taken out of them. 'I am sorry; that's all I can say in my defence.'

'Why, Cartman? Why?'

'I had to look for bin Laden or they would have killed me.'

'Who are *they*?' Miller finally moved in for the kill, his eyes hard. Having a member of the CIC admit to the presence of the Conglomerate was a big leap for him. Having the head of CIC confirm that the Conglomerate was responsible for a war aimed at taking down the American president was even *better*.

Cartman massaged a throbbing vein in his temple and buried his head in his palms. When he spoke next, his voice was broken. 'No more lies. I can't take it anymore. Screw them, screw them all to hell.'

Wilson and Miller merely gawked at the shattered man sitting in front of them.

Cartman confessed. 'I accept it. Yes, I *have* been a minor cog in an organisation called the Conglomerate.'

'And what *exactly* did you do?' Miller probed further.

'They told me to engineer a situation in South Asia...and I inserted Yasser Basheer into the area.'

'Why?'

'The Conglomerate wanted to meet some objectives. Taking you out of the game was one of them.'

That spooked Wilson. 'You wanted to assassinate me?'

Cartman was livid at the accusation. 'Of course not, sir. I would never have gone along with that; trust me. The aim was to weaken your presidency, and then give the chair to someone else.'

'But what has the president done to earn the ire of this Conglomerate?' Miller interjected.

'He's not that popular with the corporations, is he? I had no choice. They said they would kill me. What else could I have done when faced with such pressure?' With this, Cartman let out a nervous laugh, and moments later broke down completely.

Wilson could not believe his ears. He wanted to have Cartman arrested on the spot for treason, but he knew he needed him by his side now that they had bigger fish to fry. He pushed the rage out of his head, and focused on the task at hand. Wilson regarded anger as a sign of weakness, and knew it was the surest way to failure. He had learnt that on his first campaign trail a long time ago.

He tried to soothe Cartman, pushing a glass of water in his direction, and asking him to continue. 'Listen to me, Cartman, pull yourself together. This is important. Tell me, what were their objectives?'

'I'll file a full report within the hour, Mr President,' Cartman said and reached for a handkerchief to wipe off the sweat that had started to speck his forehead. He inhaled deeply and seemed to regain his lost composure. He looked at a flabbergasted Wilson and a victorious Miller and sombrely announced, 'We have bigger problems at the moment.'

'Bigger problems? Pray enlighten us,' Miller said in a mocking tone. He had not risen through ranks by being courteous to his colleagues, or by letting go of opportunities to score brownie points.

'It is true that I had been following directives from the Conglomerate...but that was in the past. At this moment, we need to unite and stop *them*.'

'Stop who?' a puzzled Miller asked. 'The Conglomerate?'

'No,' Cartman shook his head, 'the Qa'haQ.'

'The who?'

'The Qa'haQ, Mr President,' Cartman answered, as if the name was supposed to mean something.

Wilson looked at Miller, shrugged, and then turned back to Cartman. His head was beginning to ache again.

'Who or what is the Qa'haQ?' he asked cautiously, rubbing his temples.

Cartman decided to cut to the chase. 'Mr President, how much do you know about *Area 51*?' He saw Miller shift uncomfortably in the chair. For the first time that day, Cartman felt like smiling.

Wilson froze instantaneously, before slowly answering, 'Only as much as you want me to.'

'Then you do believe in extraterrestrial life?'

Wilson almost slipped off this chair. This was preposterous. 'Hang on, did you just say *extraterrestrial* life? As in aliens?'

Cartman solemnly stared at him. 'We are not alone, Mr President.'

'Aren't we?'

Cartman had come prepared for this. A tablet emerged from his pocket and his fingers danced over it till he found the file he was looking for. Without further ado, he started reading. 'Let me quote from the cult classic *Chariots of the Gods?* by Erich Von Daniken. Willy Ley told the writer that "the estimated number of stars in our Milky Way alone amounts to 30 milliards. The assumption that our Milky Way contains at least 18 milliard planetary systems is considered admissible by present-day astronomers. If we now try to reduce the figures in question as much as possible and assume that the distances between planetary systems are so regulated that only in one case in a hundred does a planet orbit in the ecosphere of its own sun, that still leaves 180 million planets capable of supporting life. If we further assume that only one planet in a hundred that might support life actually does so, we should still have the figure of 1-8 million planets with life. Let us further suppose that out of every hundred planets with life there is one on which creatures with the same level of intelligence as *Homo sapiens* live. Then even this last supposition gives our Milky Way the vast number of 18,000 inhabited planets". Can you imagine that?'

Wilson raised an eyebrow. 'Whoa!'

Cartman took this as a sign that his point was being understood, and continued, 'Daniken then wrote that "without quoting Utopian figures or taking unknown galaxies into account, we may surmise that there are 18,000 planets comparatively close to the earth with conditions essential to life similar to those of our own planet. Yet we can go even further and speculate that if only one per cent of these 18,000 planets were actually inhabited, there would still be 180 left!" A *hundred and eighty*! Do you really believe we are alone?'

It didn't take Wilson much to assimilate the information. Like most Americans born in the 1960s, he had grown up on a healthy dose of *Star Trek* and *Star Wars*. Still, the sceptic in him wasn't satisfied. 'But we are *Homo sapiens*. No other planet can have the right balances between the various forces of nature which are required to spark an intelligent life form!'

Cartman was ready with a reply—or at least Daniken had been, a long time ago. 'Intelligence is not our monopoly, sir. Even Daniken questioned this. "Why is it essential for the planets that support life to have conditions similar to Earth? The idea that life can only flourish under terrestrial conditions has been made obsolete by research. It is a mistake to believe that life cannot exist without water and oxygen. Even on our own Earth there are forms of life that need no oxygen. They are called anaerobic bacteria. A given amount of oxygen acts like poison on them. Why should there not be higher forms of life that do not need oxygen?" Life need not be like ours to be termed as life.'

'But...!'

'Sir, most of the theories that argue for the *non*-existence of extraterrestrial life are either too mired in human religions or shackled by conventional anthropocentric thought that extraterrestrial intelligence *must* always be like us. They must look like us, think like us, behave like us, and live like us. Ridiculous! If, millennia ago, life was to grow on a planet full of say, sulphur, and gave rise to a life form that thrived on sulphur, then I dare say by now that intelligence would have thrived, created civilisations, and be light years ahead of us in terms of capability, technology and thought!'

Cartman turned to Miller, curious as to what his reaction might be. Miller's face was unreadable. He simply stared at a point on the desk in front of him.

Cartman chose to go on. 'Imagine how the White House looks to an ant. Should the ant say, "Hey, there is no life here. No ant colonies, no civilisation, just a vast space with random shapes"?

Wilson whistled. 'And you're saying that in our universe, we are the ants!'

Despite his reservations, and the storm of mixed feelings raging within him, Wilson allowed a faint smile to play on his lips, thereby conveying his defeat at the hands of Daniken. Deep down, Wilson knew he *wanted* to be convinced.

Cartman nodded, sensing his victory. He pocketed the tablet, and smiled. 'I hope now you will be a bit more receptive to my revelation.'

'I'm all ears,' Wilson replied slyly.

Miller, on the other hand, kept staring at the duo impassively, unwilling to share the joke. He narrowed his eyes, and without breathing a word or twitching a facial muscle, leaned forward to listen—processing, recording, and analysing every single word spoken.

'We seem to have made contact with one such advanced civilisation, Mr President—the Qa'haQ. They are a reptiloid, sentient life form from the Horsehead Nebula, and contacted the Conglomerate some years ago. Even I don't know the details of when exactly they shouted a hello to us. Anyway, their observers have been permanently stationed on Earth since then and have been aiding the Conglomerate with its objectives.'

Wilson's reaction was not unexpected. 'Even if I do, just for a moment, mind you, believe this ridiculous yarn you've spun, tell me, why did these Qa'haQ choose to contact a chimerical organisation rather than the democratically elected government of the most powerful country in the world?'

'Sir, you've answered your own question—precisely because this government is answerable to the people. The Qa'haQ wanted to keep their presence a secret. They were unsure if a democratic government could have done that, especially when all the data these days is in some digital form or the other—and thus liable to be hacked. Controlling digital information is no longer easy—WikiLeaks proved that.'

Miller looked as if he'd seen a ghost. Wilson, ever the politician, was slightly more reserved in his reaction.

'Moreover, the aliens also believed that if they talked with a nation's government, they might give that particular nation an upper hand in global affairs. And the UN can't keep secrets, can it?'

'Fascinating,' Wilson muttered, 'tell me more about the Qa'haQ. What do they do? How do they look?'

'For the sake of a word picture, the Qa'haQ resemble an eight-foot tall cross between a giant lizard—standing on two feet—and a Neanderthal.'

Wilson wheezed; he was afraid of lizards—a phobia he tried his best to hide.

'What are they up to?'

Cartman continued, 'Qa'haQ technology is genetic in nature. Theoretically, they can transform DNA—at least activate all the dormant strands in the chromosomes, thereby leading to rapid changes in any organic life form. I have received unconfirmed reports that the Qa'haQ were responsible for helping the Conglomerate come up with cutting-edge innovations. The microprocessor, aviation technology, the IT revolution, all are products that the Qa'haQ gave to humanity way before we were ready for them. They create a technology that aids them in their colonisation of primitive worlds. They travel to such civilisations and then deploy these innovations. These technological marvels are then reverse engineered and integrated in target societies by collaborators earning them a huge profit in this game. In our case, they enlisted the help of the Conglomerate.'

'And where do we fit in this?'

'Hmm. We have been at the receiving end, Mr President. 9/11, 26/11, Iraq invasion, civil wars, you name it.'

'What?' Wilson squawked. 'That makes *no* sense.'

'Think about it. It is all a ploy to weaken humans and to divide them into warring factions. To quote Ariel Durant, "A great civilisation is not conquered from without until it has destroyed itself from within." Yes, humanity has been infighting for a long time, but this plan aimed at increasing the number of global conflicts exponentially. The intent was to soften us up before the final assault.'

Miller could no longer control himself. He burst out with an intensity that surprised Cartman. 'What...*final* assault?'

Cartman shrugged. 'This is a conjecture, but this is what Red tells me.'

'Red? Who is Red?'

Cartman saw their confused looks and immediately clarified. 'He heads the apex-decision making body of the Conglomerate, the High Council.'

'Go on...I would like to know how this information exchange between the aliens and the Conglomerate has impacted our strategic interests and national security,' Wilson said earnestly.

Cartman swallowed, as if searching for the right words. 'Red...he told me...there are other human players working for the Qa'haQ.'

'Who are they?' Wilson queried, and looked at Red with a mixture of shock and fear.

'I was told that ISIS, neo-fascists, and xenophobic, white-supremacist groups are being controlled by the Qa'haQ.'

Virginia, USA

16 hours into the invasion

Basheer's head thudded against the padded seat. His left hand shot out to grab something as the car swerved again. He gave his driver an irritated look. Here he was, snugly sitting inside an armoured car, and it felt like he was in an F-16's cockpit during a turbulent bombing run over Baghdad.

He felt sick to the core, despite having rested at a roadside motel. The file he was reading skidded off his lap and fell as the black Chevrolet Tahoe rounded another bend. Damn inertia, Basheer thought and gritted his teeth; he hoped that the Punjabi profanity that escaped his lips did not reach the driver. He had a feeling it did, despite the spotless glass partition that separated the rear of the vehicle from the front—installed primarily to lend an *impression* of privacy. Basheer knew the car was bugged with hidden cameras to record every single action undertaken in company vehicles, for the darkest of secrets were revealed in such cars.

A shrill beep jolted him back. It was a text message.

He lunged for his iPhone, and his eyebrows shot up in surprise—so did his pulse. The message was from an unknown source. Only a handful of people had access to this number of his. Receiving such a message either meant his cover had been blown or that he was being contacted by a member of the Conglomerate Council itself. Both these situations brought him closer to one thing—his death.

He carefully read the message.

Genetic Mutation has begun. Qa'haQ? – Blue.

'Wait,' he thought—a message from Blue? The Blue? Why was someone so high up in the Conglomerate sending *him* a text that made no sense?

Speechless, Basheer shrugged, and reread the message, trying hard to see a coded meaning to the text. He was still engrossed in his cryptographic endeavours when he heard a faint hiss. He would have missed it had he not trained himself to smell and hear even the faintest of variations in the air. A slightly metallic odour drove him to action.

The car was cruising at high speeds now.

Basheer immediately reached for the door. Of course, locked. Damn central locking, he thought, and looked for something to throw at the window glass. Basheer rejected that plan of action even before it fully formed in his mind—he knew the windows were bulletproof. He changed his target to the partition, hoping that it would provide less resistance. Basheer thumped at it with all his might and then kicked it with his left leg. The sole of his boot cracked the pane upon impact but the partition did not budge. He shouted irately.

Hearing the sounds of this struggle, the driver, making a conscious effort, turned around and helplessly stared back at Basheer. The chauffeur wasn't human anymore—he was thrashing wildly and turning into a reptiloid anomaly right in front of his eyes.

The message suddenly made some sense. Basheer tried to get through the partition again, this time with a frantic zeal. His kicks and punches were proving to be futile. The chauffeur lost control of the car—he could no longer drive with his DNA being rewritten at an explosive rate—and the vehicle swerved off the road, turning turtle as it slammed into a tree. Basheer felt a rib snap, and was flung hard against the roof of the rolling car. When it finally came to a halt, the doors automatically flew open, and he had a small opening to crawl out of.

Head swimming, Basheer barely realised what he was doing. He puked on his shirt and then, without thinking, wriggled out of the car.

Basheer yelped in pain. His battered body managed to clear the crashed vehicle, and then the car caught fire. He summoned the last ounce of strength he had left, and dragged himself to a tree nearby. It was only then that he could force himself to look in the direction of the car.

He saw the lifeless, mangled body of what used to be his driver burn where it lay slumped on the front seat. He felt no pity for the driver—only for himself.

Basheer kept staring at his injured hand and then bellowed in absolute terror until his voice gave out.

His blood was grey.

Panchavati, Prime Minister's Residence, 7 Lok Kalyan Marg, New Delhi, India
18 hours into the invasion

General Rohit Malhotra observed National Security Advisor (NSA) Manish Ranjan squint at Cabinet Secretary Ajay P. Mishra with an earnest helplessness. Owing to his tactical brilliance, shrewd wisdom and closeness to the current prime minister, Mishra was widely touted to become the next principal secretary in the prime minister's office, making him an even more powerful man. What sent chills down Malhotra's spine was how the two men in front of him had reacted: NSA Ranjan was not prone to overt displays of the lack of absolute surety that he just manifested. For a split second Malhotra swore he could see a chink in Mishra's cool demeanour, and within it, he saw a feeling never associated with the cabinet secretary—pure, unadulterated fear.

The men were lounging on comfortable couches in a conference room that was the location of a high-powered meet. In attendance were the service chiefs, the top bureaucrats, and Malhotra himself—in his acting capacity as the chief of Integrated Defence Staff.

Prime Minister Bipolab Roy could sense the air beginning to coagulate right in front of him, and dived right into the discussion. 'This is the best thing that could have happened. I am glad Agyaat has kicked the bucket. He had innocent blood on his hands. Moreover, if he was caught alive, it'd have been another four years till the courts granted us permission to hang him. Good riddance!'

General Rohit Malhotra suppressed a wry grin as he saw Roy flinch under the trademark, sanctimonious stare of Mishra.

Mishra cocked his head to one side and spoke slowly, 'Sir, I still think that he would have been more useful to us alive. We could have learnt a lot about Maoist operations in the Red Corridor from interrogating him. He could have helped us bring down left-wing extremism the same way Chhota Rajan helped us fight organised crime.'

Malhotra wanted to nod in agreement but couldn't. L'affaire Agyaat wasn't the only thing on the minds of those present. General Malhotra had been doubly surprised when a call came a few hours ago to summon him to 7 LKM for a meeting. One, he hadn't anticipated any major development that would require such a meeting. Two, he was even more surprised at his inclusion in it. He was under the impression that his post-war career would consist of him tending to mango orchards under house arrest at best. He wondered at the severity of the crisis that had apparently made his earlier transgressions be forgotten, even if momentarily.

The NSA's voice cut into his thoughts. 'This shows Pakistan's duplicity in the War on Terror yet again...they gave asylum to Agyaat! Now the Pakistani DGMO says the culprits were rogue ISI officers. Why don't I believe that?'

'Ranjan,' the cabinet secretary countered, 'we are forgetting the regime change in Pakistan. I am sure the new quasi-secular government sees that the jihadi elements within the Pakistani establishment are as big a threat to them as to us...Remember the attacks on APS Peshawar and Bacha Khan University?'

The prime minister shrugged dismissively. '*Arre ruko*—this meeting is not about Pakistan. Something else is afoot...Mishra?'

Roy swivelled his chair towards Mishra, who bowed his head slightly and stood up. 'Gentlemen,' he remarked, 'you are here because a zonal office of the National Centre for Disease Control

(NCDC) has detected an extremely strange contagion. The report was forwarded to our 24/7 Disease Monitoring Cell. An emergency brief was immediately prepared and sent to the Ministry of Health and Family Welfare. The Health Secretary forwarded this to me.'

Mishra paused to clear his throat and reach for a glass of water. His salt and pepper hair and white sideburns gave him an aura of professorship that went well with his greying moustache and piercing eyes. He took a remote out of his pocket and pointed it towards a 42-inch plasma screen kept in a corner of the room. The TV sprang to life, showing an image of a quarantine ward in a government hospital.

'A few hours ago, a private hospital in Delhi reported a disturbing case. A regular patient of the hospital was admitted in a serious condition. His biochemistry was changing at a very rapid level and his genetic structure was rearranging itself at almost explosive speeds. To top it all, his physical appearance was also affected.'

Ranjan could no longer contain himself. 'How is that even *possible*?'

'That is undetermined as yet. But I assure you, it *did* happen. There is something you all should see.' Mishra pressed a few buttons, played a clip, and turned around to study the faces of those around him.

The clip was shot in a poorly lit hospital room. A human male, around 60, lay on a bed, moaning. He kept thrashing wildly as two pairs of hands tried to restrain him. The man was changing into something which, by all fair accounts, could not be classified as a human being.

Roy heard a few loud gasps, followed by a confused, shocked silence.

'This is for real?'

Mishra nodded. 'It has been authenticated. I have seen this myself.'

'Carry on, please.' Roy said.

Mishra continued, 'The patient was immediately shifted to AIIMS Quarantine Ward, as health regulations demanded. The patient is currently comatose—barely alive—and under constant surveillance.'

Mishra held out a hand and cautioned, 'I would have dismissed this as a freak accident had I not come across something that might explain what had just happened.'

'What?' Roy was suddenly inquisitive.

Mishra continued, 'We were in the process of studying this event, when we got another call.'

The bureaucrat played with the remote. The image on the screen changed.

'This is the video of a conversation between staff at Genomics and Integrative Biology Research Institute, Delhi.'

'Video?'

'GIBRI is regarded as a critical installation and is thus under constant video surveillance, pursuant to sub-clause 16f of the National Defence Act, 2016. This is a conversation recorded by a security camera. It was forwarded to us by the institute and *this* is what made me apprehensive about the matter.'

Without any delay, Mishra pressed a button and a clip started playing.

***

A large room. The camera is positioned high above on the wall; it is trained at a cluttered desk and a bulky cabinet kept in a corner. Doctor 1, a balding man in his fifties, is sitting on a chair and slowly typing something on a Toshiba laptop.

A few seconds later, a door flies opens and Doctor 2, a scientist in her early thirties, comes into view. She seems agitated and almost screams her first words.

Doctor 2: Sir! We have a Code Red in my Lab!

Doctor 1: (Looks up slowly, blood draining from his face) What? Are you sure?

Doctor 2: Positive! (Sits down on the chair in front of Doctor 1)

Doctor 1: Okay, calm down. (Hands her a bottle of water that she gulps down). Which project are you talking about? What were the parameters?

Doctor 2: Project Alpha12, sir. I was trying to locate the effects of cell phone radiation on human DNA. Overexposure leads to mutation!

Doctor 1: How long did it take?

Doctor 2: No abnormalities were reported till 2200 hours last night. Before logging out for the night, I accelerated the radiation dosage so dynamic models could predict the outset of mutation, if any. It seems that something in the atmosphere is accelerating the rate of mutation.

Doctor 1: How did it happen?

Doctor 2: I am not sure.

Doctor 1: Working hypothesis? Speculations?

Doctor 2: The radiation present around us—the radiation emitted from cell phone towers and the wireless signals that connect the cell phones we use with their network hubs—has somehow been amplified. If the situation remains the same, it will start triggering changes in our DNA within 27.6 years of regular cell phone usage.'

Doctor 1: (Sniffles but tries to remain professional) Suspected mutagen and prognosis?

Doctor 2: Mutagen is definitely EM radiation. Even low levels spread over time can do the trick if the current atmospheric conditions of radiation-amplification persist. Such radiation will mutate the human double-helix DNA strands into another configuration. Physical manifestations of this spontaneous mutation will include transformation into class Reptilia.'

Doctor 1: (Rubs his eyes) God, this is too much! Repeat all of it; I am having trouble processing this! Are you absolutely sure?

Doctor 2: (Frantic by now) Positive, sir. I was researching the effects of prolonged exposure to electromagnetic radiation in the microwave range on the nucleotide sequence contained within human DNA. But something has changed! Short-duration exposure caused no anomalies, but long-term exposure to that sort of radiation activated some dormant gene in the human DNA, one which resulted in instantaneous genetic mutation. Death may or may not follow—though I need to study the sample more for a detailed prognosis. For the moment, see this!

(Doctor 2 passes a cell phone to Doctor 1 and plays a video. The cell phone had captured a black, organic, gecko-like entity moving on the screen.)

Doctor 1: Hai Ram! How much time did you say we had? (He suddenly realises he is holding a cell phone and seems to flinch.)

Doctor 2: The dosage of radiation I concentrated on the tissue could be analogous to roughly 28 years of human time using a cell phone. This is catastrophic! What do we do?

Doctor 1: We need to warn the others. Make the call!

***

The screen went black.

Part II: Little Green Men

No one would have believed in the last years of the nineteenth century that this world was being watched keenly and closely by intelligences greater than man's and yet as mortal as his own; that as men busied themselves about their various concerns they were scrutinised and studied, perhaps almost as narrowly as a man with a microscope might scrutinise the transient creatures that swarm and multiply in a drop of water.

H.G. Wells

Uri, Jammu and Kashmir, India

20 hours into the invasion

The projectile smashed into Sonya with a sickening thud and exploded into a thousand tiny fragments.

Sonya had heard a bone-chilling, premonitory shriek before she was hit squarely on the head. She automatically closed her eyes, sank to the ground, and waited for the red-hot stab of pain that usually followed such shrapnel impacts.

It never came.

Sonya slowly opened her eyes. She was still alive!

She muttered a short prayer and tried to stand up—she knew this would be difficult. Sonya was glad as her body obeyed without a sliver of protest. She whirled around to face her assailant, her hand immediately reaching for her press credentials. She stared in the direction where the projectile had come from, and got ready to throw her body around.

A snarl died down in her throat.

Sonya found Imran standing a few feet away from her, another snowball waiting dangerously, tauntingly, in his hand. She eyed him uncertainly.

'Are you okay?' he asked.

Sonya was about to reply in the affirmative when she felt another snowball crash into her face again. It disintegrated and covered her jacket with powdery snow.

'Got you again!' Imran grinned triumphantly.

Sonya, dressed in a flashy maroon overcoat, felt a flash of impatience, which was then immediately replaced by relief.

'How old are you, Mr Imran?' she sneered, still stinging from the hit. 'We are here for a story, not this goofing around.'

'Come on!' Imran pretended to be hurt. 'You don't have to be a kid to have a snowball fight!'

'Huh? You're forgetting that I grew up amidst snow. Whatever you can do with snow, I can do better.'

Is she seriously challenging me, the Artillery man in Imran thought. The gunner in him focused on the projectile, guessed its weight and dynamics, and then calculated the parabolic trajectory, and was about to apply the right amount of force to send it flying bang towards her face. But then, he realised, she did not know who he really was, and that was exactly how it he wanted it to be.

He gave her a helpless shrug.

'Fine,' he mumbled, red-faced. 'The story it is, then.'

Sonya nodded a bit too coldly for his liking. 'That does sound better.'

Imran smiled weakly and scurried towards Sonya. 'I'm cold,' he muttered, and ensured his teeth were chattering.

'Oh.' Sonya walked to him, and playfully slapped his forearm, trying to compensate for her earlier coldness. 'Losing already? Let's sit down and have some *kahwa*.'

Imran forced himself to shake his head. He extended her his arm, bowed slightly, and used the best British accent he could muster. 'I say, let's walk around first, shall we?'

Sonya just nodded in response.

They were far away from Uri, with its bustling tea corners, handicraft showrooms, and antique shops. The mountain was covered with a thick blanket of pristine snow, and they soon found a secluded spot for themselves. They climbed the snow-clad slopes a bit further, careful to avoid the gorges, crevasses and precipices that were so common in these parts.

Imran climbed the mountain and Sonya followed him—they were trying to get to the top and click a good shot of the village from a decent vantage point. Sonya wanted to supplement her report on a Kashmiri village with photographs that would make her readers go 'whoa'.

Imran was, by now, furiously wondering how he had landed in this soup. A part of him kicked himself again. This was supposed to be a critical mission, yet at times he felt like a giggling teenager. Meeting Sonya had made his foray into India worthwhile, Imran confessed to himself, but it was distracting him a lot.

Four months ago, ISI had deputed Imran to cross the border and establish a base of operations near the LoC. Perhaps it was his record, his degree in Chemistry, or maybe his knowledge of local language and customs, that had ensured he was handpicked by the ISI top brass—and later asked to stay back in India.

He had.

However, a few days ago, everything had changed. This mission had suddenly become high-profile. Following a phone call from Dubai, he had walked to a small hotel nearby. A locker in its vault room doubled as a dead-drop location used by the ISI in exceptional circumstances. An envelope was waiting for him there, containing a watch and a piece of paper.

He had looked around to ensure he was not being followed, settled in a corner, and rummaged through the envelope. The coded message it had contained was simple.

Objective: *Locate, extract and transport 'Sinium' to Islamabad.*
Tech Brief: *Sinium, a new element, atomic number 109; classified as an actinide, sits next to Plutonium. Found in crystalline form.*
Info: *Sinium can be used as a clean fuel with a negligible carbon imprint—might be the answer to Earth's energy crisis. Deposits near Uri. Use the instrument contained in this packet to locate it.*

Rem: *Must not fall in Indian hands. Approach with caution.*

Following standard operating procedures, Imran had burnt the note right after reading it. He had memorised the information and strapped the instrument he found in the envelope to his wrist. It looked like a cross between a compass and a watch. The message had contained detailed instructions on how to operate it.

That was when his task actually began.

Post a rigorous search, Imran had finally stumbled upon the rough location of Sinium as evident from the levels of radiation it was emitting, thanks to the device he was supplied with. Since it was in the middle of nowhere, and Indian forces did not take lightly to Kashmiri youths wandering alone in the hills with strange instruments beeping on their wrists, Imran had lured Sonya into coming along—promising a lovely trek and breathtaking photographs for her next byline.

It had not been hard to convince her. Even if the tourist in Sonya could have refused this offer, the journalist in her couldn't have. She had said yes—which was why, hours later, she was trailing Imran as he negotiated the treacherous mountain paths.

Imran and Sonya inched across the mountains. Flakes of snow kept drifting out of the skies—making the view even more spectacular. There was white as far as his eyes could see, and snow-covered peaks provided an extremely romantic panorama, even if unrequited. A part of him felt bad for involving Sonya in all this, but her presence was necessary. Her being there with him made the needle of suspicion swing away. Imran, thanks to her, became another tourist guide helping a foreign reporter in the state.

In between careful strides, he furtively glanced at his 'watch'—Imran had an inkling that it was supplied to him by Pakistan's National Engineering and Scientific Commission (NESCOM), though he was sure the device was not of indigenous make. He had, on a few occasions, overheard his Battalion Intelligence Officer—a devout chap who refused to touch his scotch on Fridays—mention en passant something called the Conglomerate. This omnipresent organisation, if Imran's sloshed colleague was to be believed, sometimes liaised with the top brass of the Pakistan Army for reasons God alone knew. However, Imran felt that this was nothing more than a stupid conspiracy theory fed to young officers to give them something to talk about apart from national politics and Islam.

Imran stared at the device—it tracked the radiation emitted by Sinium and was bound to lead him to his quarry. The instrument beeped faintly and directed Imran to search in different directions—its finesse and craftsmanship dazzled him.

'Come, I want to walk towards that side. The view from there looks lovely!' Imran led the way and Sonya followed, absorbing the sublime beauty all around.

After an hour of trekking under the direction of Imran's wonder watch, they were almost there. The mountain passes and trails were steadily getting more dangerous.

'Let's go back, Imran,' Sonya dragged him back to the present. 'We've had the shots, and it's getting colder.'

Imran heaved a sigh of irritation and continued climbing.

'Hey, I'm talking to you.'

'Just a few hundred metres more,' Imran snapped.

Sonya gave him a quizzical look.

He immediately regretted his outburst. 'I'm sorry, Sonya. I just want to go a bit further. You see that little cave in the distance? It looks so mysterious!' Imran gazed at Sonya, who merely nodded unhappily, looking unsure.

They reached the cave, which was almost invisible from the main trail, and located right at the precarious edge of the mountain. A few feet away, Imran could see a long drop below. Snow covered the cave's entry and Imran realised that it was almost impossible for anyone to find except those specifically looking for it.

He almost jumped in glee, and then used a few rocks as handholds to hoist himself up—moments before the biting cold froze his fingers. The watch hand went mad the moment he entered the sinister cave.

Imran had found the Sinium.

The Oval Office, White House, Washington DC, USA

20 hours into the invasion

The hallowed portals to the office of the most powerful man on this planet were opened by a harried-looking Sean Miller. He poked his head in—without knocking—and muttered, 'May I come in, Mr President?'

'Come right in, Sean,' Wilson said from where he sat, gesturing at Miller to make himself comfortable on the chair opposite him. 'We've no time to waste on pleasantries. We have a world to save!'

Miller smiled strenuously, knowing fully well the president was being kind, and trying to put him at ease. He also knew he had to make amends for his earlier lapses and oversight. 'Sir, I have something for you—on the Qa'haQ!'

'On the Qa'haQ?' Wilson leaned forward and muttered, 'Finally! What about them?'

'The Qa'haQ have...' Miller's voice trailed off.

Wilson suddenly understood. Sean Miller was not a man accustomed to being kept in the dark, that too for so long. It was his job to know everything that was going on around him, especially issues pertaining to national security. This time though, he had failed—spectacularly. The Qa'haQ had made first contact with Earth and had contoured humanity's development without the CIA ever finding out. It had bruised Miller's ego in ways more than one.

'It is okay, Sean,' Wilson said. 'We're dealing with an ultra-secretive, omnipotent organisation. There's nothing you could have done.'

Wilson cursed inwardly. This was a bad time for the Director of National Intelligence to be on administrative leave due to a political scandal. He got up and poured Miller a drink. 'Here, this'll help.'

Miller downed the whisky in one go and looked gratefully at Wilson.

'Now tell me about the Qa'haQ.'

'Yes, Mr President. After our last meeting, I directed all the resources at my disposal towards finding more about the Qa'haQ. It's surprising how important, even crucial, information gathered by us from all over the world gets buried in the terabytes of data filed daily at Langley. We had received a report from our man in Paris, but we did not pay it much attention. It was only when I red-flagged some words like "Conglomerate" and "Qa'haQ" that this report showed up on our central databases. I assume full responsibility for this failure and accept any...'

'That will not be necessary,' Wilson cut him short. 'What did you find out?'

'Er,' Miller stalled and coughed, 'I think I can explain the cases of genetic mutation we have witnessed over the past few days. They are not freak accidents, despite what the lobbyists have told us.'

'Then what are they?' Wilson was quite visibly distraught at this new nugget of information.

'The answer is right here, sir.' Miller pointed at the file. 'Why don't you read it yourself?'

A flustered Miller handed Wilson a black file with the CIA logo and the words 'Classified Omega 3' emblazoned on the cover.

'What is this?'

'The transcript of a conversation one of our agents recorded.'

'Why are you giving it to me?'

Miller softly whispered, 'Please *read* it, sir.'

Wilson raised his eyebrows, put on his spectacles, and leaned back into his chair. He opened the file and felt the sharp stab of a paper cut.

He cursed and started reading.

After an hour, a wheezing Wilson shut the file with a thud and slapped his forehead.

He could not digest it all in one go, and shook his head in a shocked stupor. He had to warn the Indians.

At a signal from Wilson, his chief of staff reached for a secure line and dialled a number. Within moments, the Oval Office was connected to a flabbergasted, sleepy-sounding secretarial staff member posted at the US embassy in Delhi.

The last thing Wilson clearly remembered from that day was asking Miller and Cartman to get on a military transport bound for India.

Peshawar, Pakistan
22 hours into the invasion

He was no longer Parvez Chaand Mahmood.

PCM's previous identity was discarded the moment his assignment—exposing fringe elements within the ISI—had successfully been executed. Agyaat had been assassinated in Pakistan right under the glare of the media, and American financial and military support to Pakistan was in the process of being reassessed by the US Department of State even as Pakistan's Foreign Ministry tried (rather unsuccessfully, this time around) to distance the rogue ISI officers from the mainstream Pakistani establishment.

A few years ago, the CIA had realised that the ISI was not telling them the whole truth about their role in the fight against terror. Classified information—known only to American and Pakistani two-star generals and above—was somehow making its way to the terrorists. Vital convoys were being intercepted, targets were inexplicably absent during predator strikes, and funds were being redirected to fatten the coffers of those against whom such allocations were to be utilised in the first place. Having the CIA infiltrate the ISI would have been too risky. Exposure would have risked America losing a valuable partner in the war against terror—a partner they desperately needed to wage war in Afghanistan as the other border country, Iran, was even more antipathetic towards the Americans.

In an intense, high-stakes gamble, the CIA had requested the RAW (Research and Analysis Wing) to put an agent inside the Islamic Republic. A deep-penetration RAW agent within Pakistan's core establishment gave the Americans plausible deniability—and the Indians a chance to strike back. The idea had got the Indian National Security Advisor, a former head of RAW, all fired up, and he had approved this plan with gusto, despite the risks. The CIA had liaised with Israel's Mossad, which had been more than happy to process—and conjure up—the required documentation for PCM. For this operation, they had created a new identity for him, complete with a new airtight background. The cover was that of an ISI double agent who had 'pretended' to defect to Mossad—while giving ISI its first glimpse into the dark underbelly of solid Israeli intelligence in the Middle East. It was gambling the life of one man for critical intelligence that could shape decades to come. It all sounded rather ridiculous—*so* ridiculous, in fact, that it just could have worked.

And it did.

Once inserted, PCM had seamlessly blended in with the Pakistani intelligence apparatus, thanks to the CIA's ruthless efficiency, Mossad's painstaking thoroughness, the ISI's paranoid compartmentalisation, and PCM's own abilities to improvise and think on his feet. He was welcomed as a triumphant Case Officer of the ISI returning after a spectacular stint in Tel Aviv, and was immediately posted to ISI's elite SS Directorate.

For the past few months, PCM's primary objective had been to act as an acute observer and to locate the extent to which generals and politicians sympathetic to Islamic fundamentalism controlled the Pakistani policy-making institutions. He was to take minute notes, draw profiles, and then leave the country with one final act exposing Pakistan's duplicity.

PCM had just exercised that option. The extraction plan had been initiated by the RAW attaché at the Indian Embassy in Islamabad, thanks to a simple phone call made to an asset within the international media in Pakistan.

He had chosen the safest route out of Pakistan. Instead of crossing into India via the heavily fortified Punjab border or the even deadlier LoC in Kashmir, PCM had hitched a ride to Peshawar in a truck carrying supplies to the frontier town. Just as his idol Netaji had dressed as a Pathan and escaped the dreaded British CID, so had he, though in a different country and time, PCM thought and grinned despite himself. The best thing about PCM, as his superiors used to say, was his flair for languages and his 'stock' appearance. His fair skin, chocolate eyes and brown hair ensured that he could pass as Indian, Latino, Arab and sometimes, even a white person. This combination had saved his life more than once.

Once PCM reached Peshawar, he merged with the milling Afghan refugees. It wasn't particularly hard since daily-wage earners crossed the Durand Line quite often. PCM pretended to be an uncouth, illiterate adventurer-cum-worker returning home to Kabul after trying his luck with a cousin's transport business in Peshawar.

He scrutinised the surroundings of this terror-attack prone city, kept a low profile, and navigated using the landmarks he had been made to memorise. He rarely spoke to anyone, or made eye contact. PCM made his way across the city, walking along the clogged main roads until he reached a nondescript madrasa. He stared at the structure: it was nothing special to look at, just a red-bricked, two storey building, tucked away in a corner, right next to a busy ammunitions market.

PCM stood outside the main gate of the dilapidated school, fished out a handkerchief, and wiped his face thoroughly. He was doing this for a few moments when he realised that a school teacher was staring at him through a window. PCM quickly stuffed the handkerchief back in his pocket, and walked away.

Two floors above, the wiry school teacher—a sturdy Pashtun with a bushy brown beard—saw a middle-aged man wiping his face outside the school and surreptitiously stealing glances in his direction. He instantly dismissed his class, went home early, and made a call from a burner phone he had been given for emergencies.

He dialled a number saved on the phone, and it was picked up after three rings.

No one spoke from the other end until the school teacher introduced himself. 'This is Gul Gulshan Gulfam.'

'Yes?'

'He was here.'

'Who?' The curious voice of the duty officer sitting far away cut through the line.

'He.'

'When?'

'He left 15 minutes ago.'

'Are you sure it was him?'

'Yes.'

'Good work.'

The school teacher hung up; his job was done. The voice at the other end, he realised later, had a strong 'South Indian' accent. He recalled the accent from old Bollywood movies—from the time when he could still watch them without being labelled a traitor by the Taliban. One of the reasons why he did what he did was because he felt the Talibs had ruined an entire society with their dogma and superstition. As a student of science, he had rebelled against fundamentalist doctrines, and had vowed to teach physics at moderate madrasas spread across Peshawar.

Like almost every other Pakistani, he did hate the Americans for what their drones did to his country, but unlike many other Pakistanis, he could also identify the deleterious impact of the jihadi mentality on the people and institutions of his country. He knew it first hand. His only son had been executed by the Taliban for running a music shop.

Meanwhile, PCM had started walking in another direction, smiling to himself. With his actions outside the madrasa, he had conveyed to RAW's only asset in Peshawar that he was still alive, and that the next stage of his extraction plan should be initiated.

PCM kept wandering around the city, continuously checking whether he had a tail. The cramped, noisy streets of Peshawar were no longer bustling. Terror, and the War on Terror, had taken an equal toll on its people. Many chose to stay indoors unless it was necessary to go out. However, the spirit of this fighting city, the capital of Khyber Pakhtunkhwa, was still unbowed—PCM could feel it in the roadside eateries, the markets, and the *chaupal*s, in what he would have called *adda*s.

With his shoulders hunched, senses wary, and gaze lowered, PCM kept pressing deeper inside the city, until he reached dusty, crowded Karkhano Bazaar bus stand.

A Pakistani Army picket just outside the bus station made PCM instinctively duck away into a nearby tea shop, which was half-empty. He sat down on a wooden bench, and quickly ordered some chai. As he sipped his drink, PCM studied the body language of the personnel manning the checkpoint. After a few moments of observation, he sighed in relief. The guards were not anxious, jumpy or paranoid: simply bored, he concluded. The fighting had shifted to FATA, thanks to the Army's Operation Zarb-e-Azb aimed at culling tribal support to jihadism. Peshawar had become a lot safer than it used to be.

PCM kept a 10-rupee note under the finished cup, and slunk out. He made his way straight inside the terminal, right past the picket. He did not even glance at the sentries, and nobody challenged him.

He went inside, scanned the timetables and went to his desired departure gate. Without second thoughts, PCM confidently boarded a rickety, half-empty bus bound for Torkham, the border town. The bus started moving westwards along the N-5 route, stopping only briefly at Landi Kotal, where PCM simply stayed put in his seat, pretending to sleep.

A couple of hours later, he reached his first destination: Torkham checkpoint. This was a border crossing which connected Afghanistan's Nangarhar province with Pakistan's Federally Administered Tribal Areas. Since it was busy port of ingress and egress, PCM knew he would be out of the reach of Pakistan's law enforcement agencies the moment he crossed over. He knew the Pakistanis would be looking for him, but hoped his earlier misdirection might have thrown the ISI off his scent.

It had. Pakistan had concentrated all its might on the LoC and the international border between India and Pakistan in an attempt to locate the rogue ISI agent. Fortunately for PCM, the Durand Line, the border between Afghanistan and Pakistan, was as porous as always.

PCM walked to the border post, and joined a serpentine queue of those trying to get into Afghanistan. He casually glanced around to see if the post was on high alert.

It wasn't.

The metal detectors were still malfunctioning, the Pakistani Army presence was still symbolic, and the ferocious guard dogs were still caged. PCM thanked the gods and inched forward. The pace was slow, but steady. He kept to himself, and avoided any conversation with those around him. When his turn came, he gently reached in his pocket, took out the required documentation, and wordlessly handed them over to the Pakistani border guards.

The brute-faced Frontier Force sentry gruffly grabbed PCM's Afghan passport, eyed him warily and asked him a few questions. He, rather unsuccessfully, inferred that PCM was a fellow Yousufzai since his Pashto used the softer sounds of 'sh' rather than the harsher 'kh' of the southern dialects, and waved him through. PCM could have been a mujahid or a mercenary, for all the guard cared. The Pakistanis, feeling the bite of terror, were more concerned these days with who was coming *in*. After all, the Americans were already out there to take care of those who exited.

PCM, trying to suppress a wave of sudden jubilation, walked into the Afghan border control and repeated the drill. In another half an hour, PCM emerged: he had crossed over into a neutral country from a hostile one.

He chose not to board the waiting taxis bound for Jalalabad and Kabul, and started walking on the highway instead. To many, he was just another Afghan labourer returning home, choosing to save some money by not buying a bus ticket. It was after a couple of miles that he started to falter. What if the school teacher hadn't conveyed his message, he thought. PCM was debating whether or not to flag down the next taxi to Jalalabad, when he saw something in the distance.

His heart skipped a beat, and he started walking faster. Moment later, PCM found a grey, battered Toyota Corolla pulled over at the side of the road, its dented bonnet wide open. This was the sign he was looking for. He whooped with joy. The driver, who seemed to be a reticent Tajik lad, immediately understood who he was, and held open the door for PCM without exchanging a word.

Registered to an Indian engineering company, the Corolla was PCM's ride to Kabul. He slid into the passenger seat, gratefully sipped from a canteen he was provided with, and fell asleep.

After a four-hour non-stop drive, PCM finally woke up to see an Indian flag fluttering atop a building. He had reached the Indian embassy in Kabul.

A man was waiting for him right outside the fortified gate. PCM nodded at the RAW chief of Afghanistan, who smiled and shook his hand. At a signal to the sentries, the concrete doors swung open, and PCM was driven straight inside. Instead of the diplomatic building, PCM was ushered into the Indo-Tibetan Border Police (ITBP) barracks inside the vast embassy complex.

PCM was so tired by now that he had entered a dazed state, reserved only for safe locations reached after a treacherous mission. He was given a fresh pair of clothes, the opportunity to shower and a meal comprising piping hot parathas with white butter.

Within a few hours, he was issued a new passport and put on an Air India flight to New Delhi.

The moment the flight left Afghan airspace, PCM went to the bathroom and wiped his silent tears. Home was where the heart was.

Panchavati, Prime Minister's Residence, 7 Lok Kalyan Marg, New Delhi, India
22 hours into the invasion

The room felt nauseatingly claustrophobic. It seemed to be getting smaller with each passing second. Most of the people present there would have laughed had they not been sure about the veracity of the message—and the competence of the specialists making that claim.

'My God!' The NSA Manish Ranjan was aghast at the mutation he just witnessed on screen. 'What just happened?'

'The unthinkable. Behold what happens to a human body once the mutation is triggered,' Mishra replied with a clinical serenity only a medical-doctor-turned-bureaucrat could have summoned at such a critical moment.

'How long does it take?' said the prime minister, his senses suddenly alert. Whatever was happening, Roy had to ensure it did not spread.

'As per the briefing I got from the Director General of the National Centre for Disease Control, once a human is exposed to around 27–28 years' worth of electromagnetic radiation, the process begins. Also, this mutation might affect as much as one third of the world's population...something to do with their genetic make-up. To top it all, someone or something is accelerating the mutagen,' summarised Mishra. With this admission, even his usually calm demeanour was beginning to fray.

'I...I still do not know how this is possible. *This* radiation? Cell phone radiation?' the minister of defence stammered, and then whipped out his cell phone and threw it on an empty chair nearby.

'I do not follow,' said the Health Secretary. 'WHO has classified cell phone radiation into Group 2B on the IARC scale.'

'2B? That's possibly carcinogenic, but not outright dangerous,' supplied Mishra, another man who knew his conventions by heart. 'Though, yes, the WHO *did* want to conduct more tests.'

'Tests which were then blocked by global corporations. Cell phones are no longer about communication alone. They're modes of advertising, tools of navigation, devices for tracking, and means of social networking. Not to mention catching Pikachus!' General Rohit Malhotra added.

Everyone nodded in agreement. A cacophony of 'The perfect money minters!', 'We should have listened' and 'What do we do now?' rang through the air.

The PM raised a hand and asked for silence. 'Ranjan?'

'Thank God we carried on with it and funded the GIBRI to conduct research on this, with whatever limited resources we had at our disposal, sir. I just hope it's not too little, too late!' Ranjan said haltingly.

'So what are we going to do about it?' asked the PM. For all it mattered, he thought, the scientific theories could go bury themselves in manure as long as the ground realities were controllable.

'I don't know. We cannot just dismantle all the cell phone towers in the entire world. I can see no...' He trailed off at the sound of a gentle tap at the door. The PM's Private Secretary (PS) rushed into the conference room. With a brief nod to the rest of the group, he crossed straight to Roy and handed him a slip of paper.

Roy, irritated at the intrusion, snatched the chit from his hands and scanned the contents. His eyes widened and he looked at the messenger quizzically.

'You may want to see her, sir,' the PS bent low and whispered in his ear.

'We're in the middle of an important meeting here,' PM Roy fumed. 'Why did you let her in?'

'She says she has some vital information regarding some sort of...what was it...err...mutation.'

The room fell silent as the words hung in the air.

'Bring her in,' Roy heard himself say as the information sank in.

The PS heaved a sigh of relief, nodded and rushed outside.

Moments later, the group stared at a business-suit clad American diplomat who had requested an immediate audience with the PM during an emergency meeting.

'Hello, sir. Thank you for seeing me at such short notice.'

'Mutation,' Roy decided to come straight to the point. 'You said you know something about the mutation.'

'Yes, sir, we do happen to know something,' the woman replied calmly. Her eyes shifted uncertainly.

'Who did you say you were?' asked Ajay Mishra, trying to get the conversation back on track.

'My name is Rhea Varma, sir,' the woman replied. 'I am the Assistant Counsellor for Agricultural Affairs at the US Consulate in...'

PM Roy was genuinely surprised by now and cut Varma short. 'A *consulate*? Not even the embassy?'

'Yes, sir. I have my orders. The president of the United States wants to talk to you—through me.'

The Minister of External Affairs was not pleased. 'This is highly irregular. Why wasn't the MEA informed in advance?'

'Security reasons, sir,' Varma defended herself. 'The president wishes to maintain a low profile here.'

The PM was not fully convinced. 'Even then, why is the ambassador not telling me this? Why is an Assistant Counsellor talking directly to me?'

Varma looked at her shoes and said, 'Sir, I have been asked to hand over a classified dossier to you, and convey that the president has dispatched two special envoys to brief you on the situation—they are already en route and would be arriving shortly.'

'Envoys? Coming to us?' the MEA secretary shot back. 'Let me call your ambassador to coordinate.'

Varma turned to his interlocutor. 'I request you not to. The diplomatic staff doesn't know about this visit.'

The penny dropped.

NSA Manish Ranjan slowly stood up from his seat and asked incredulously, 'The ambassador doesn't *know*?'

'No, sir. Only I have been briefed on this.'

'Only *you*?' countered Mishra disbelievingly. 'Pardon me; I find this hard to swallow. We must call the American ambassador right away.'

A spark seemed to fly in the room. In a single moment, Varma changed. The harmless, slightly flustered woman who had walked in a moment earlier, acting as a lowly messenger, suddenly became a lot more serious. Her eyes acquired a steely resolve, her shoulders went straight, and her hands crossed themselves behind her back. 'That would not be a wise move, sir. I request you to exercise caution,' she said coldly. 'This is a top secret meeting that must not come to public notice.'

The NSA was the first to notice this. As a career intelligence officer, he could spot an operative switching skins. Ranjan also knew that the next generation of American spooks in India would be those who could fit best amongst indigenous crowds and local populaces. Second- and third-generation South-Asian Americans, he thought, were the best intelligence assets for the US in the new millennium, especially when deployed to the lands of their forefathers. At least, this is exactly how *he* would have done it if he had such a diverse human arsenal at his disposal.

Ranjan decided to test his theory.

'Why is a minor diplomat telling us all this?' he began. 'I find this extremely disturbing. Tell me, how can you, as an Assistant Counsellor of Agricultural Affairs, know about all this? How come you are chosen to be the bearer of this information when even your embassy doesn't know of your presidential envoys' visit? Something fishy is going on here. Give me one good reason why we should believe you.'

The PM nodded in agreement, a confused expression plastered on his face.

'I think you should listen to me, sir,' replied Varma in a matter-of-fact tone, 'as I also happen to be the Delhi Station Chief of the CIA.'

Hybrosol Medical Labs, Virginia, USA
24 hours into the invasion

Basheer felt a strange, surreal presence up close—and shuddered when he realised that the feeling was somehow coming from *inside* him.

He tried to shout but an inhuman croak emerged out of his mouth. His brain burst into a hundred questions. What had happened? Where was he? And why was he enveloped in darkness?

Random, scattered memories of the past few hours assaulted him. Basheer's body went into spasms as he started to recollect the specifics of what had transpired. The car crash. The mutating driver.

Blood.

He tried to move but realised he was tightly bound to a bed. Basheer craned his neck and looked around but could not see anything. A knot of panic started to unfold in his stomach. He closed his eyes, tried to shut out the voices in his head, and inhaled deeply.

Basheer felt a sudden tingling in his right hand; he swore he could feel microscopic worms moving inside his body. He started to sob, no longer able to bear the pain, or the horror.

A lone teardrop ran down his sunken cheeks, and reached his parched lips. Basheer grimaced as his taste buds made sense of the liquid. The teardrop tasted strange; it was not salty, but sickly sweet, like the sugarcane gur he loved as a kid.

'Is this another side effect of the procedure?' he thought. Aching inside, tied down in a dark room from which he saw no escape, Basheer was thrown back in time.

Many years ago, Basheer had considered himself to be an extremely lucky man. He had a bright future ahead as a rising star in the Pakistan army, an amazing wife who loved him, and a beautiful daughter on the way. Everything had changed the day he had received a phone call from the base doctor with the results of a routine check-up that, it turned out, wasn't routine at all.

He was dying. His immune system was being ravaged by a cruel, unforgiving virus. There was no cure. His job, his family, his reputation and his life were at stake.

Basheer was a fighter, a man not prone to losing hope so easily. He had consulted the best hospitals, the best doctors, and availed the best treatments, until his money and insurance both ran out. His wife, Sara, was racked with trepidation that their baby would be born infected with the same disease.

She need not have worried: the baby never lived. Sara could not take this and died soon after. That was the day something wilted inside Basheer. It was then, in those dark times, when despair ruled his life, that an agent of the Conglomerate had approached him. Basheer should honour his family's memory by living, he was told. He could still be saved. The IMIC, or the Conglomerate, as it was called, was working on an experimental procedure to cure people like him. This was a virus affecting millions and it was high time the world's cutting-edge scientific research was pooled and directed towards finding a cure. Interestingly, it wouldn't cost Basheer a dime. He would just have to join the Conglomerate, and do what was asked of him from time to time.

Basheer was an intelligent man—and that made him afraid of dying. He knew once he was in, he'd have to serve one and only one master—the IMIC. There was no turning back, but then there was nothing else left to live for. He had relented, knowing that there were far worse things in this world than serving a transnational master who perceived humankind from the lens of purchasing power alone.

Basheer had been placed in the experimental treatment programme. Using a technology far ahead of its time, his DNA had been altered to target the virus. He was injected with a serum that would make him produce specialised antibodies that could take on the virus hell-bent on destroying his immunity.

Miraculously, this treatment worked. He had recovered within months.

Basheer had been injected with a Qa'haQ medicine to combat the virus—the Conglomerate had succeeded in creating a cure for one of the world's deadliest diseases and plans were afoot to market it soon. It was only much later that he realised that what he had been injected with may not have originated on this planet.

Basheer returned to the present as alien alphabets began to race inside his head. He squawked as the letters glowed in the darkness of his altered subconscious like tipsy glow-worms. He closed his eyes as an unnatural drowsiness caught up with him.

It was nightmare time again.

Uri, Jammu and Kashmir, India

24 hours into the invasion

The darkness beckoned.

Imran tried to take stock of his surroundings. The cave was not very big; it was hardly 20 metres in length and about 10 metres in width. The polished interiors shone so smoothly that they lent the cave an eerie artificiality.

He reached forward and touched it. The blackish rock was warm.

Imran immediately withdrew his hand. Maybe someone lived here, he mused, or maybe it was a storm shelter.

Sonya had climbed up by now. She stood at the mouth of the cave and frowned. 'I am not going any further. Who knows what might be inside?'

Imran laughed nervously. 'What do you expect? A yeti?'

His watch beeped thrice but Sonya did not seem to notice it.

'No problem!' Imran continued smoothly. 'Hope you don't mind if I go in and look around. You can sit outside '

'I don't know...' Sonya replied haltingly. But then, noticing a change in Imran, she mumbled, 'Okay...you go on. I'll wait for you right here.'

With this, she sat down at the mouth of the cave, threw her trekking rucksack to the ground, and starting rummaging through it for something to eat.

Imran pretended to be unhappy at being deprived of her company. He nodded morosely and plunged in, but not before throwing a glance downwards. He had earlier observed specks in the distance but had ignored them. Now the clear visibility and the height ensured that he could see quite far. Imran spied a cavalcade of vehicles on the main road. He also saw a few snowmobiles being revved as a mass of people prepared to make way towards them.

He noted the distance they were still at, and focused on the task at hand. Imran had barely gone a few feet inside the dark cave when he realised that the temperature had risen drastically. His eyes started watering and visibility was hindered by a strange reddish-brown vapour. Imran could no longer see the entrance of the cave, even though he was just a few feet from it. Sounds disappeared too. It was as if he had stepped inside the vacuum of a different world altogether.

Imran felt a deep unease. The cave walls started to glow cerise red.

He had to be hallucinating, Imran muttered to himself. How could rock glow? Perhaps it was some natural phenomenon.

Imran stood rooted to the spot for a few moments, and just when he had made peace with the fact that what he saw was a one-time occurrence, the walls start glowing again. He swore loudly this time, and instinctively started reciting *Ayat Al-Kursi*.

When nothing happened, Imran tore his gaze away from the walls, drew up courage with his chants, and started pressing inside, again. The cave walls were beginning to get narrower now. Imran breathed in deeply.

He started counting his steps. He heard a faint humming in the distance—coupled with a terrible feeling that he was being watched. He was about to panic when he saw the walls start to quiver. He stopped as he saw some random shapes appear on the wall.

He was horrified at first, and readied himself for a dash towards the entrance, but curiosity got the better of him. Imran drew in a sharp breath, and walked to the surreal shapes projecting through the cave walls. He touched them, afraid but inquisitive.

The shapes disappeared as soon as they had appeared. Imran stepped back, this time more puzzled than rattled. He decided to keep going deeper inside. Within moments, he reached the centre of the cave—again, random shapes and colours played on the walls, and again, Imran touched them, this time careful to do so in the same order he had before.

With a mechanical hum, a circular hole appeared in the floor. Imran, no longer scared, cautiously inched towards it. The orifice in the ground turned out to be an entry to a dark tunnel that extended deep down into the heart of the mountain. Imran strained to see inside it. Pitch darkness stared back at him. As he squinted further, he heard a metallic, grating noise emanate from below.

Imran jumped back.

Unknown to him, Imran had just proved his identity. Memory scanners at the first screening tier had assessed him—and he had confirmed his identity with the second screening by touching the colours and shapes in the correct order. Luckily for Imran, the trusting AI of the Genetic Transmutor now saw him not as a threat, but as a visiting Qa'haQ technician.

This proved to be its undoing.

Imran, in an attempt to investigate further, approached the opening and studied it further. It was big enough for a man to enter. He was in the process of deciding whether he should go in, when he realised the tunnel was not natural—it had a distinct metallic texture.

The walls of the hole that had opened up before him were slightly different from the cave walls. If the cave walls merely looked artificial, the tunnel walls were definitely so. They were jet black and had the same markings as the walls, though more pronounced.

He fished a yellow glow stick from within his jacket and threw it inside—but it fizzled out almost as soon as it went in. Imran tried again, but any attempts to throw any object that could shed some light on the depth and nature of the tunnel suffered the same fate.

Curiosity got the better of Imran. He sat next to the opening of the tunnel, and did something his mother had always warned him not to do—he thrust his left hand deep inside the hole without knowing what was inside.

He could only feel his hand grasp at a cold nothingness. Imran bent down further and started swinging his hand—eager for any touch at all. His hand came in contact with the tunnel wall—he was about to whoop in excitement when he was struck with a searing pain. The tunnel walls were burning hot.

Imran screamed. When his hand came up, he realised his index finger was scorched. His skin had been bloodied, just a bit—his thick gloves were now torn and burnt. Thankfully, they had saved his fingers from any significant damage.

Before Imran could back off, the walls of the cave started glowing again. An alien hissing filled the chamber. Shapes appeared again; Imran could swear they constituted some sort of an alphabet system he was unfamiliar with; the letters stayed this time. He ogled at the walls, his eyes wide with wonder. They reminded him of some sort of a digital console staring at him. After moments of intense deliberation, it occurred to him that when his flesh had touched the bare walls of the tunnel, it seemed to have initiated some automatic procedure to get to the Sinium.

It was then that it hit him—he was not supposed to go down into the tunnel. All he had to do was recall the piece of machinery humming below, and get it to emerge through this tunnel. For that, he had to decode the symbols that were now shimmering on the cave walls.

He got to work.

The micro-operations were taxing, but Imran was a trained cryptographer—it was a mandatory course for all ISI field officers. He kept trying different combinations of the symbols, touching them with his uninjured hand, and made notes in a small diary he always carried.

After what seemed like hours, Imran felt he was finally getting somewhere. He knew Sonya was waiting for him outside—she could come barging in any time. Imran took out his smartphone and recorded a video of the walls, just in case. Then, needing a break, he closed his exhausted eyes, and tried to rest leaning against the cave wall.

He closed his eyes, tried to picture what lay below, and imagined it rising to the surface.

Luck was on his side—it actually *did*.

Imran jumped up in excitement. He rationalised that his flesh, when in contact with the cave walls, had created a conduit where his thoughts became capable of operating the alien equipment. Maybe those who built the cave thought intruders would never be able to use their minds to operate this piece of complex machinery, he thought.

Within minutes, a sweating, panting Imran saw alien equipment rise from the bowels of the tunnel.

He gaped at it in wonder.

It was a black container—about three feet in length, and two in breadth and height, that sat atop a white table which seemed to be made of Italian marble. The container and the table emerged from the hole in the ground as if on antigravity beams.

A surreal glow filled the cave.

The heavy-duty lid of the container automatically opened as it came to rest—four feet above the ground. Imran tiptoed to it and peered inside. The contents reminded him of a DJ console he had once seen in an underground NYC club, except that this machine had in the middle a slowly rotating crystal. It was glowing silver. Moreover, the crystal turned in thin air, sans any support, just like the machine—it hovered a few inches above the machine, and sparkling beams of light shot through it and made a lattice pattern around the container.

Imran understood in a flash that this was the Sinium crystal. It was logical to assume this crystal was the power source of this machine. He touched the wall with his bare hands and imagined that the crystal stopped rotating and disengaged itself from the apparatus.

Within moments, the machine stopped working: its lights dimmed and the laser-grid seemed to power down. With the last laser gone, the Sinium crystal fell on the console, and tumbled to the cave floor.

Though Imran was intrigued by the machine, his primary target was the Sinium crystal. It was not exactly as the brief had determined, but it looked pretty close to it. Plus, it was clear this crystal was a power source of some kind, some sort of a fuel cell, since the machine had stopped working the moment the crystal fell out of its socket. It had to be the Sinium he was tasked to find.

Imran had barely picked up the crystal when he heard light footsteps.

Sonya had decided not to wait any more.

'Imran,' Sonya heaved, 'what the hell is that?!'

Imran cursed under his breath. Sonya assaulted him with a barrage of questions even before he turned to face her. Damn, he swore, how could he forget she was here with him?

'This cave is so weird!' Sonya began. 'You didn't respond when I called out, so I came inside. What is this place? You got something interesting?'

'I guess so,' Imran grinned as he held up the crystal for her to see; it was large enough to fill his palm. The crystal had stopped glowing the moment it was out of the 'DJ Machine'. Imran suddenly remembered the tunnel and whirled around to prevent Sonya from seeing the container and the table which had arisen out of the bowels of the cave. He needn't have bothered—the console was gone; it had automatically withdrawn back into the tunnel the moment the Sinium crystal was taken out of it.

'Looks like a crystal of some kind!' Sonya tried to grab it from Imran but he resisted.

'It must be some sort of...snow. Yes, snow polluted by some chemicals, most likely,' he lied. His mind was whirring by now.

'*Wunderbar*! Let me see.' Sonya finally snatched the crystal from Imran's hand and eyeballed it closely. 'Isn't this...?'

Sonya was cut short by a faint rumbling in the distance that got louder with every second.

Something sounded wrong to Imran. He looked towards the mouth of the cave. Maybe, he speculated, the security protocols guarding this installation were reacting to Sonya's presence, who had come charging in without being authorised by the first and second tiers of identification.

A grating noise accosted them again, like grinding metal gears, one which made Imran shudder. The cave, suddenly, started shaking.

Imran, without thinking, positioned himself behind Sonya, and with all his might, pushed her towards the entrance, away from the dark belly of the cave.

That was what saved Sonya.

The very next second, a cave 'wall' to Imran's right collapsed. It was there one moment; the next it just disappeared. Next, the ground beneath his feet gave way and formed an incline—the mountain itself rose to trip him over into the hole that had appeared out of nowhere.

Imran lost his balance, slipped and fell down. He felt himself being sucked towards the cave wall—which had ceased to exist by then. It happened so fast he could do nothing to prevent it.

Within a few seconds, he passed through it and emerged on the other side of the mountain, his clothes covered in snow. He rolled to a stop next to a ledge that led to a sheer drop. Thankfully, he stopped just in time.

He heaved a sigh of relief.

However, fate had other plans for him. The ground beneath his feet rumbled and moved again. Imran lost his balance for the second time in less than five minutes. He thrashed his legs and tried to stab the rock with the pickaxe he produced from his holster. Imran tried to arrest the fall, but to no avail. It seemed he was going down the sheer drop.

Imran opened his mouth to squeal as he began tumbling down the steep slope, falling towards the edge of the mountain. He wasn't able to breathe, and sounds got stuck in his throat. No air, no words.

As Imran rolled down the mountain and hurtled towards the edge—and a painful death at the bottom—something wonderful happened: he was able to draw in a rare, rejuvenating breath, and managed to caterwaul at the top of his lungs.

Islamabad, Pakistan

26 hours into the invasion

An inconspicuous man, black-haired and dressed in a spotless white kurta pyjama, climbed out of a green Land Rover Defender, and slammed the door shut. He was in his late fifties, of an average build, and had one of those unremarkable, easily forgettable faces. This was something he knew very well but did not seem to mind—at all.

The man started walking and then stopped. He realised that he had left his pack of cigarettes in the car. He whirled around, ready to let out a commanding shout, but the car was already gone. He muttered an expletive under his breath, unsure how the SUV had managed to disappear so soon into the crowded lane.

Shaking his head, the man turned back and started walking towards a nondescript building visible in the distance. Sometimes he chose to be dropped off a few minutes away from his office—and walked through the market. He learnt more about the current mood of the Pakistani middle class on this short walk than from an entire stack of the carefully prepared briefs his staff presented to him daily.

The man's starched kurta gleamed in the sun as he ambled towards his destination. Only a select few recognised him and hesitatingly salaamed as he passed; he ignored them. It helped that people at large did not know him. Or to be more precise, people who did not matter did not know him. Knowing the right people was a science—not being known to the wrong people was an art.

Brigadier Tahir Jamal Agha of the Inter-Services Intelligence was an expert at both.

A better part of Agha's life had been spent with the ISI—a powerful state within a rather emaciated one, and which had more than 25,000 active men on its payroll. The ISI had informants and assets spread all over the globe on accounts of jingoism, funding and pan-Islamism. Though the ISI recruited from the military, police, paramilitary and civil service, civilian employees could rise no higher than a Major. It recruited its top brass solely from the armed forces, a move aimed at cutting civilian flab and petty morality. However, above that rank was where sizeable profits actually lay.

The secrecy that the ISI maintained brought with it great power, responsibility and even greater profits. Among other things, Agha was responsible for bugging the phones, mobiles and emails of politicians, civil servants and industrialists. He was unwittingly privy to personal conversations, which had business tycoons, governors, chief ministers and secretaries eating out of his hands. It was not blackmail; it was professional advancement. However, what really set Agha apart from many others was his intelligence acumen. He always knew which bad guy to strike a deal with to catch an even worse guy, a policy that had helped him score from Kashmir to Chechnya to Xinjiang.

Agha kept walking on the now much less crowded road. A four-storey building with a fresh coat of paint came into view. It was still a five-minute walk away. The entry was through an alley hidden from the main road. Agha had taken this route thousands of times before. There was no sign of security anywhere near the building; it was guarded solely by a military checkpoint a few hundred metres from it. The building resembled one of those medium-sized business establishments in Pakistan that provided low-cost accounting services, which effectively meant that they assisted in tax theft.

In between slow strides, Agha kept reaching in his pocket for almonds, which he threw in his mouth every few minutes and chewed thoroughly. Almonds were good for the brain, he knew, and the chewing helped him think. He mentally listed the important tasks he had to execute that day. One, he had to somehow disentangle himself from the memo-gate scandal that had recently rocked the Pakistani establishment. He had merely been trying to have the age-old policy—to appoint only those officers who had never served in the ISI before to head it—repealed. His promotion was coming up and he wanted someone who had served in the ISI to lead it to glory. He knew he had to make a few calls to politicians and judges to correct the situation. Or the details of their intimate phone conversations would spill out to haunt their happily married lives and upright political careers.

Two, thanks to his contacts in Afghanistan, he had to inform the Americans about a secret meeting of Taliban warlords. Once that was done, he'd have to ensure that those TTP and Taliban leaders who were beginning to question his directives were invited to the meeting so he could personally address their concerns. Sadly, Agha would never show up—American drones would, instead. His political opponents would bite the dust and the Americans would laud him for securing important intelligence in the War on Terror.

Three, he had to send some more kids to the other side of the border. Things were getting too quiet for his liking. The surprise visit of the Indian PM to Pakistan had suddenly made the civilian government rethink making India bleed from a thousand cuts, as envisaged by General Zia, God rest his soul. One Pathankot was not enough—he had to continuously keep prodding, hoping for a response. After all, it was only with a sabre-rattling India in the neighbourhood that the ISI would get more power, funding and respect. Otherwise, the insipid fools of the Pakistani middle class might go do bhangra with the enemy across the border. He pitied those who wanted to make peace with the Indian-Zionist aberration that was hell-bent on destroying the very foundations of an Islamic Pakistan.

Four, he had to get Yasser Basheer. The bastard had double-crossed the ISI and defected to the Americans. He would pay for it, Agha swore. Also, he received word from a source in the Chinese Ministry of State Security that there was a foreign agent placed inside ISI itself. This was more than serious: Agha would have to weed this persona non grata out or it would set a dangerous precedent.

Five, he had to order his men to stop attacking mining corporations in Afghanistan. He had already been paid for it. He rubbed his hands in glee as he imagined his coffers in Switzerland swelling up.

Six, he needed to talk to Imran in Kashmir. The crystal must not be allowed to fall in the hands of civilian scientists; it was to be examined by the military first.

Brigadier Agha was so lost in thought that he missed the first sign that something was wrong. The sentries at the military roadblock had not saluted as he crossed them. They had just stared at him with curiosity.

Agha had reached the building by now. The main gate swung open noiselessly. Agha confidently started walking towards the small door at the side of the building which led to the main lobby. As always, it was Suleiman, a heavily built, moustachioed SSG Naik from Lahore, who was on duty. Agha knew him from the time he had commanded an SSG battalion. The bond between the two men was forged not amongst the filing cabinets of ISI, but in the snow-laden slopes of FATA and Kashmir, where they had shed blood together.

Agha looked up fondly. Suleiman was dressed in civvies, as regulations demanded. His light blue shirt and black trousers were spotless despite the heat. Agha smiled encouragingly at him. Suleiman stared back, his brows furrowed, and mouth muttering something inaudible.

Agha glanced at his watch and stopped dead in his tracks. His hands were greenish brown.

He gasped. What was wrong with him?

Suleiman stared at Agha, and his eyes narrowed. He seized the brigadier and politely said, 'Sir, are you okay?

Agha felt something move inside his stomach, something alive. This was insane, he thought.

Before he could take another step, his nose started to bleed. Agha staggered back—stunned.

His white kameez was, by now, spotted with dark patches where the blood dripped off his chin. It was as if a faucet had been opened in his nasal passage. A crowd was beginning to gather. Military police eyed them nervously, weapons drawn.

What was happening? Agha could make no sense of his surroundings. Was this a bad dream?

A few guards from the military post nearby came running. Agha was in no position to care. He looked up in a state of shock at Suleiman. The Naik had, by then, called for a medical team. Agha felt his face melting, quite literally, as a pain, the likes of which he had never felt before, hit him. Agha had been stabbed, shot, bayoneted, and tortured, but nothing trumped the agony he was in presently.

He saw his reflection in a nearby windowpane and yelped in horror. A strange entity glared back at him, a blue-green being with the face of a lizard, and a rapidly growing tail.

He shrieked again.

Agha did not know what was more painful as he hurtled towards the sudden end of his life—the angry, dark force that roiled inside his body, eating it from within, or the cold, suspicious stares from those who had saluted him for 30 long years.

He heard a gunshot near him, and eternal darkness fell over his eyes.

Panchavati, Prime Minister's Residence, 7 Lok Kalyan Marg, New Delhi, India
26 hours into the invasion

'What?'

General Malhotra heard the NSA Manish Ranjan burst out. Whatever was bothering the Americans, Malhotra realised, was enough to make them forget the age-old, time-tested, standard operating procedures of the intelligence community. Or maybe the American government had finally included India in its kitchen cabinet and declaring the CIA station-chief was the first of the benefits to reach Indian soil under this new arrangement.

'I know you're facing bigger problems,' Varma said, her eyes betraying distress that her professionalism concealed. '...So are we.'

'You know about the mutation?'

'It came to our notice quite recently,' confessed Varma, her shoulders stooping slightly. 'We're working on it. As far as I can tell, you will soon be introduced to two words: Qa'haQ and Bio-forming.'

'What do you mean?'

'I can't tell you much. The first is a proper noun and the second is analogous to terraforming, only this process is undertaken on organic tissues, not the atmosphere.'

'I still don't get the hang of it!' Roy exclaimed.

Varma whipped a file out of a bag she carried. 'I am sorry, sir, I was just asked to hand this over to you. You can direct further queries to the envoys who will be with you shortly.'

The NSA took the file from Varma and gave it to the PM, who had taken out his glasses.

Roy opened the first page of the file and started reading.

Office of Russian and European Analysis
NHB, George Bush Center for Intelligence,
Tscpt/14/FR/Ag080/++CDG/TS/0085857383
- start conversation; 7 subjects -

'What? The Qa'haQ have decided to invade Earth?'

'Yes!'

'But how?'

'Through genetic mutation, of course.'

'So you mean the human gene pool...'

'Compromised.'

'How do you know? What happened?'

'We have received word from our associate in South Asia. The Qa'haQ have deployed their weapon. The Genetic Transmutor.'

'What? How? Where?'

'One of our members, whose house was the first to receive the cell tower design the Qa'haQ gave us, started exhibiting signs of spontaneous genetic mutation.'

'And what exactly does that mean?'

'It means that there has been a change in the nucleotide sequence of the genome of an organism, in this case a human. Mutations usually stem from damaged DNA/RNA genomes. This one seems to be caused by radiation.'

'What sort of radiation?'

'Cell phone radiation.'

'But did we not give the world cell phones?'

'Technically no, the Qa'haQ gave the concept and technology to us. We merely operationalised it. And we erected mobile towers in every locality—which have suddenly started emitting something my science team calls Omtronic radiation.

'What does that do?'

'The Qa'haQ may not be as munificent as we thought them to be. I had our specialists analyse the emissions from the tower. It acts as a communication beacon that renders mobile telecommunications possible, yes, but another signal rides piggyback on the waves it emits. My people weren't very sure what it did but now it seems we do: it is a genetic rearranger. It targets human DNA and transmutes it into something quite different at a highly accelerated level.'

'How did this happen?'

'Each mobile tower we installed suddenly seems to be getting a strange feed from an unknown device located somewhere in Asia... this device amplifies carcinogenic radiation and causes spontaneous genetic mutation in humans!'

'Oh my God!'

'We should never have allowed them to give us the technology!'

'But look at what it did for us. It helped humanity grow so much!'

'You defend them still?'

'Hang on; you said that the radiation from the Qa'haQ tower piggybacked itself on wireless communication waves to change human DNA into something quite different. What exactly is this "something different"? I mean, what does one mutate into?'

'Based on preliminary reports, I'd say the Qa'haQ themselves.'

'What? Why on Earth will the Qa'haQ want us to become them?'

'Now that I think about it, I think it's the perfect invasion plan.

The invader doesn't need to do anything except genetically engineer the native populace of a planet in the invader's own image! There can be no resistance to it. One can't hate his or her own self forever, right? Perfect bio-forming, I say. Win without firing a single shot.'

'But...how could you trust them in the first place?'

'Why did you?'

'No, you did. We followed your lead!'

(Minor scuffle)

'Ladies and gentlemen, this is no time to fight amongst ourselves. Earth cannot be allowed to succumb like this. We need to talk to a few governments. However, word must not get out to the public or there might be mass panic.'

(Murmuring)

'As head of this council, I'm invoking my right to cancel the vote and arrive at a decision on my own. And I've decided. Blue, you need to leave right away and come up with a solution. The rest, please think about how best to play this: we need to repel the invasion, and simultaneously strengthen our global standing. I want ideas. Let's conference in 24 hours. Thank you for coming.'

(Silence)

- end of conversation -

ANALYSIS: Inconclusive

Ref: NSA/DIA.

Notes: Processing

Fwd: PMO, INDIA (by hand)

(This file contains classified information intended only for the recipients mentioned above.)

Roy exhaled and closed his eyes. He wanted to bang his head on a wall till both ceased to exist.

Uri, Jammu and Kashmir, India

26 hours into the invasion

Sonya suddenly felt alone, as if Imran was just *gone*.

She had cried out when she saw a gaping hole appear out of nowhere and swallow Imran. Without losing a second—or her head—she had extracted a small coil of rope from her bag, taken a deep breath and rushed inside.

With a few leaps, she reached the hole. The rock had been shattered at that point—and then snow had covered it, hiding the gap from view. Somehow, the snow had melted, and Imran had fallen out.

She ducked and emerged through the narrow hole. It opened up to a steep, snow-clad slope that ended in a cruel drop. And there was Imran, clinging to a boulder, minutes, maybe seconds, from slipping and disappearing forever. Sonya sprinted as fast as she could, and where the slope became too steep for a decent foothold, hit the ground, dug herself in and threw the rope at Imran with all her might.

Imran lunged at it, and somehow caught it after a fumble. He clung to it for dear life as he had stopped barely a foot from the edge. Sonya tied the rope to a rock and tried to pull him up.

But he was too heavy. She struggled, but he was getting closer to the edge.

Imran slipped a little bit further. His fingers were numb by now.

Suddenly, Imran felt a couple of powerful jerks. The rope went taut and he felt himself rising. He was being pulled to safety. Imran thanked God and almost wept with joy.

Soon, he was back on terra firma. Imran found out that he wasn't alone in the cave now. Before he could think or say anything, Sonya hugged him. He hugged her back, unsure of what to say.

Imran's eyes turned to his saviours. They were two Kashmiri teenagers, dressed in long, brown robes, with coarse wool mufflers wrapped around their heads. One of them clutched a wooden stick in his hand. Herders, most likely, Imran thought.

'*Shukriya* for saving my life.' Imran put his right hand over his heart and gave a slight bow. The two boys just smiled good-naturedly and pointed at the heavens. It was all Allah's doing, the two boys conveyed; they were merely His instruments.

The four started clambering back towards the cave, reached the freshly revealed opening, ducked and crawled back inside, muttering about a structure that wasn't here till last week. The cave looked much less menacing now. The vapours had dissipated, the walls looked normal, and the shapes had disappeared. The group walked all the way to the original mouth of the cave through which Imran had first entered, and emerged on the other side. Imran limped at the rear—his leg was bleeding by now. The two lads helped carry him out, talking to themselves in rapid Gojari.

When they were out on the other side—back to a somewhat gentler slope that led down—one of the boys looked at Sonya and spoke up with hesitation, 'You must leave now. This area is not safe. *Fauji* patrols come here often.'

Sonya was confused. She shot back, 'So?'

Before the boy could open his mouth to explain, Imran realised what he meant and his eyes turned sorrowful. He placed a gentle, reassuring hand on the boy's shoulders, and said, 'Relax. We are the press, you see. They...'

A shout made him stop and turn around. The people who Imran had seen in the distance had reached them.

*Khaki*s.

Sonya sensed a dozen guns trained on her. She spied three stars on the shoulders of the gaunt, strapping man walking towards her with a slight frown on his face. He was an inspector of the Jammu and Kashmir police, she could make out by the epaulettes.

'You!' Inspector Mohammad Mir barked and pointed at Imran before Sonya could say anything. 'Get lost! This is government property.' Mir was attached to the CID of Jammu and Kashmir Police, and had been tasked with sanitising this area.

Sonya flared up. A public servant talking to her this way was more than what the First World citizen in her could swallow.

'You've no right to use that tone with us!' she thundered.

Mir turned and shamelessly leered at her. 'And...you are?'

'Sonya Loewe, international media,' a defiant Sonya snapped as she flashed her Press I-card at the Inspector. Imran visibly shrank back—he wanted to have no trouble with the authorities. It was the fastest way to blow his cover.

Inspector Mir studied the press card thoroughly, and softened his tone. Bloody foreigners, he thought. They think they own this place.

'Look, Madam,' Mir tried a different approach, 'I am giving you a formal warning. The SSP has ordered this area to be brought under police control immediately. Please leave now or I will be forced to arrest you...'

'This is private land,' one of the boys drew up the courage to interject.

Mir clenched his teeth—his eyes went hard. However, before he could do anything, a deferential constable who accompanied him thrust a beeping phone into his hands and muttered a respectful, '*Janaab*! Superintendent *Sa'ab*!'

Mir dropped his belligerence and lunged for the receiver. His body language underwent a drastic transformation, Sonya noted to her amusement. From a haughty, arrogant man, Mir became a humble, soft-spoken hunchback while talking to his senior, even on the phone. Taking advantage of the sudden vacuum, Imran inched closer to Sonya, took her hand and muttered something in her ear.

That was when two things happened simultaneously. It started to snow again, and another flurry of vehicles reached the group. When zeroing in on Imran and Sonya, the policemen had created such a ruckus that it looked quite menacing from a distance. A Rashtriya Rifles (Grenadiers) platoon was on patrol and Lieutenant K.P. Meitei, the squad leader, had decided to investigate. He thought it might be an encounter and had come to lend a helping hand.

Lt. Meitei hurried towards the group. Mir was still talking on the phone, but managed to eye the army men with distrust. He was sick of ceding his turf to the olive green. The two boys stiffened at the approaching army units and dropped their earlier defiance.

'You guys okay?' Meitei asked Sonya the moment he reached. He had concluded that this was no encounter or ambush. Only the police helping some injured tourists.

A confounded Sonya pointed towards the bleeding Imran.

'Hamid, first aid,' Meitei motioned to one of the Grenadiers to bring out a medical kit.

The medic got to work. He cleaned and bandaged the wounds and gave Imran a painkiller.

'You'll be fine, *sa'ab,*' Hamid said merrily. 'Here, eat this!'

Imran looked at him gratefully and washed down the tablet with warm water from the soldier's canteen. He hadn't even gulped it down fully when the mountainside was filled with the sound of revving engines.

Within moments, five snowmobiles ground to a halt near them. A man in a green military jacket and brown jeans got off the first one. He was around 40, with a wheatish complexion. His lips were chapped from the cold. It was his eyes that caught Imran's attention—they were chillier than their sub-zero surroundings.

'That will be all, ladies and gentlemen. Please leave now,' he said softly, and gestured at them to disperse.

Inspector Mir, having touched base with his seniors, gave him a quizzical glance.

'That includes you too, Inspector. And you, Lieutenant. Your men didn't see anything.'

'You're asking me to leave? I'm from the CID, you mangy dog.' Mir howled angrily.

Meitei, too, was not pleased. He looked at the newcomer and snarled, 'Who the hell do you think you are?'

The man stopped where he was, and stared at the duo. 'Walk with me,' he said with a sadistic smile, addressing the inspector and the lieutenant. It was not a request.

The moment the trio was together, the newcomer placed a paternal hand on Meitei's shoulder. 'Son, I'm Lokesh Pratap Singh, IPS.'

The inspector's eyes widened in surprise. 'This is no longer a state subject. The Centre is involved now. Your men will immediately withdraw. This area is under the supervision of the Research and Analysis Wing now. And no, don't salute!'

The inspector, his shoulders drooping, nodded vehemently, whirled around and started walking back. He approached his men and told them to pack up. The lieutenant nodded as well, shaking Lokesh's hand and turning back to his troops.

'Let's go. We're done here,' Mir told his constables, much to their surprise.

The Grenadiers, on the other hand, acted as if nothing had happened when given the order to retreat. There was a time to question the decisions of the *paltan* commander—in hell.

Sonya gulped as Lokesh motioned for her to step forward. Imran was horrified to see his hands jerk up to her shoulders protectively, of their own accord—a gesture that did not go unseen.

Lokesh asked the pair, 'Are you together?'

'Yes,' Sonya replied defiantly.

'What were you doing here?'

'German media,' Sonya flashed her ID card. 'He's my cameraman. We were just taking a walk when he slipped.'

Imran felt like kissing Sonya right there and then. She just might have saved his skin.

'Sonya Loewe?' Lokesh read out loud from the I-card. His gaze switched from Sonya to Imran's right leg. Imran gave Lokesh a sheepish smile, while at the same time trying to project pain on his face.

Lokesh scrutinised Sonya's I-card and Imran's injury again. This couple was clean, Lokesh thought. They were just two people at the wrong place at the wrong time. Sometimes, love could get people killed. This was one of those times. He smiled inwardly—he, too, had experienced similar emotions in youth. Why blame them?

'Hmm...all right...You can leave. But stay clear of this area in the future,' Lokesh said, and motioned to his men to let the couple leave.

Sonya thanked them and helped Imran as he limped towards the main road.

Lokesh saw them struggling and shouted out to them, 'Take my snowmobile. Leave it by the road. I'll have it collected later.'

Imran and Sonya conveyed their thanks, and sat on the snowmobile. They revved the engine and sped towards the main road. Imran moaned, as the pain was now getting to him. Sonya shot the snowmobile forward, accelerating. Within minutes, Imran and Sonya reached their vehicle. Their hands subconsciously brushed each other's, and the two struggled into a waiting Mahindra Xylo, the taxi which had gotten them there in the first place.

'Help me get him in,' Sonya told the driver. 'He needs help'.

The man saw Imran bleeding, and loaded him in. He knew better than to ask questions. Information was always a dangerous thing for civilians in the valley, especially since the law enforcement and militants both, quite often, came looking for it.

Within moments, the car was racing towards a government hospital nearby. Thankfully, Imran was admitted just in time. He went into a deep sleep, having lost quite a lot of blood.

The next few hours were a blur. Sonya filled the paperwork, paid for Imran's treatment, and got him medicines.

After some time, when Imran was stable and sedated, Sonya told him that she was going out to get some fruits and that he should just try to relax. Imran merely nodded in drugged gratitude and fell asleep.

Sonya came out of the hospital, her coat pocket bulging with her prized catch. She navigated through the seemingly familiar streets she had heard so much about as a little girl growing up in Germany. A red pashmina shawl was wrapped around her head, and her eyes were fixed on the ground in front of her; she was careful not to maintain eye contact with the locals, the police or the military. She passed a few checkpoints, and a sudden aroma of roasting *kabab*s wafted in her direction, reminding her about her empty stomach. She went to a nearby cart and purchased a few apples, but did not go back to the hospital. Instead, Sonya took a taxi to her house, where she quickly packed a few essentials, and then asked to be dropped off at the nearest airport. Once there, she purchased a one-way ticket to Delhi, and boarded the last flight that day out of town.

Sonya thought she had pulled it off without being seen or noted by anyone, as she was instructed.

She couldn't have been more wrong.

Unknown to Sonya, the CIC South Asia Liaison and Deputy Station Chief of the CIA were holed up in the sat-recon room of the US Embassy in Delhi, tracking Sonya's every move over the past few days. The men had been following her via the ultra-high-resolution cameras on a US military satellite poised directly overhead. They also knew something that no one else did.

When Imran and Sonya had come out of the cave to meet Inspector Mir, no one had noticed Sonya surreptitiously stuff the Sinium power crystal—which she had taken from Imran's coat moments before he had pushed her towards a lucky escape—into the inner lining of her jacket and walk away as if nothing was the matter.

It seemed the Deutsche-Welle was not the only organisation Sonya was indebted to.

Hybrosol Medical Labs, Virginia, USA

28 hours into the invasion

Basheer roused himself with a start, and gasped for air.

He had been drifting in and out of consciousness for quite some time now. He saw he was still connected to a strange machine, and then felt someone had entered the dark room. A pungent odour assaulted him.

As he peeked through half-closed eyes, a silhouette towered over him and something cold touched his bare arms. Terrified eyes immediately flew wide open—he could no longer keep them shut. Basheer *had* to see what was plaguing him, and tried to wriggle out of his restraints.

'Calm down,' someone responded in a soothing murmur. 'You're safe now.'

'Safe?' Basheer's tone vacillated between disbelief, discomposure and anger.

'Yes,' came the calm reply. A voice used to being obeyed.

'What have you done to me?' Basheer shrieked. 'Why can't I see?'

As if in answer, Basheer heard footsteps going towards a wall. A switch was flicked and the room was flooded in light. It stabbed Basheer's eyes, forcing him to shut them again.

'Relax. No harm has come to you.'

'What is wrong with me?'

The man took his time to reply. 'The Qa'haQ mutagenic radiation is affecting you more than anyone else—though ironically, thanks to the rDNA inside you courtesy the experimental procedure, you are immune to its final effects.'

The voice contained a hint of amusement at Basheer's overt paranoia.

Basheer peevishly looked around, and tried to slowly open his eyes. 'Where am I?'

He saw that he was in a small room with no windows. The walls were plastered with white tiles and he was connected to medical equipment that he did not recognise.

'Somewhere safe,' the voice said.

'*Who* are you?' Basheer croaked with a dry throat.

'Someone who wants to help.'

Basheer's eyes had fully adjusted to the light by now. He saw a man with wavy brown hair and a thin face sitting on a chair right next to his bed—too close for comfort, yet too far for Basheer to lunge at him. Suddenly, Basheer was able to link the face with a name, and the conclusion made him recoil in terror.

'Blue! What is going on? The last thing I remember is that I was in a car crash...What happened to me?'

'We are investigating the matter,' Blue said and looked away.

Basheer felt a chill. 'What...what am I doing here? What do you want from me?'

'I am only here to help you, Basheer—nothing else.'

Basheer eyed him uncertainly. 'What *is* happening to me? You told me the procedure was harmless.'

'Mate,' Blue chuckled, '...don't be unfair. I think the serum injected in you during treatment might have saved your life today too. Look how quickly your wounds are healing.'

Basheer shrugged uncertainly. 'What do you really want with me?'

Blue kept mum for a few moments, studying the man lying spreadeagled in front of him.

'Okay, to be honest, I believe the serum in you will shortly react to the radiation...'

'And?'

'And that,' Blue continued, 'might provide us with an insight into the Qa'haQ's brain.'

'What *exactly* did you do to me?' Basheer asked, horrified as thoughts of grey blood accosted him.

'We were trying to create artificial stem cells we could use in humans transplants—using alien DNA on humans.'

Basheer was stunned into silence.

'Alien DNA? *Damn you*...you never told me the serum came from ET sources!'

'Would you have consented to the procedure had I told you the truth? Plus, our scientists did wonders with that serum. The recombinant human DNA thus perfected is a wonderful thing! It has the same overall structure, but the minute differences in nucleotide sequences give it wholly new properties. That is what we used on you—courtesy Red. A new age of eugenics!'

'Bullshit!'

Blue chortled. 'How else do you explain the grey blood?'

'Mutation? Haemoglobin deficiency?' Basheer clutched for straws. 'Medical sciences can explain...'

Blue did not let him finish. '*Cannot* explain it.'

'But...' It suddenly struck Basheer that others too knew of his freakish anomalies, and that made him even more nervous. 'How do you know?'

'Come now,' Blue said dismissively, 'don't insult my intelligence. You know we monitor our vehicles quite closely.'

Basheer shrunk back in horror. 'Then it was you who tried to have me killed!'

Blue placed a gentle hand on Basheer's shoulder. 'I wouldn't *be* here if that were the case. The driver just lost it—he became a Qa'haQ. I don't know how he was targeted thus.'

'I don't follow. How did this happen in the first place?'

Blue, who had been fidgeting with a black, diamond-studded Visconti pen till now, stopped. 'Red had an alien serum injected in your body, as you know. He said that would make you fight the virus.' Blue looked deep in his eyes and said, 'It seemed to have worked. What you *are* right now is a result of that experiment.'

Basheer was incredulous. 'But why go through all this trouble? For me?'

Blue just leaned back on his chair, calm. 'The Conglomerate did not do it for you but for *us*. You were our first *willing* test subject. We were trying to use alien technology to cure humanity of life-threatening diseases and then sell the medical treatments for a huge profit, of course. Think about the military applications of this procedure—the profits we could have made! Governments would pay billions, even trillions, to possess that sort of technology. Plus, Red wanted us to go ahead with it.'

'But why...why...me of all people?' Basheer mumbled.

'Heroes are made of ordinary matter...and right now, we need you.'

'What now?'

Blue laughed despite himself. 'You know more about the Qa'haQ than any man alive, thanks to your rDNA.'

'But I don't!' Basheer screeched in protest.

'You will, soon enough.'

'How?'

'Your unconscious brain is in the process of analysing and assimilating the rDNA inserted in you—which contains traces of Qa'haQ DNA that has now been activated by the radiation,' Blue explained. 'Yes, others will suffer, too, but they don't have Qa'haQ serum in them—those little doses of serum have now given you immunity.'

Basheer was silent for a few seconds. 'So just as small doses of poison can make one stronger, my immune system has been boosted by the treatment I received?'

Blue slapped an armrest in zeal. 'Exactly! Ergo, you might feel sick, but you will never transform into a Qa'haQ. On the contrary, you will become a resident expert on them soon.'

'So that I can disclose their weaknesses to you and you can use this information to make a buck?' Basheer asked bitterly, conscious of the fact that he was yet another pawn in a game he couldn't really comprehend.

For the first time, anguish spread over Blue's tanned face. 'You do not understand, Basheer; this is not about money. This is about survival. We need to fight back. With *him* no longer with us, you are Earth's last hope.'

Basheer moaned and sank back in his bed. He could feel the walls closing on him, making his claustrophobia stronger. 'What do I do?' he groaned.

'Go and warn the Indians—they can get to the Genetic Transmutor before anyone else can. It is located in their territory.'

Basheer opened his mouth to say something but could not.

Blue continued. 'I have a private jet waiting to fly you to Delhi. You *have* to go. We need you. *He* can no longer be trusted.'

The first part made Basheer anxious but the latter part made him even more confused. 'He? Hang on...this is the second time you have referred to a "he". Moreover, something just struck me—you said I was the first "willing" subject who acquiesced to this procedure. Who was the first?'

Blue didn't answer. He got up from the chair and started pacing the room.

'Tell me!' Basheer implored. 'Please.'

Blue stopped in his tracks and then turned towards Basheer's bed. 'You were the first one we tried to cure of life-threatening diseases,' he said tenderly, '...but there was another before you. The Qa'haQ had directed us to experiment with him...this time, the issue was mind control. The Qa'haQ wanted to observe whether a human would serve an alien master and follow him blindly if the DNA of such a human slave was changed bit by bit into a Qa'haQian one...' Blue dropped the bombshell.

Basheer started. 'There's someone else like me?'

'Even worse. You were merely a test subject for a life-saving medical drug. He, on the other hand, was a subject who was modified genetically and conditioned in a manner so as to remove every human emotion in him. He's an earlier prototype where alien DNA was directly inserted into a human subject with the intent of creating a perfect soldier-slave who obeyed instructions without question and was beyond the petty laws of humanity.'

'Then what happened?'

'By agreeing to it, we failed as humans, but succeeded as scientists...The prototype was ready for deployment. The Qa'haQ gave him a series of instructions and let him loose on the world—taking care to control his mind whenever he strayed from their objective.'

Basheer was repelled by this. 'Why did the Qa'haQ want such a being?'

'We earlier thought it was just a hyper-intelligent race testing the Faustian frontiers of knowledge...but I now suspect the Qa'haQ created this man to sow discord amidst humanity, and unleash suffering on mankind. Yes, even more than mankind had already inflicted upon itself with the artificial barriers of nations, colours, castes, religions, and creeds. Much, *much* more.'

'Why?'

'Don't you see? We are weak when we fight amongst ourselves. The Qa'haQ want a World War III—where our top powers destroy each other, leaving a battered Earth open for external attack.'

Basheer could not believe his ears. '*Ya Allah*! Why did you go along with it?'

'We did not interfere or bring this to light as it implicated us. After all, we helped the Qa'haQ create this monstrosity! Moreover, as Red convinced us, whatever this man did was horrible, but it somehow allowed our Conglomerate to register profits the likes of which we had never seen before...War is good for business, as they say.'

Basheer could no longer contain himself. '*Who*? Who is it?'

Blue sighed. 'Why do you want to know?'

Basheer gritted his teeth and hollered, 'I just do!'

Blue shook his head morosely, as if mentally washing his hands off this entire affair. He unbound Basheer's restraints, placed a hand on his bandaged shoulder, and remarked, 'We refer to him as Subject X/1/F".'

'X1? F?'

'"X" stands for the crossing of genes. "1" was his serial number. "F" stands for failed—the experiment went out of hand. We could not control what we had created. The being served its own Qa'haQ masters, sometimes not even them. He brought chaos into this world—more than what the human race was ready to handle—which is saying a lot judging by how destructive we have been for the planet. Yes, the wars he provoked were obviously good for business, but there comes a time when even a businessman must stop and think. This man...no, *being*, almost caused a nuclear meltdown.'

'Who...who was he?' Basheer was by now not sure if he really wanted to know the truth about his predecessor and what horrors he had unleashed on modern civilisation.

Blue laughed mirthlessly, himself horrified at what he had helped achieve.

'We call him X/1/F. You know him as Osama bin Mohammed bin Awad bin Laden.'

Air Force Station Palam, New Delhi, India

32 hours into the invasion

Squadron Leader Bishwanath Barua appreciated the swift decisiveness with which the convoy had moved out. He gestured to the sentries to seal the gates and turned back towards his quarters.

Barely a couple of hours ago, Barua—an ace chopper pilot with a master green rating on multiple aircrafts—had been summoned by Air Commodore N. Venkatesan, the Commanding Officer (CO) of the Air Force Station.

'Once more unto the breach, BB,' the dramatically-inclined Venkatesan had remarked to Barua with a smile. 'Once more.'

Barua liked the informal jokes his CO made. They put men like him at ease, provided them breathing space, and allowed them to give their best.

'Sir?' Barua enquired. He was the security officer of the AFS, and it was his job to handle such assignments.

'See for yourself.' Air Commodore Venkatesan had thrust a fax in his hands.

Barua had only glanced at it cursorily but had immediately grasped its importance. He opened his mouth to say something but was cut off by his CO.

'Yes, I know,' Venkatesan shrugged, '104 directive, all the way from *Raksha Mantri* himself. Go Protocol III.'

Barua nodded and tried to refresh his memory in babu-talk. With the rise in ranks came the chair of a military administrator in Vayu Bhawan or the Ministry of Defence (MoD). He knew the sooner he forgot the pre and post take-off checks of a Mil Mi-35 helicopter and familiarised himself with the Secretariat building, the better it would turn out for him. Barua recalled that 104 was the metonym for the Minister for Defence, whose office was located in Room Number 104 of the South Block in the Central Secretariat Building. South Block also harboured the Ministry of External Affairs and the prime minister's office.

Barua tried to make a mental map of the corridors of power—right opposite the South Block, flanking the Rashtrapati Bhawan, lay the North Block, which housed the Ministry of Finance and the Ministry of Home Affairs. Interestingly, just as Room Number 104 in the South Block was allotted to the Minister of Defence, Room Number 104 in the North Block belonged to the Minister for Home Affairs—two 104s that jointly oversaw the internal and external security of India.

Air Commodore Venkatesan had received specific instructions from the MoD. Barua was to receive the incoming VIPs, and ensure that their aircraft reached a secure military hangar. He was then to hand them over to a waiting embassy team. Protocol III meant no customs or immigrations were to be involved or intimated, no questions were to be asked, and no records were to be kept.

The painfully thin, good-natured Squadron Leader had done all he was supposed to do. An hour ago, Barua had contacted the Air Traffic Control about an incoming VIP transport, told them to give it priority to land, and had ordered the station's main gate to allow certain embassy vehicles to be allowed till the hangar itself—though with an Air Force Police escort, of course.

The hush-hush nature of it all didn't startle him. Technical Area Palam was a vital air force base located in the heart of Delhi and was thus preferred to a far-away Hindon for such operations. Public figures and high-ranking diplomats didn't always want to be seen on their visits. The prime minister's office and the Ministry of External Affairs often requested the station to host such covert receptions. However, they usually gave the station 36–48 hours of notice to process such requests. In this case, Barua was barely given a couple of hours, and the request had come from the Minister's office itself. As far as Barua knew, the incoming VIP was actually a VVVIP.

Things had gone like clockwork. About half an hour ago, a Gulfstream G650ER jet had landed at Palam. The ATC asked the jet to taxi straight to an isolated military hangar, where it was then towed inside. The massive doors clanged shut.

The sky was, by now, deliciously overcast—the hill dweller in Barua rejoiced, and simultaneously, almost paradoxically, the pilot in him realised that clouds led to low visibility and that implied daunting and dangerous conditions for sorties. Pushing these thoughts out of his head, Barua glanced at the aircraft with renewed interest, though careful not to look too inquisitive. As demanded by his job, Barua jotted down the identification markers on the jet's tailfin, whipped out his phone and surreptitiously typed a message.

'Req details AS23K Gulfstream G650ER Arr VIDP.'

He clicked 'send' and turned to deal with the jet.

The text ended up on a military-issue cell phone inside Vayu Bhawan. It was processed within four minutes and Barua received a call, not on his cell, but on a secure line located inside the hangar. After confirming Barua's identity, the caller mumbled just one word and hung up. 'Company.'

This had truly piqued Barua's interest. Acting under standard operating procedures, he had sent the serial number and markings of the aircraft to the Directorate General of Air Intelligence (DGAI). The information was cross-referenced with multiple databases to locate the identity of the aircraft. Barua's counterpart at the DGAI had sifted through India's integrated security database of the National Intelligence Grid—which collated all the intelligence collected by Indian or friendly agencies—and had responded quickly.

Barua hadn't taken long to put two and two together. The jet was registered to a business corporation that was a CIA shell company. Perhaps now the '77 CD' vehicles that were waiting for the VIP in the hangar made sense.

The jet came to a full halt. Its doors opened, stairs were lowered and security personnel escorted the passengers to waiting cars.

He escorted the convoy till the main gate, waved them away and then turned towards the Air Traffic Control building to ensure no logs were kept of this flight, either by the civilian AAI air traffic controllers or the Indian Air Force personnel who were monitoring the skies. He could handle the military, he mused, but some civilians had the unfortunate knack of being ultra-competent *only* at times when national security demanded utter incompetence on their part.

Barua smiled to himself, and then thought about his impatient son, who had already called him thrice in the previous hour. He knew he wouldn't be able to focus on the *Halo* match with his son because of whom he had seen up close that day—and he was duty-bound not to tell anyone who he'd seen, except his immediate seniors. Barua reported back, conveying that the task was done, and started jogging home.

Jason E. Cartman of the CIC and Sean D. Miller of the CIA had finally landed in India.

New Delhi, India
34 hours into the invasion

Radiant blonde streaks ran through his dark, shaggy hair. A chubby youth in his early twenties, dressed in a red tee shirt and blue, baggy jeans, bobbed up and down on his bike whenever it hit potholes. Through the visor of his helmet, a silver eyebrow piercing glinted in the sun as he gunned his black Pulsar 220F down the road.

Nonchalantly, his left hand drummed his thigh as he rode. His right hand was still on the motorcycle handle as he hit a hundred kilometres per hour on a rather busy intersection, missing a car by a whisker. He swerved with panache, cut across traffic, and glared at overtaking drivers with a patrician arrogance only a Delhi driver could have mustered. Quite a *jugaadu* chap, he persistently stuck to the tail of the diplomatic convoy, knowing fully well that the police would give it way—and him with it.

He opened the throttle and the bike leaped forward. The Pulsar's power delivery had kicked in. The convoy was now just five feet away. He reached the bumper of the last car and abruptly slowed down.

An insect splattered on his helmet. He felt a slight thud. He winced, and felt something shift inside him. He pushed the accelerator again till he cleared the tail vehicle of the convoy in a vroom of dust, soot and carbon monoxide.

His hand snaked inside his jacket as if to locate something, and then withdrew it. In a quick motion, the rider raised his left hand to his helmet and adjusted it. He then leaned forward to his right, unmindful of a Ford Endeavour with diplomatic plates just behind him, even though he had been admiring the car for a long time.

In a quick motion, he turned and spat out the illegally procured gutkha he was chewing so fondly. He cleaned his lips with the handkerchief that he had taken out of his pocket, readjusted the helmet lest another policeman fine him, and disappeared into the crowd. He had not slowed down for this delicate manoeuvre, which was, by now, second nature to him.

On the other hand, the driver at the receiving end was not pleased at all.

'What the hell! Asshole!' the man driving the lead vehicle of the convoy, a Ford SUV that was currently transporting a VVIP, swore angrily. The red spit from the biker had splattered on his vehicle's left side view mirror. He looked at his partner, who just bared his teeth in a taunting smile that seemed to say just one word: 'Indians'.

Blissfully ignorant of what had transpired in the first car, the specially modified silver Cadillac SRX unsuspectingly followed the lead vehicle. It carried Jason E. Cartman, DG of CIC, and Sean Miller, Director of CIA—special envoys of the president of the United States of America sent to India.

The Cadillac made its way to Central Delhi. Necessary security arrangements had already been made, though hastily, but they had worked like a charm. No complications were reported when the American envoys stepped inside the prime minister's residence, barely an hour after landing at Palam airport.

The meeting that was being chaired by Prime Minister Roy earlier had been put on hold, though members were still assembled in Conference Room-I of the PM's residence, eagerly awaiting news of the emergency that had got Wilson's ambassadors to India.

A total of two men separated from the American delegation and headed towards the meeting place. Miller and Cartman were taken straight to the personal office of the prime minister of India, and its doors closed to the outside world.

The office of the Indian prime minister inside 7 LKM was a fancily decorated, 40-by-40-foot room. Plush red curtains adorned the windows and a spotless light-blue carpet covered the floor. Sunlight filtered in through huge, bullet-proof windows that overlooked a grassy lawn. The room smelt of fresh roses and, in accordance with democratic symbolism, a teak elephant stood in the east corner of the room, an oak horse in the south, a Makrana-marble bull in the west, and a Sundri lion in the north. A wooden board with the names and tenures of all Indian prime ministers was placed behind the PM's shining mahogany desk. On the right wall of the room was hung a calligraphic representation of *Satyamev Jayate* in Devanagari. The left wall was studded with framed pictures of important state occasions and Madhubani paintings. A framed picture of Mahatma Gandhi, hung just behind a couch and gazed down—almost ironically—at the luxurious surroundings.

Prime Minister Bipolab Roy got up from behind the desk, and closed the blinds. With a faint smile on his lips, he walked to the red sofas and asked the Americans to come join him.

The first words out of Miller's mouth constituted an apology rather than a greeting. 'Mr Roy, please accept my apologies for visiting you like this.'

Roy motioned his guests to sit with a sweep of his hands and spoke in a warm, friendly voice. 'Come on, it's great to have you here, Mr Miller. Why didn't you tell us you were coming? We would have made slightly more elaborate arrangements.'

'That is precisely what I was trying to avoid. Let's keep this visit off the books, as I requested your protocol officer earlier, too,' Miller replied, having made himself comfortable. He reached for the glass of water in front of him, downed it in one go, and muttered, 'I will come straight to the point. We have a very delicate situation on our hands.'

'A situation?' Roy immediately tensed. 'Is Pakistan thinking of nuking us?'

'Nope,' Miller said, 'it is an even bigger problem this time.'

Roy wanted to retort, 'What is bigger than a nuclear war bound to go global?' but he caught the drift of the discussion and mumbled, 'China?'

Miller slowly shook his head. 'China might have caused a recent Indo-Pak war as our intelligence agencies tell me.' He quickly glanced at Cartman and the signal was understood in a split second, '...But not this time. We are in immediate danger—mortal peril, I daresay.'

'We?'

'Yes, we. The entire world faces a threat of unparalleled proportions.' Miller paused to let it sink in and then continued, 'And if something is not done right away, we will all perish.'

'And you come to us? In all fairness, why didn't you go to Russia or China?'

Miller looked at Cartman, who was sitting right next to him. Cartman entered the discussion by speaking hesitantly, almost guiltily. 'Because the answers lie *here*.'

'I'm sorry, I do not understant what you're talking about.' Roy was confused, and it showed.

Miller leaned back on the sofa and stretched his legs. 'Let me introduce the man sitting with me—for what he actually is.' He turned to the other man. 'This is Jason Cartman, the current Director General of the CIC.'

A flicker of surprise played on Roy's face. He had heard of this name before, and with it, seen enough proof to trash such rumours.

Roy was about to say something when a bearer knocked, and brought in tea. He served it steaming in small transparent glasses rather than porcelain cups (Roy preferred his tea desi style), enquired about sugar, and disappeared.

Roy felt the delicious smell fill him with renewed energy. He reached for a glass, and gently twirled it in his hands. 'So the CIC *does* exist!'

'It won't for long if things continue the way they're going.' Miller stared hard at Cartman, who looked more like a portly school teacher than a secret agent.

'What *things*?' Roy narrowed his eyes suspiciously. 'What is happening?'

Cartman licked his lips, and said, 'Mr Prime Minister, the world is changing.'

'How?'

'The mutations—you know of them. You read the file.'

'Yes, I did. So?'

'The mutation is not a random phenomenon. Somehow this mutation has been weaponised!'

It took Roy a moment to process it. 'But this is suicide! No one will do this—or can. Even ISIS cannot be *so* brainless! No power on Earth is stupid to *that* extent, or technologically advanced enough, to execute what you are proposing.'

Cartman looked at Miller, who went red in the face. Miller looked away.

'What?' Roy barked. His eyes narrowed in suspicion at the looks exchanged by the Americans. He managed to warily croak, '*Now* what?'

Cartman cleared his throat, leaned forward and placed a comforting hand on Roy's shoulder, as if to provide his support. 'That's an even more convoluted issue, Mr Prime Minister,' Cartman began with a deadly seriousness on his face. 'The perpetrators of mutations may be manipulating humans to do their bidding...but they aren't from Earth.'

Bipolab Roy shrank back and did not respond for a full minute. His office seemed extremely strange all of a sudden. Roy could not believe that these Americans were actually briefing him about extraterrestrials. He clamped his mouth with his left hand to prevent himself from sighing, and then raised the chai glass to his lips with his right.

Roy realised that the Americans were waiting for him to speak. He started fidgeting nervously, opened his mouth, and mumbled, 'You mean...they're...as in...*aliens*?'

Miller merely nodded, a part of him still mentally shaking his head at his own ridiculous, laughable thoughts.

Cartman continued in an undecipherable tone, 'Yes, sir. They are extraterrestrials.'

'Fu...But why?' Roy asked. 'Why do they want to destroy us?'

'We don't know yet. But we're trying to get in touch with them to find out.'

Roy wasn't sure he had heard right. 'Hang on. You're in *communication* with them?'

'We are not,' acknowledged Miller hastily, '...though we know someone who is.'

The hairs on the back of Roy's neck stood up. 'Who?'

'The IMIC, Mr Roy, the International Military-Industrial Conglomerate,' Miller spoke in a hushed tone. 'Or as it is referred to by some others, the Conglomerate.'

A stunned Roy looked at them incredulously for a couple of seconds. Then he started to laugh. Just when he thought it couldn't get any more ridiculous, the Americans had raised the ghost of another legend. 'Come on, Mr Miller! I would have expected the Chinese premier or the Soviet Politburo to indict this evil, diabolical capitalist entity. There is no such thing as a global, ultra-covert secret organisation that commands the entire financial wealth of this planet. No one single body that controls, shapes or directs human behaviour. No one can! IMIC is a paranoid myth spread by conspiracy theorists and delusional communists.'

'That's what I thought too till quite recently, Mr Roy,' said Miller, 'until some facts came to light.' He looked squarely at Cartman, who flinched under his gaze.

'Anyway, whatever we know about this invasion till now is all thanks to a Conglomerate source who contacted us via Cartman. I just wish that they had given us this information a long time ago. Maybe then we would have been able to do something to prevent this from happening.' Miller sighed and continued, 'However, I am happy that the Conglomerate *did* share some crucial information with us. They're the only ones in contact with the aliens.' His tone was sad by now, almost spent. 'God knows why the aliens chose to initiate contact not with the US government but with a secretive group of financial princes.'

Cartman asked, 'Do you know why these mutations occur?'

Roy immediately responded, not wanting to miss any opportunity to show the Americans that he was slightly less clueless than they thought he was. 'I do, actually. The mutations seem to be the result of prolonged exposure to EM radiation emitted from cell phones—this radiation somehow activates dormant DNA in our bodies and triggers mutation in the nucleotide sequences. However, we did not know that it was the Qa'haQ who were behind this.'

Miller and Cartman nodded. 'And?'

'My specialists tell me that an average human can go up to 27 years using a cell phone without any adverse side effects. However, after that, one out of every three individuals who regularly use a cell phone would be susceptible to genetic mutation '

'What do they expect us to do?' Miller asked, irritated. 'Stop using all wireless communication devices?'

Cartman was about to answer when Bipolab Roy's personal phone, whose number was known only to his family and close friends, burst into an old Hindi melody. Roy jumped in his seat, regained his composure and slowly reached for the phone. This might be important, he thought. Maybe someone from his family had started to exhibit signs of mutation. He desperately hoped not.

He sank deeper in his chair as he saw the Americans discuss something amongst themselves quite animatedly. Roy looked at the number flashing on the screen of his vintage clamshell Motorola. It was an unknown number. He pressed 'answer' and put the phone near his ear. '*Haan*?'

He jerked his head up in surprise as the colour drained from his face. It was a familiar voice, a voice he had grown to mistrust and hate. Incidentally, this was the last person he expected to call at this moment.

'Mr Roy,' a deep, male voice rasped at the other end, 'if you want your country to survive this madness, you're going to listen to me very, very carefully.'

'Who...' Roy spluttered. 'Who are you?'

'Don't you recognise me, Mister Roy?' The voice at the other end was cold as ice. 'My name is Yasser Basheer.'

Film City, Noida, Uttar Pradesh, India
36 hours into the invasion

Pooja Srivastava stomped her feet, snapped her make-up kit shut, and muttered an invective that her Lucknow-bred mother would never have approved of. Her rotten mood was a result of one simple event—or the lack of it. She had been shooting since early morning and the catering staff still had not provided her with anything decent to eat. When she had complained, the incompetent clowns had appeared with oily samosas—while behaving as if they were doing her a favour. Did they want her to start playing *Baa*?

Pooja stared at the fried snacks, oil seeping through the paper plates in which they were served. She scoffed at the cold tea handed to her and got ready to throw a fit. She was one of the leads on this serial and the absolutely disgusting way in which she was being treated was simply unacceptable. Pooja may not have made it to the silver screen yet, but she was the rising star of *saas-bahu* soaps in India. Barely 22, she played similar characters—shy, obedient, and resilient bahus—in five Hindi serials.

She was a dusky, doe-eyed beauty with shoulder-length black hair that she tied into a domesticated bun. Pooja's amiable demeanour projected an incorruptible daughter-in-law who did not snatch sons away from their mothers, nor brothers from each other. In *Kyunki Saathiya Rishta Nibhana*—the serial she was presently shooting for—Pooja played a strong yet demure character who passed the litmus test for an ideal middle-class woman. In the TV serial, Pooja was well educated though not working; pretty, yet not arrogant; intelligent and smart, yet not crafty and manipulative, and a girl who, despite belonging to a well-to-do family, was not averse to facing financial difficulties with her slightly selfish husband. No wonder the serial was lapped up by listless housewives all over the subcontinent.

Today, Pooja was in the NCR to shoot for the 500th episode of this super-hit series. The gala, celebratory atmosphere made her all the more hungry. The fact that the other three daughters-in-law on the show had already been delivered hot meals had not cheered her up one bit. In fact, she saw a sumptuous-looking Greek salad delivered to another bahu right in front of her. The production assistant assigned to look after Pooja was sick. No one had bothered to tell her that.

She felt background noises on the set drill into her head. She forced her eyes shut to lock the noises out—but it was futile. Pooja carefully lifted her green sari, got up from the foldable metal chair she was sitting on, and began walking towards the doors of the studio, taking care not to stain or smudge her garments. She wanted some fresh air.

Pooja swayed as she walked and felt a gentle hammering in her temples. A groan escaped her lips but she controlled herself: last night's party was still coursing through her veins. The liquor had given her a hangover, dancing had made her tired, and the early morning hour-long call from her jerk boyfriend had her irritated. He was in some trouble and had wanted to talk—the selfish bastard cared little for the state *she* had been in, she thought. 'Asshole,' she muttered, and hurried away as she felt the roving eye of a slimy spot boy trail her.

Pooja reached the door, swung it open, and stepped out, leaving the huge air-conditioned set behind.

Her sandals met moist earth. It had rained recently. A refreshing breeze was blowing from the east and the wind felt good on her parched skin. She folded the script in her hand and tried to locate *Baa*, hoping to get someone sane to talk to.

Baa, the deeply devout, soft-spoken matriarch of the family on screen was a certain Mrs Meera Mistry in real life—a cheerful, 45-year-old woman with no immediate family in the country. Her industrialist husband was often found touring the world, and her only daughter was studying medicine in England.

Pooja located *Baa* standing with her right leg bent, resting on a tree trunk. *Baa* had a shot later in the day and she hadn't changed yet. She still had on a knee-length, yellow dress with floral patterns that she had worn at the hotel—a striking pearl necklace hung from her neck. Pooja stared at her with concealed jealousy—and hoped she would be half as pretty as her when she reached that age.

Pooja hurried towards Mrs Mistry. Perhaps it was something in Pooja's gait, the hard-pressed look on her face, or the dark circles under her eyes, that made Mrs Mistry look up at her with marked concern.

'Hello, darling,' she cooed and giggled. 'Late night, eh?'

'Don't even go there,' Pooja replied sullenly and eyed Mrs Mistry as if to gauge the level of trust she could place in her. Pooja didn't want a solution to her problem; she just wanted someone to talk to.

'Aww, sweetie,' Mrs Mistry blew another smoke ring in the air. 'You look so tired!' Then she lowered her voice and asked conspiratorially, 'Where was the party?'

The tone soothed Pooja, making her smile. 'Kitty Su,' she found herself saying.

'You sure could use some Hello Kitty right now.' She laughed at her own joke, and offered Pooja a bottle of water. 'Let's sit down the grass. Why stand? We have to stand for the next five hours *vaise bhi*, no?'

Pooja smiled and did as she was told. Then she forced herself to take a sip of water. She needed to rehydrate her system, Pooja told herself, and gulped it down. She gave the bottle, half empty by now, back to *Baa*. Out of its own accord, her stomach rumbled.

Mrs Mistry eyed her with concern. 'Hungry?'

'No—I mean yes. They did get me some oily samosas. Probably the same they got for the light boys. Ugh! I didn't touch them. I was like, come on, you want me to die?'

Mrs Mistry listened sympathetically and touched Pooja's left arm. Perhaps she had detected the slight slurring. 'Here, have some cucumber sandwiches.' She then reached for a flask kept by her side, poured Pooja a cup of coffee and handed it over. Pooja accepted it gratefully and smiled. 'Thanks. I needed it.'

'Now tell me what's wrong.'

Pooja could contain herself no longer. 'Abhishek is being a jerk again. He calls me up at odd hours and bitches about his work. He expects me to be there for him when he's not there for me. I don't think a long-distance relationship is working for us.'

'*Arre baba*! He's an investment banker—they stay quite busy. I am sure he must be dealing with a lot of stress in his on-site posting. You should behave with him the manner you behave with your hubby on screen. Putting up with him is worth it, *trust* me!' Mrs Mistry smiled wickedly, and flashed her perfect teeth.

Pooja's eyes suddenly teared up.

'Relax, Pooja,' Mrs Mistry said, 'Come, let us rehearse our lines. It'll take your mind off things. Some things, I have learnt with age, only get sorted out with time. The catch is to make your today worthwhile—the tomorrow will take care of itself.'

Pooja nodded at her gratefully, and then gave Mrs Mistry a weak smile. She wiped a tear from her eye—careful not to mess her make-up.

They started rehearsing.

In an hour, Pooja was standing in front of the lights. She was back on the set. A spot boy had come to fetch her as the production team was getting ready to shoot her sequence. It was a soliloquy about how she was being victimised by another bahu in the family. Pooja knew she was in real life too. That bitch even gobbled up the meals meant for her, Pooja snorted.

Pooja sat right next to the assistant director, who was buried in his script. The teleprompter wasn't working and she had to memorise the entire speech.

She heard a shuffle behind her. It was Mrs Mistry talking to Radhika, another daughter-in-law on the show. Radhika was Pooja's main rival, both on and off the set.

'What's wrong with her?' Pooja heard Radhika grunt at Mrs Mistry. The object was Pooja, of course, and Radhika was oblivious to the fact that Pooja, hidden from view, could hear them.

Pooja had expected Mrs Mistry to defend her but her reply made her blood boil. 'Come on, Radhika, you know how much of a crybaby that Pooja is. Even today she was whining about the second-class treatment she gets here. The way you're treated depends on how you perform, right?'

Radhika sniggered as Pooja went red.

'I agree. I would be surprised if she's re-signed for this. She brings so much negativity to the show,' Radhika said sweetly.

Pooja couldn't believe her ears. She walked up behind the duo. Her flapping sandals alerted them to Pooja's presence. Mrs Mistry and Radhika whirled around. Radhika beamed as she saw Pooja.

'Hey, Pooja,' Radhika crooned and hugged her. 'How are you doing, babe? Are you ready to dazzle us with your acting skills?'

Pooja just stared at her incredulously. Then she smiled warmly, and hugged Radhika back.

'Oh you're already in the role, I can sense it. No wonder they're talking of re-signing you. We want you back! *Chalo*, got to go change, babe. Mwah!' Radhika leaned forward, perfunctorily kissed Pooja on her right cheek and sauntered off.

Mrs Mistry somehow noted the way Pooja's eyes bored into Radhika's back—and realised Pooja had overheard them talking about her.

'Oh don't mind her,' Mrs Mistry began hastily. 'She's just jealous. What a vixen, that one! But you *do* know whose side I'm on, *na*?'

Pooja opened her mouth to retort but she was silenced by an authoritative voice that rang out over the set.

'Silence on the set!'

The command repeated itself.

'Silence! Switch off your cell phones. *Sab apni jagah per. Koi nahi bolega*!'

A sudden frenzy descended on the entire set. People rushed to their posts, spot boys threw their *bidis* away, and production teams jostled for better views.

The voice shouted again. 'Characters! Position!'

Pooja took the cue and stifled a sob. She hurried forward and positioned herself on the couch, right in front of the camera. She held on to her anger at her backstabbing colleagues so that the momentum of her victimisation in real life somehow manifested itself in her reel life. This was called show business for a reason.

At that precise moment, her cell phone started ringing. Pooja cursed and lunged for it: it was Abhishek. Damn, this was too much, she thought. They were talking a *lot* on the phone these days, more than what could be considered healthy.

Pooja switched off her cell phone, red-faced. She stowed it away in her purse, and shied away from the producer's irate gaze.

She returned to her position and after a few moments of composing herself, nodded. It was time.

'Lights! Camera rolling! Action!'

She stared directly into the camera and began speaking. Pooja was pissed: at Abhishek, at Radhika, at the production assistant, at Mrs Mistry, at herself for drinking too much and at life in general. Not one to give up so easily, she channelled her fury into putting up a better show.

The producer's eyes lit up.

Pooja could sense this was a good start—things were going better than expected. She was in the middle of her act when she saw the lights start to dim—and ultimately go out. Something was wrong. She wasn't even finished but the director chose to call a cut.

She stopped speaking, her mouth hanging open in amazement.

Pooja heard alarmed, urgent noises in the background. She wanted to say something but her head seemed to explode with the ferocity of a bomb. The pain blinded her. She clutched her forehead, slapped her temples, and shrieked.

By now, Pooja had fallen to the floor, and was writhing in pain. She screamed at the top of her lungs as the indescribable agony seemed to spread to other parts of her body. She tried to move but remained rooted to the spot.

Pooja bellowed again, and instinctively tried to reach for her cell phone to call Abhishek, before everything went black.

Mrs Mistry, who had been observing the shoot with much interest, stared in horror as Pooja's skin started to release a dark-brown liquid that spread out from her pores. It shortly evaporated into blue-green vapour.

Pooja had begun changing. Her smooth skin started turning coriaceous—scales sprouted on her torso. Her deep, dark eyes were now sinking into her face and her irises changed shape and colour. Her teeth became enlarged and pointed; her face grew a snout and a leathery tail sprang from her lower back.

The last thing Mrs Mistry heard was the executive producer shouting at his spot boys to fall back as Pooja, now a reptiloid, thrashed her tail and reached for Mrs Mistry's pretty dress with two sharp, gleaming claws.

Once Pooja was satisfied with Mrs Mistry, she hissed menacingly, sniffed around the set, and wildly lunged at the Greek salad *inside* Radhika's stomach. It smelt delicious.

Blood splattered the camera lens, and the director fainted.

The camera kept rolling.

Panchavati, Prime Minister's Residence, 7 Lok Kalyan Marg, New Delhi, India
36 hours into the invasion

Beads of sweat glistened on Bipolab Roy's forehead despite the steady hum of air conditioning. He wiped them away just in time to prevent them from running into his wide-with-disbelief eyes, and continued listening to the tinny voice coming from his cell phone.

Miller was the first to notice that something was wrong. He looked in Roy's direction with curiosity. Roy had, by then, pressed a switch on his desk. Although every call in and out of the prime minister's office and residence was recorded for security purposes, pressing that switch meant that the PM also wanted the caller tracked and apprehended—for routine questioning, of course—as soon as possible.

'Yes,' Roy mumbled, '...please continue.'

The voice sounded as if it came from far away.

'You can put me on speakerphone, Mr Roy,' Basheer remarked snidely. 'I want the Americans to listen, too. Yes, I know they're there. And no need to hunt me down. I am doing this to help you.'

'Ah...okay,' was all a dumbfounded Roy could mutter. He put the call on speakerphone and motioned to the Americans. They stood up from the sofa and approached the mahogany desk.

Basheer spoke, 'You know about the Qa'haQ?'

'Yes,' Roy replied.

'Hmm, I am sure it wasn't the Conglomerate who told you about them, was it?'

'Er...no...It was the CIA.'

'Oh. The Conglomerate is full of bloody pathetic fools. They're still controlling information and playing a dirty game to further their own petty agendas. I'd be careful dealing with them if I were you. The most wretched of all those scoundrels is their leader, Red. How I wish I knew his true identity. I would have snapped his neck myself,' Basheer spat out angrily. 'Ask Cartman. I'm sure that even he, a lowly, yet loyal, member of this precious Conglomerate, has been kept in the dark about the full facts.'

Cartman forced himself to wince and looked away, wary of the careful, studying gaze Miller shot in his direction. He acted as if the Conglomerate keeping secrets from him actually pained him deep down.

Roy was silent for some time. 'So, the Qa'haQ? What...what about them?'

Basheer's cold laugh made Roy shudder. 'The mutation is caused by exposure to a certain spectrum of EM radiation associated with cell phone usage, but it was deliberately turned into a potential weapon by the Qa'haQ.'

Roy rubbed his head and tried to stay calm and rational. 'I have a rough idea about that, but if the Qa'haQ are really so superior to us in technology, why don't they just attack and colonise us?'

'Let me ask you something,' Basheer responded. 'Suppose you're at grade school. You pick a fight with a classmate who hates you. How will you go about that?'

'I'd beat the shit out of him,' Roy replied slowly as realisation dawned on him even before Basheer explained it.

'Exactly!' Basheer continued triumphantly. 'That's the way *we* think. Our weapon systems, conditioning, and aggression are based on inflicting physiological and psychological damage. We use force on our enemies. It may be punches, projectiles, bombs, or even financial and psychological warfare, depending on who we are and what we want. But we're dealing with an *alien* species here, with different models of thought altogether—they have different notions of what constitutes force. The Qa'haQ do not even possess the sort of weapons we have. For them, war is focused on different premises and waged by different mechanisms.'

'How...?'

'The Qa'haQ have successfully fused organic tissues with inorganic matter. They attack their enemies by genetic manipulation. The enemy itself *becomes* you.'

'My God!' Miller moaned.

'But why us? Why Earth? Surely, the universe is big enough for all our needs.' Roy was livid.

Basheer kept silent at his end for some time. 'Evidently, it is not. They feel they are doing this for the benefit of this planet.'

'What do we do? We cannot hope to match their firepower!'

'We may not have to.' Basheer smiled mysteriously.

Cartman started at this. Roy looked at him and then focused back on the call. 'What do you mean?'

'I mean that there still is hope.'

'How?' Roy was curious.

'How did these mutations begin?'

'Cell towers, of course!'

'But they have existed for decades...what triggered them to belch out noxious radiation?'

'Hmm...something is different now, right?' Roy tried to focus on what exactly had changed.

'Indeed. The Qa'haQ have activated their Genetic Transmutor. It converts all the mobile-telephone towers to become Radiation Amplifying Devices—which in turn affect the people around them and turn them into human-Qa'haQ hybrids.'

Miller cawed; it made sense now.

Roy couldn't fathom the end of it. 'But...but how can we destroy every cell tower in this world within the stipulated time frame?'

He started pacing the room.

'We don't have to,' Basheer spoke up. 'We just need to get to the Genetic Transmutor and shut it down. The Radiation Amplifying Devices will automatically stop functioning without the Genetic Transmutor guiding their operation—and things should return to normal.'

'And how do you propose we find this Genetic Transmutor?' Roy mouthed the words that were on everyone's mind.

'The Conglomerate tells us that it is located somewhere in Jammu and Kashmir...near Uri...buried in the mountains by the Qa'haQ...'

'And we can track it by the high levels of Omtronic radiation it emits?'

'Precisely,' Basheer confirmed.

Still, there was one more thing that kept nagging at Roy's head. 'But why Uri? Why J&K?'

'I heard something about Uri being located over a strategic spot where the earth's magnetic field amplifies the Genetic Transmutor's own functioning capabilities.'

Roy nodded.

'Do you get what I'm saying?' asked Basheer with sudden strong emotion.

'Yes. We'll send our best men to locate and destroy it,' Roy muttered. 'Anything else we need to know?'

'Yes. You will need Osama bin Laden.'

Those sitting in the room shot up.

'Excuse me—what?' Roy was not sure whether he heard correctly. *'WHY?'*

'The Qa'haQ *control* him. We need to end him forever, and with him, the alien plans to egg humanity towards a World War III. Perhaps the Conglomerate failed to tell you this but I now believe that OBL is the result of a cross-breeding between Qa'haQ and human DNA. We need to find him to be able to guess what the ET plans are.'

'But he's passed away! This is preposterous. The Americans killed him in Abbottabad!' Roy bellowed into the phone.

Basheer lowered his voice and whispered conspiratorially, 'That's exactly what *they* want you to believe, Mr President. OBL may look like a human but he's not—thanks to the alien DNA inside him. Let me tell you a secret. The American raid on Abbottabad was not entirely successful. Yes, OBL *was* captured. He was barely alive, profusely bleeding, and quite unconscious when he was taken to a secure location aboard a US aircraft carrier. Then something disastrous happened.'

He took a deep breath and continued. 'Within a few hours, OBL's wounds healed mysteriously. He rose from the dead, broke past the heavy security, and jumped into shark-infested waters. He was rained with bullets when he swam away but his body was never found. The SEALs thought he died and thus "buried him at sea". Days later, he washed ashore and contacted the only two organisations who could still help him—Al Qaeda and the Conglomerate.'

'My God!'

'His altered rDNA gave him resilience, massive strength and tremendous regenerative powers. As we speak, he sits in a secure marine facility the CIC runs—at the behest of the Conglomerate.'

'How do you know all this?'

'I know this because I was tasked by the CIC to capture OBL again—and I did. That is how he reached an American detention facility. You must know, Roy; your government facilitated the extradition. The unnamed terrorist you gifted to the US was you-know-who himself in disguise.'

Roy didn't know what to say. 'Why should we believe you?'

'Oh, don't trust me, but trust your own man. Ask Cartman.'

Miller looked pained. Cartman stared at the floor at muttered something that sounded like 'Ragnarök'.

Basheer let out a hollow laugh. 'Don't blame him. Poor chap. He's just another puppet of the Conglomerate.'

Roy felt his head spinning. 'Basheer,' he softly asked, unsure of whether he wanted to know the truth, 'just how do you know all this?'

There was an uncomfortable silence at the other end of the line. Roy persisted. 'How do we know you're telling the truth? Cartman, tell me!'

Cartman replied guiltily, 'Because like me, Basheer, too, is a lowly, disgruntled member of that godforsaken Conglomerate.'

Roy looked at Cartman and then back at the phone. 'Why are you helping us?'

Miller decided it was time to jump in the fray. 'Basheer, this is Miller. What you are telling us is highly detailed information. If you really are a protector of mankind, then why didn't you tell this to us before it was too late?'

Basheer sighed.

'Go on, tell us,' Roy said.

'Don't ask me how I know, what I know...' Basheer answered. 'When I go to sleep, I feel alien voices whispering inside my head, inundating it with senseless information I cannot comprehend. Every morning I forge a new memory, a new feeling, and a new perspective—a memory that I never knew existed before. I feel like someone who's recovering from amnesia a bit at a time. Except in my case, I *know* it is not my memory—or experience!'

Roy was frankly puzzled. Was he supposed to trust the word of a schizophrenic? He wouldn't have, but Roy trusted Cartman, who, in turn, corroborated everything Basheer told them.

Basheer moaned. 'You don't get it, do you? The reptiloid Qa'haQ have both collective unconscious and conscious memories. I seem to be getting glimpses of their collective memories as I transform into something non-human with each passing day, thanks to an alien serum injected in me by the Conglomerate. I am now an impossible hybrid—swinging between Terran and Qa'haQ DNA like a pendulum.'

Before the horrific implications of Basheer's condition could sink into Roy's already overwrought brain, he heard a bone-chillingly inhuman wail at the other end and the line immediately got disconnected.

All India Institute of Medical Sciences (AIIMS), New Delhi, India

38 hours into the invasion

A moustachioed, henna-haired head constable of Delhi Traffic Police—dressed in a white shirt gallantly battling the soot—waved his baton at the autos standing near the AIIMS bus stop. He blew hard on his whistle and started jogging towards the parked public transports clogging the street. He had received word of VVIP movement over his radio and he could not let traffic come to a halt. After all, *bandobast* in this area was his responsibility and he did not want to piss off his SHO again.

By the time he reached, the serpentine queue of autos had disappeared, kicking up a plume of dust that made the masses milling around the bus stop start coughing. He smiled in satisfaction, and then motioned vehicles to stop as he heard sirens wailing in the distance.

Only passingly aware of the arrangements being made for the safe, expedient journey of the American delegates to the airport, Ajay Mishra sat inside the armoured Ford, immersed in a conversation with Sean Miller. The doctor-turned-bureaucrat had been deputed to brief the American diplomats on whatever the Indians had learnt about the mutation. As the delegation was in a hurry to get back home to ensure its own house was in order, Mishra had readily agreed to accompany Miller to the airport. Cartman had decided to take another flight—the heads of the CIA and CIC preferred not to travel in the same aircraft together, thanks to General Zia's exploding mangoes. While geopolitical exigencies had forced them to arrive together to the PMO, but once their task was completed, standard operating procedures were back in place.

Miller sank back in his seat, sipping a local drink he had found really enjoyable: packaged, spiced buttermilk. He focused on the road, and then on the tablet he held. The beggar girls peering excitedly at his convoy from a fair distance intrigued him. The chief of spooks thrust the image out of his head, and continued questioning the top bureaucrat. 'So, Mr Mishra, how were you able to determine that this Qa'haQ radiation can affect a significant part of humanity?'

Mishra thought for a moment before replying in a careful, measured, tone. 'Our scientists created dynamic models by studying how this particular radiation affects the gene sequence. We've had a few live models. In fact...' Mishra pointed at a multistorey building right across the road, 'that government hospital is where we've quarantined the subject. He's one of the first. I'll go pay him a visit after I drop you off.'

'Did you study the patient? Who is he? Maybe this is nothing but a random genetic anomaly?' Miller knew it was not. He was testing Mishra to see what degree of the truth he'd be willing to tell him.

'I'm afraid not.' Mishra scratched his right ear. 'We've run all possible diagnostics. This *is* a contagion and certainly not a natural phenomenon. I read a brief case study on the subject. His reports, taken from a routine check-up merely a week ago, are totally ordinary. Someone, or something, triggered this immediate mutation.'

'Can we control it? Cure it?' Miller asked.

'I can foresee no solution till now. Needless to say, we're working on the case the best we can. The patient—or Subject-

Zero—is Madhav Khanna. He is around sixty-five, otherwise quite healthy, and is currently quarantined there.' Mishra pointed again towards 'Medical', as the AIIMS-Safdarjung complex was known to the residents of Delhi.

'Any others?' Miller asked.

'As per the latest reports, we have had another four males admitted till now.'

'Anything special about them? What are their names? Where are they from? Might they be connected in some way?'

Mishra flipped open a tablet and accessed some files. 'There is no common thread as far as I can tell. Aneesh Gupta, Eddy Samuel, Dhaval Shukla and Abhijat Jain are all young men in their late twenties with a spotless medical record. It seems all four of them have been infected by...someone...something...and presently show signs of deadly contamination. They're currently in stasis, fighting for their lives.'

'What common factor can affect four young, healthy men in their prime and make them so ill; that is the question...' Miller stopped speaking as he looked out of the window to see a traffic police constable running towards their car. He was swinging a cane his hands and seemed to be shouting something.

Mishra followed Miller's gaze, and tensed as the car gave a slight lurch. Something did not seem right. Just as the pilot vehicle crossed the AIIMS main gate, there was a loud bang. The gate opened and a large mob streamed out. Mishra stared at their faces to see if they were going to attack, but instead of rage, hatred or determination on their sunburnt, broken faces, he saw disbelief, confusion and fear.

Miller's security chief, who had been calmly riding shotgun with the chauffeur, got visibly agitated and asked for a short burst of speed. The car gained momentum as the driver stepped on the gas. Mishra felt his back digging into his seat due to inertia as he reached for his cell phone. He wanted to know what was happening but stopping to find out was not an option due the precious cargo he was ferrying. The American delegate was on a secret visit, but Mishra could not be a hundred per cent sure terrorists had not found out about this—maybe this was an Al Qaeda module targeting them.

The American spook, meanwhile, reached for a hidden compartment and withdrew a Walther PPK, a semi-automatic pistol he had fallen in love with as a young soldier in Vietnam. Mishra watched uneasily.

At that precise moment, something heavy crashed against the left C-pillar of the car—right where Mishra was seated. The vehicle shook, and the armoured car spun twice before coming to rest. Glass shattered, metal screeched, and windows caved in.

The impact was so tremendous that it left the occupants dazed; it jerked them around against their seat belts. Mishra was the first to come around. He rubbed his eyes, tried to sit up, and reached for the door. He could smell something burning under his seat. Confused at what could have been powerful enough to do this to an armoured car, he cautiously peered out to see what had happened.

Ajay Mishra, cool, calm and composed in all situations short of a nuclear holocaust, screamed at the top of his lungs at what he saw through the broken glass window.

Through half-shut eyes, Subject-Zero was leering at him. Madhav Khanna was in a mood to kill.

Before Mishra could react, 'Khanna', or the reptiloid creature that had once been him, slithered to the door. Khanna thrust an arm in—it scraped against the glass, but the ragged edges did not slow it down. A claw slowly unfurled from his leathery, yellow-green reptilian paw, and traced a nasty, bloody gash across Mishra's forehead. An immobile Mishra closed his eyes in terror and wailed as he felt a slimy paw hit him again.

Mishra, still in shock, was about to say his prayers when he felt a gun fire right next to him. The sound almost deafened him. Mishra's body went rigid as he felt the bullet fly inches from his ears—and buried itself in Khanna's arm.

Malhotra sighed in relief as he saw Khanna pull back as Miller fired again—this time at his face. Khanna staggered back and sank down. A low hiss escaped his lips. He was about to get up again when a hardy wooden stake hit it firmly between his eyes.

'*Raa harami*!'

The Delhi police constable had reached the spot. He growled angrily, ballistic at a VVIP being accosted during his watch. He repeatedly, mightily, hit Khanna with his well-oiled wooden baton with a frenzy only a desperate man could have mustered.

Miller, too, joined in—so did his security detail. They pumped lead into the creature till it sank on its knees.

Miller, his face leached of colour, was unable to believe what had just happened. He was helped by two security men, and Mishra, still shuddering and bleeding slightly from the forehead, turned around and thanked Miller for saving his life.

Miller and Mishra were ushered into a secondary vehicle, and the convoy—or what remained of it—screeched away.

Only then did the people present gather the courage to go near the *shaitaani* creature that had caused this commotion. The giant lizard being had collapsed right in the middle of Ring Road, quite aptly in front of a gate marked 'Emergency Only'.

Responding to this event, the Delhi Police was quick to arrive. The mob was dispersed, and the area cordoned off.

As shocked NIA teams rushed to collect samples from the crime scene, the creature, who once had been Madhav Khanna, lay deathly still—never to move again.

Command and Control Centre, Prime Minister's Residence, 7 Lok Kalyan Marg, New Delhi, India

40 hours into the invasion

Manish Ranjan squirmed in his chair. 'This does not look good at all. An American delegation attacked in the heart of Delhi! What have things come to?'

At the insistence of the SPG, the prime minister and other key personnel had been shifted to the newly constructed Command and Control Centre (CCC), a subterranean emergency bunker located under one of the five bungalows which made up 7LKM. The war room of the CCC they were deliberating in was a blast-proof, concrete-reinforced structure that was meant to serve as the nerve centre of the Indian state during a major crisis. The CCC was a self-sustaining four-storey building—which was buried almost half a kilometre underground—and contained computer labs, conference areas, a cafeteria, storage areas, a dormitory and even a hydroponics bay of its own. It was equipped with state-of-the-art communication devices, power generators, water recycling facilities, and stocked with long-term survival gear. Currently, a digital map of North India was displayed on a huge screen.

'No one was seriously hurt—thank God for that. But it raises serious questions about our security protocols. Moreover, Subject-Zero, I am sorry to say, has been terminated,' the defence minister reported.

'I'm yet to understand what this means,' Ranjan snorted.

'It means war!' Roy thundered and banged a fist against the table. He turned to service chiefs, who were huddled together, comparing notes. As Roy looked at them, they straightened their starched uniforms and focused on the PM. 'Take necessary action and sanitise the airspace. Have armed troops do the same on the ground.'

'Yes, sir!'

CR Prasad, head of RAW, coughed—a bit unsure about the plan of action, thanks to recent events. 'Sir, the Qa'haQ might be harmless...or very powerful. Either way, a full-frontal assault might not be our best option.'

Roy replied dismissively, 'In case you forgot, they attacked us first—with their mutagenic radiation. We did nothing to hurt them.'

At that precise moment there was a small commotion outside. The group turned their heads towards the source of the noise, which was coming from an adjoining corridor. After a polite knock, the doors parted and a rejuvenated Ajay Mishra made his way in. The men and women in the room were quick to express their surprise at seeing Mishra return to work so soon—he might have been suffering from post-traumatic stress disorder, after all.

Mishra, when asked if he'd like to take the day off, shrugged and settled down. He informed the gathering that after the incident, he had ensured that the American delegates had safely boarded their flight, and then returned to the PM's side after a quick health check-up at AIIMS—sans any jitters. Even an alien attack was unable to batter the chainmail of bureaucratic protocol that Mishra adorned with such panache.

The people present in the room understood that the fight was now personal for Mishra—and to take the opportunity of revenge, nay, justice, away from him was unfathomable. Thus, after a brief round of pleasantries and enquiries about Mishra's health, the group returned to their unfinished business—with Mishra taking his place near the PM.

Malhotra was the first to get the conversation back to point. 'What do we do?'

Ranjan jumped in. 'We need to strike at their master weapon. Destroy their Genetic Transmutor. With that weapon offline, they will not be able to inflict further damage and we can hunt them down.'

'Status on that? We first need to find out where to hit them!' Roy said.

'Yes sir, we have located high concentrations of Omtronic radiation,' Malhotra said.

'How does that help us?'

'Since Omtronic radiation is a by-product of Qa'haQ technology alone, human devices cannot generate it. Thus, it is logical to conclude that the location of Qa'haQ headquarters on Earth would be the area with the maximum Omtronic flux,' reported Ajay Mishra. Rather than making him jittery, the accident with the Qa'haQ had galvanised him into action.

Prime Minister Roy stared quizzically at the maps. 'Please continue.'

'The DRDO had provided specifications of the Omtronic radiation to friendly countries so that we can pool our resources and locate the source ASAP, and thus neutralise the Qa'haQ device. We have a hit, thanks to the VKO.'

'VKO?' The PM inquired.

'Voyska Vozdushno-Kosmicheskoy Oborony,' replied Air Chief Marshal Vikramjeet Sharma. 'I mean, the Russian Aerospace Defence Forces,' he corrected himself immediately when he remembered that not everyone in the room was as fluent in Russian as he was—thanks to his training with the Soviet Air Force.

'Oh! What did they find out?'

'The Russians, I must tell you, have been very touchy about aerial threats since the February 2013 meteor explosion in central Russia. They constructed a specialised early-warning Lekhtusi Radar Station near Leningrad Oblast to keep an eye on such matters. Based on our request, the Russians detected two extremely strong sources of Omtronic radiation. They then triangulated their locations using their Kosmos 2480 military satellite and forwarded the data to us as a goodwill gesture.' Sharma continued, 'Our own readings have confirmed this. The radiation is strongest in our own country.'

'Where?'

'The epicentre is Uri.'

Malhotra turned, nodded and an NTRO engineer operating a console pressed a few buttons to zoom in further on the map. An area near Uri was marked in red, merely 15 kilometres from the Line of Control.

'Neutralise this radiation,' Roy commanded, having had enough of this. 'Get a team to Uri. Find and destroy the Qa'haQ device there. Also issue orders to the IAF Aerospace Command. I've something specific in mind.'

At a signal from the PM, chairs were immediately moved, telephones were picked up, and faxes were sent.

Within moments, a private secretary appeared bearing an executive order and placed it in front of Roy. The prime minister signed it, marked it directly to the air force chief for further action, and started thinking about what to do next. The state apparatus and chain of command would take care of the rest.

As the orders were sent, authenticated and obeyed, pilots stationed in the Operational Readiness Platforms in various Air Force bases across the country heard a 'scramble' command.

Having given the order, Roy could feel something at the back of his mind vying for attention. 'You mentioned two sources? Where is the other one?'

There was a brief pause.

General Malhotra cleared his throat. The confounding phone call he received a few minutes ago made sense to him now. 'Sir, I recently received a phone call from an old friend, a Colonel General of the Russian Federation, pledging his support in case we decided to act.'

Roy couldn't follow. 'Act? On what?'

'He also said Russia stands with one of its oldest friends in this hour of need.'

'What is that supposed to mean?'

Malhotra decided to drop the bombshell. 'As per Russian reports, *this* is the secondary source of the Omtronic radiation, sir.'

The camera zoomed in further on the map, highlighting an area in red, and Roy could only gag in consternation. Just when he thought the day couldn't get any worse, *this* had happened.

The epicentre of the secondary radiation was the Great Hall of the People, Beijing.

Incidentally, this also happened to be the meeting place of the National People's Congress—the name by which the parliament of the People's Republic of China was known to the outside world.

Part III: The Beginning

Now this is not the end. It is not even the beginning of the end.
But it is, perhaps, the end of the beginning.

Winston Churchill

Kamala Nehru Ridge, New Delhi, India
42 hours into the invasion

A deafening din of rotors ate into the still silence of the university ridge. A sparrow beat its little wings furiously, and disappeared amongst the trees.

'Waypoint 3 clear. En route to 4,' Squadron Leader Bishwanath Barua gruffly reported over his radio and returned to his scans.

The Mi-35 'Akbar' gunship glided over the green, rocky ridge with a predatory grace. The Delhi Police was in the process of emptying the area—and had already cordoned off the entry points. Eager joggers, bored students, frisky lovebirds, and amateur bird enthusiasts raised their eyes to the skies. A menacing shadow swept over them—a coiled snake ready to strike. Those watching from down below suppressed a shiver of excitement; had they truly known about the firepower on board, their zeal would have been replaced by dread.

At the entrance to the ridge the onlookers simply stood rooted to their places—their bitterness manifested in long, irritated sips of lukewarm coconut water, and curious stares at the low-flying IAF helicopter hovering over their usual haunts. Most of them were used to aircrafts passing overhead, but this chopper was almost skimming the treetops: in fact, it flew so low that it must have been looking for something *very* specific—which it was.

The camouflage-liveried attack helicopter, belonging to the No. 125 'Gladiators' Squadron, was being piloted by Barua. On board was also a young flight lieutenant who acted as the weapon station operator, a flight engineer who was huddled over a special console fitted in the cargo hold, and a JCO. The chopper, operating in tandem with 11 others, was tasked with a grid search of Delhi. They were on a unique Seek-and-Destroy mission.

Target: extraterrestrials.

Barua knew about the enormity—and importance—of the task allotted to him, and thanked the fact that the Mi-35 was armed to the teeth. The chopper carried radio-guided supersonic missiles, 80mm rockets, 23mm cannons and nose-mounted four-barrelled 12.7mm Gatling guns.

His quarry had evaded him till now. All 12 helicopters had scrambled from Hindon and Palam Air Force Stations following an urgent message from the Ministry of Defence, and were ordered to rendezvous over Raisina Hill after a thorough search of Delhi. To top it all, the flabbergasted air marshal, head of IAF's Western Air Command, had been personally telephoned by the chief of air staff a few minutes ago, and given a specific task.

The message was numbing—a foreign dignitary had been attacked by an alien hybrid in the heart of Delhi. The government could no longer sit idly by as its authority was challenged under its very nose and its sovereignty violated with such impunity. In response, the air marshal had scrambled all available gunships near the National Capital Region (NCR), and ordered a grid search even before the birds were airborne. Even more birds were en route to Delhi from Sirsa, Ambala and Adampur to locate the alien vessel as soon as possible and provide close air support to ground units.

This was why Barua was where he was: sitting inside the cockpit of an aircraft he had grown to love.

'Any signs yet?'

'No, sir.'

Barua motioned for his co-pilot to get on the radio and ask for a status update from the other gunships covering different parts of the NCR. The co-pilot nodded, and spoke over the radio on a military frequency. Meanwhile, Barua busied himself with the radar.

Everything looked normal. Barua swore, and kept looking for the needle in the haystack.

There!

Barua's head shot up. He thought a saw a blip on the radar to the left. The crew craned their necks to see something shimmer in the distance, but it was gone before it fully registered. Barua checked his heads-up display, and tapped the radar screen with his fingers: the blip returned neither in the radar nor in his line of sight.

'Negative, sir,' his co-pilot, who had been busy with the radio, reported to him. 'The others have found nothing unusual.'

Barua grunted. He'd better confirm this.

'Rome,' he spoke over his radio, and contacted ground control to verify if he really did see a sensor ghost. 'This is Gladiator 1. Request airspace status. Two clicks. Bearing 120. 100F AGL.'

Barua waited as the controller focused on the surroundings with a much more powerful set of eyes—the newly-procured, Israel-made IAF radars, which sifted through mountains of external sensory data to determine if anything was present where it shouldn't have been.

A short reply came within five seconds.

'Gladiator 1, airspace clear. No activity.'

Barua could swear he had seen something—yet all instruments told him he was alone in the sky for miles. A good pilot always knew when to trust his instruments, and when to trust his instincts. This combat pilot decided to cave in to his sixth sense.

'Req satlink R2,' he snapped over the radio.

This was sure to send the ATC into overdrive, he realised. Barua had asked for an uplink with the orbiting RISAT-II, India's newly launched spy satellite, and hoped that the request would be expedited. In fact, Barua was counting on the fact that Air Commodore Venkatesan would be nearby, listening to every word being exchanged on the radio; he'd know that when an experienced pilot asks for something mid-air, especially during a vital combat mission, then he must really need it.

'Standby.'

The radio went silent for a full minute—confidence started to seep away as Barua realised that his request might have been turned down. Or even if it was accepted, and he found nothing, he would have to answer some pretty hard questions on the base of having made that call.

The voice that came next was of Commodore Venkatesan, not his fighter controller. 'Uplink with R2 in 30 secs, Biswo. Shift to Channel Cactus for live feed.'

'Wilco.' A visibly relieved Barua turned to look at his co-pilot, who gave him an enthusiastic thumbs up.

'You have the controls,' Barua told him and switched on the newly integrated video monitor present in his cockpit—one that was directly linked to incoming satellite imagery from RISAT-II.

'I have the controls,' the co-pilot spoke out loud, so that no mistake would be made in this transfer.

Barua increased the magnification, and squinted at the feed, his eyes half closed in concentration. It helped that he knew the ridge like the back of his hand, having spent many free evenings here during his BSc days at Delhi University: hanging out on this very ridge, drinking, playing and gambling with friends. If there was someone who could have cracked it, it was him.

At first he could see nothing out of the ordinary. Not one to give up so easily, he zoomed in further. After a few tense moments, Barua saw a shape emerge. His instruments still did not read anything, but when seen from a top view his eyes could make out a slightly sunken patch on the damp ground—as if something heavy and invisible was kept on it. Barua would have dismissed it had he not seen this sunken patch from the skies; the knee-high wild bushes around this particular spot were perfectly stationary, whereas the foliage just a few metres away was swaying wildly in the wind. The simple fact that the ridge was emptied of people had ensured no one had stumbled across it till then.

There was only one explanation—there was something lying on top of the grass, keeping it still, something which no instrument could pick up and no eyes could see. Something cloaked. Something extraterrestrial.

Barua almost whooped in joy; he lunged for his controls and decided to inform the fighter-controller. 'Rome, I have a visual. Bearing 124.'

'Acknowledged,' the ground-controller replied.

'Analyse intent?' Barua double-checked his orders.

'Hostile,' came the prompt reply.

Barua smiled in spite of himself. 'Permission to engage?'

'Area cleared of civilians. Happy hunting!'

'Copy!'

Barua motioned for the flight gunner to get ready as he swerved his chopper *away* from his quarry. He did not want the bogey to know it had been spotted. The moment Barua thought he was in a comfortable position, he thrust the helicopter in a high-g roll; the steel shrieked and screeched in protest, but held. Barua somehow felt that the primary weapon of the aliens was stealth, and he had managed to see past its defences. He only hoped the offensive capability of this entity was not as potent. He locked on his target, fired a few rounds from his Gatling gun and let loose two *Shturm* anti-tank missiles at the depression in the ground.

He waited with bated breath as the deadly projectiles streaked towards their unsuspecting target. He counted the seconds as the missiles slammed into nothingness and exploded. As the dust and smoke settled, he could see the air ripple and something shimmered into existence.

Barua patted the altimeter in excitement—he had it.

As far as he could make out, the Qa'haQ craft was spherical, around 50 metres in diameter and had flashing lights that were disorienting to look at. Fortunately for Barua, the first assault seemed to have taken out the cloaking capacity of the ship—he had taken the *D'bHin* totally by surprise. The Qa'haQ had never imagined that humans would be able to see through their chameleon shields.

Barua slapped his console, took careful aim, and pressed the trigger again. Tracer bullets raced towards the alien ship, their trajectory a treat to the staring eyes of those present onboard Barua's chopper.

Little known to him, he had done more damage with the first salvo than he could ever have hoped for. The Qa'haQ ship had been cloaked when lying on the ground—which meant that it had diverted all its power to cloaking shields. The actual energy shielding, the mechanism that could easily have stopped incoming projectile and energy weapons, was offline. Consequently, with only the cloaking shields and inertial dampeners in place, the *Shturm* anti-tank missiles from the Mi-35 inflicted significant damage to the alien shuttle's outer hull.

However, once hit, the shuttle automatically raised its energy shields and plotted an escape course before the second salvo struck home. Moments before Barua could request for fighter protection, he saw the sphere noiselessly rise into the air, and then dart forward with such a speed that it became a blur. The AI of the Qa'haQ vessel had decided to take the ship into orbit to conduct repairs. Thus, the bullets plummeted and fizzled harmlessly into the ground, its target long gone.

The alien craft rose to the skies—it had gone from a stationary position on the ground to an Earth orbit in a total of seven short seconds. Barua swore in amazement—the UFO had disappeared before his very eyes.

Barua cursed again, this time audibly over the radio, and promised he'd be back for it—and the next time he would not waste conventional weapons on this alien ship, for now he had realised that the only way to end this forever was through a tactical nuclear warhead.

However, he was ecstatic for one simple reason: for air forces and radars across the world, the UFO had just become an IFO.

An *Identified* Flying Object.

Uri, Jammu and Kashmir, India
44 hours into the invasion

PCM had arrived home to much fanfare in his professional circle. Post a much-needed R&R, he was asked to pad up for a second innings and head to Srinagar. PCM was to lead a security detail of 20 commandos from the Special Frontier Force (SFF) to escort a group of scientists around Uri.

SFF was a paramilitary force that operated under the direct supervision of the RAW, and PCM was an optimal choice. Before he had been absorbed by the Research and Analysis Service, he was a crack IPS officer of the Jammu and Kashmir cadre, one who had served, trekked and skied in the mountains of Uri as a young deputy superintendent of police. Moreover, during his early tenure with RAW, he had been associated with the commando wing of the SFF.

PCM, en route to his next destination, remembered his days with the J&K Police with nostalgia. The midnight oil he had to burn to clear the Civil Services Examination was only slightly less than the copious amounts of sweat and blood he had to shed for his commando training with the SFF. This had taken him to *ghatak* camps and Special Forces training institutions in India and abroad. In fact, PCM knew the British SAS and Israeli Sayaret Matkal had taught him a few tricks due to which he was still alive. Not to mention, his training abroad had made him develop contacts with the Israeli intelligence, which he had fully exploited when he was sent to Pakistan as a deep-penetration asset.

He looked out of the window. The blue skies and the cascading mountains of wool made PCM sleepy. The serene IAF Antonov-32 flight from Delhi was followed by a bumpy Mi-17 chopper ride from Srinagar, landing him in Uri within a few hours.

Seconds, minutes and hours had fused together. PCM barely remembered meeting the team and the hurried, formal introductions before they were piled into a waiting army truck that took them to the sly slopes. After an hour of climbing, he could feel his nerves getting distraught. He was not ready for another mission so soon—thankfully, he had no time to think, and could only stare at the group he led struggling with the deceptive, snowy paths.

The mountains were beautiful—yet PCM knew just how deadly they could be. He and his men had formed a basic defensive circle, and in the middle walked the scientists they were supposed to protect: Prof. Kavita Aggarwal from DRDO, Dr Revathi Balakrishnan from GIBRI, and two bald, male scientists in their mid-forties, representing the National Chemical Laboratories and National Physical Laboratories whose names a fatigued PCM had totally forgotten.

PCM suppressed a shiver and scouted the area. The world around him was a comforting, pure white. The company inched forward, equipped with special Omtronic detectors that were given to India by an unnamed source from the Conglomerate. Dressed in high-altitude hiking gear, they constantly checked the instruments' readings and kept altering their direction to try and find the source of the Omtronic radiation.

Suddenly conscious of the biting cold and tiredness, the group stopped chatting and trekked in silence. They kept climbing for another hour. It wasn't a steep slope, but the snow made it slippery and dangerous. To top it all, PCM thought disdainfully, these people were academics: they were used to a life of temperature-controlled laboratories and classrooms, hot, endless cups of tea, and oily conference food—not the cold, cruel, unforgiving mountains where second chances did not exist.

The scientist from NPL was the first one to break the silence. 'When will we find it?' he moaned.

'Tired so soon? You should start exercising!' his counterpart from NCL taunted playfully.

'Hmm...what will we do once we find the Qa'haQ device?' Prof. Kavita Aggarwal interjected from up ahead, glad she had the opportunity to divert her mind from her mildly rheumatic knees.

An instrument beeped and startled them, saving them the trouble of thinking about what would happen when they located their target. PCM whipped out the detector, pointed it in various directions, and then cross-referenced it with the newly inducted GAGAN—India's answer to the American GPS and Russian GLONASS.

The beeps grew louder, and the intervals between them decreased as the team circled around a spot. Within a few minutes, they found it. The readings pointed to a dark, ominous cave a few hundred metres from the main trail.

They cautiously filed inside—darkness made them reach for their fluorescent illuminators. They had been asked not to meddle around: they were to locate the device, torch it and leave ASAP.

As the men and women went deeper in, warm, moist vapours seemed to emanate from the ground. Their boots clanged on metallic surfaces, and their eyes darted on eerie walls.

The group suppressed shivers and pushed on.

After a few tense moments, PCM's voice reverberated in the cold cave. 'Hey! Take a look at this!'

The group bent down and peered at the discovery. The radiation seemed to be coming from a hole right in the centre of the cave, a black tunnel that spiralled and disappeared into the ground.

PCM shone his flashlight inside. It seemed to be a drop of about 50 metres—at the end of which PCM could see a small console. His first impulse was to ask for a rope and climb down—but then his instructions had been explicit. 'Do *not* go near the device,' he was repeatedly told. PCM knew when to follow orders, and when to skirt around them. This, he realised, was a situation that demanded the former. The radiation could kill him, he rationalised.

'I say: let's bomb this and get the hell out of here!' the man from NPL growled.

'But should we not study it first?' muttered Dr Revathi Balakrishnan softly.

There were a few murmurs of agreement.

'This is an alien *weapon*.' PCM decided to step in. 'Every second we delay, the radiation build-up gets stronger. We need to destroy this now!'

PCM had operational command: the scientists were there to observe, and assist in case he had trouble disassembling the device. The mission was to get the Sinium crystal, and to destroy the machine. He was about to go down when a shout stopped him.

'Wait!' Aggarwal shouted.

'What?' PCM was suddenly hesitant.

'Don't you see? Look at the Omtronic readings!'

PCM raised a confused eyebrow. 'What about them?'

'Oh my God,' Revathi exclaimed. 'For the first time in hours, they are not rising!'

'So?'

'The machine looks like it is powering down!' Aggarwal stabbed the air with her index finger. 'I would even suggest that it might be missing its power source.'

PCM stared as this development sent the scientists into a tizzy—they started talking amongst themselves excitedly, unmindful of the presence of PCM and his men.

The scientist from NPL broke away from his colleague, faced PCM, and nodded in agreement. 'Hmm…that would explain why the Omtronic radiation is holding steady and not rising.'

'If that is the case, we should not destroy it. We can call for back up, have the device relocated, and study this Genetic Transmutor in detail,' Revathi spoke up again.

However, the man from NCL was not sure this was such a good idea. 'But won't that be too risky? I mean, there still *is* enough radiation around us to cause yet more mutation…'

'But the levels of radiation will soon start falling. This machine has no power source!' Revathi countered.

'Okay, tell me,' PCM had other things to worry about. 'Where did it go? The power source?'

'The only reasonable explanation is that someone took it.' Aggarwal shook her head in despair and sighed. 'I would love to know what could power a device with such massive and wide-ranging capabilities.'

'I am not sure we should delay… '

'Hang on,' Aggarwal stopped in her tracks and shouted. 'See this? Do you see this?'

She had a tablet in front of her, tuned to certain frequencies. The team crowded around to see what she was talking about.

'What?'

'See? There *is* Omtronic radiation around us, yes, but that is not *all*!'

Revathi shook her head. 'What do you mean?'

PCM was the first to decode what was displayed on the tablet screen—he had seen similar signals during his radio-operations training.

'But it cannot be!' PCM gulped.

Aggarwal smiled triumphantly.

The man from NPL, on the other hand, swore and disentangled himself from the group. No one paid any attention to him—there were bigger concerns at the moment.

'I still don't get it,' Revathi confessed. 'What is wrong with the radiation?'

'It is not the radiation, Revathi,' Aggarwal spoke up. 'It is the presence of something else.'

'What?'

'A radio uplink has been established between the Genetic Transmutor and something up in the sky—and this link is still operational,' Aggarwal supplied.

'You mean the Genetic Transmutor might have stopped working due to its power source now gone, but an emergency-locator beacon is still reporting its status and position to something above us?' Revathi summarised the event.

'Yes,' Aggarwal nodded.

Revathi looked concerned. 'Are you saying one of *our* geo-stationary satellites is controlling this Qa'haQ device?'

Aggarwal shook her head rather vehemently. 'The satellite might not be ours in the first place.'

'You mean...'

The scientist from DRDO had said the unthinkable.

PCM echoed her. 'Yes, there has to be an alien mother ship in orbit—towards which this beacon is directed.'

Revathi shuddered. 'Which in turn means the ship we engaged in Delhi was but a shuttle. A larger, more powerful mother ship is orbiting us.'

'And this can be disastrous!' PCM grunted, unsure of how this information could affect the current mission parameters.

'Or the break we were looking for!' Aggarwal opined. 'If we can follow this radio signal, triangulate the position of the mother ship, and take it down first...'

PCM eyes lit up. He liked how the professor thought: she had the heart of a warrior, going directly for the jugular.

'Yes, let's report this immediately and I...' The man from NCL was not able to finish his sentence. He just stopped and stared at something in the corner.

PCM followed his gaze. Before he could react, a blur emerged from the corner of his eyes and a claw slashed his face, bloodying his cheek in the process.

It was PCM's instinct that had saved his life—time slowed down as he whirled around and tried to throw himself out of harm's way.

He looked back to see the man from NPL wriggling in a corner—sprouting a scaly tail.

PCM moaned in astonishment as he realised that, while the group had been talking, the NPL scientist had actually transformed into a Qa'haQ hybrid.

Within the blink of an eye, the Qa'haQ hybrid had impaled one of PCM's men on a set of sharp, gleaming claws.

The SFF commandoes opened fire as the thing scurried away into the darkness of the cave. Sharp incisors shone in the flashlight beams—and a soldier standing near Dr Revathi Balakrishnan was swept off his feet by a tail and disappeared into the darkness.

She screamed in alarm—another man was writhing on the floor, his features changing. He was transforming, too.

PCM understood what was happening. Without a power source, the Genetic Transmutor had become even more dangerous. The AI of the Genetic Transmutor knew it was dying—and like a wounded animal, it had suddenly started emitting every last bit of energy it had. What would have taken hours was now taking seconds to happen.

PCM chased the creature deeper inside the cave. The monster lizard jumped into the tunnel, drawn by the Qa'haQ device.

Without thinking, PCM reached for a grenade, removed the pin, and ran to the tunnel's entry. This was no time for science—if he did not do something now, he would lose all his men. He took a deep breath and dropped the three 36mm grenades in quick succession into the tunnel.

They disappeared into nothingness. PCM counted seconds—there was no need to run. If intelligence reports were correct, he speculated, this tunnel was but a piece of Qa'haQ hardware buried in the belly of the mountain. It was a Qa'haQ shell chamber that housed the Genetic Transmutor; hence, any explosion would not cause any avalanches.

PCM inhaled deeply; after a few seconds, he heard three explosions in rapid succession shake the ground beneath his feet. Thankfully, the cave did not collapse, and snow did not bury them all. He was still alive—the intelligence was correct. He peered down—he could see the smouldering remains of the machine, and a torn hybrid limb. The Genetic Transmutor had been blasted to smithereens and the Omtronic detectors had suddenly stopped beeping.

PCM first checked on the scientists he was supposed to guard, and after ensuring their well-being, apart from one metamorphosis, turned towards his men, feeling a bit shaken. There were three casualties. As he reported back to base, he realised, rather embarrassingly, that he did not even want to think about *why* the alien mutagenic machine had stopped working in the first place—or where the fuel cell had been taken and by whom.

Before he could say or do anything, Prof. Kavita Aggarwal walked up to him and said something that forever changed his attitude towards blowing things up.

'Congratulations, PCM,' she remarked in a stern schoolteacher voice, 'you didn't just destroy a natural formation. You did much, much more.'

With this, she pointed at the cave and it suddenly struck PCM. Now it all made sense: the artificiality of the cave, its location, its security systems, and its weird walls with the strange symbols.

This was no cave.

This was an automated alien craft.

CCC, Prime Minister's Residence, 7 Lok Kalyan Marg, New Delhi, India
46 hours into the invasion

Every disoriented, stumped member of the National Disaster Response Council leaned forward in their chair and strained to hear what was being said.

'How do the Chinese fit in this?' Akash Gupta, director of the Intelligence Bureau, narrowed his eyes and asked his present company. 'Is this a Maoist conspiracy?'

The room suddenly went mum, horrified at the possibility.

Mercifully, a phone rang a couple of seconds later. The somehow still unruffled Cabinet Secretary Ajay Mishra reached for the receiver and spoke in short, clipped sentences. A minute later, the bureaucrat hung up, and looked at PM Roy, beaming. 'Yes sir, it is confirmed,' Mishra said. 'PCM has destroyed the alien machinery in Uri.'

'Some good news, finally!' Roy exclaimed. 'Thank God!'

'However,' cautioned Mishra, 'the Genetic Transmutor was not working to its maximum capacity. Someone had already taken its fuel cell, the Sinium crystal.'

'What do you mean taken?' Roy thundered and stood up. The conference room got a lot more cramped as waves of outrage radiated from the PM.

Before the sentence could be finished, the door swung open and Yasser Basheer trudged in, followed by an agitated deputy secretary. Security had already been given instructions to escort Basheer directly to 7LKM when he landed in India.

'Where is Miller?' Basheer asked as he strode into the meeting.

Roy looked at him, half-amused, half-furious. 'Hello to you, *too*. The Americans have already left the country. Not without incident, though. Miller was attacked by an alien-human hybrid on his way back.'

Basheer shrugged uninterestedly. He had left the facade of morality and petty, genteel mannerisms far behind.

Roy glared at Basheer and felt a lump in his throat. A man who had caused him so much suffering was standing right inside his home and there was nothing he could do about it. Damn diplomatic immunity, he thought, and clutched his chair so fiercely that his knuckles went white.

Basheer didn't seem to notice. His beaked nose and sunken eyes gave him the appearance of a bird of prey engrossed in hunting down his target. A greenish tinge had already started spreading over his face.

'The crystal,' Basheer muttered. 'Where is it?'

'We do not have it,' Roy replied.

Basheer took a seat and stared at a point on the opposite wall. For all that he cared, there were only two people in the room—Basheer himself, and anyone authorised to take the decisions he wanted them to.

Basheer looked squarely at Roy. 'Find the crystal. The Qa'haQ have got only one. If you locate it and they won't be able to activate the Genetic Transmutor again—till they get reinforcements from their home planet, which are not likely to come if they fail the first time...'

Roy felt his stomach drop. 'What do we do with the crystal?'

'Destroy it, of course! And wait for him to call.'

'Call? From whom? And what about China? How come the secondary source of radiation is in Beijing? Is this a Chinese secret weapon?'

Basheer shrugged. 'I don't think so. The Chinese seem to be totally unaware of what they have under their noses.'

'But why *China*?' Roy asked emphatically. 'And why Beijing?'

'I can hazard a guess,' Basheer mumbled. 'Every weapon has two components—software and hardware. While the artificial "brain" behind this Omtronic radiation is located in Uri, it requires hardware—lots of it—to affect the world the way it's meant to.'

'And you think they're somehow using China's hardware?'

'Yes. Where do you think the majority of hardware used in cell phone towers around the globe is manufactured? By placing the hardware controller in China, the software housed in Uri could imprint the metal with a specific code that can activate itself when the time is ripe.'

'Do the Chinese know of this?'

'You would not have been here if they had,' Basheer replied laconically.

Roy was about to let loose a stream of expletives when his cell phone starting ringing. An unknown number had flashed on its screen.

He reached for it but then shirked away; Roy could imagine the cell radiation permeating every cell in his body. However, he also knew this could be an emergency. He steeled himself and picked it up.

'Hello?'

'Ah, Mr Roy. Glad to finally be able to talk to you,' a voice said. The accent was a bit nasal, though Roy had trouble assigning a nationality to it.

'Who? Who is this?' Roy asked and snapped his fingers at the officer from the National Technical Research Organisation who was sitting in a corner taking notes. The message was instantly understood: trace the call.

'You can call me Blue. Don't bother finding out my real name, though.'

'Who the hell is this?'

'I hope Basheer has reached you?'

The voice made Roy uncomfortable. 'What? First tell me who you are, sir?'

'I am a member of the Conglomerate. I have some information you might want to use.'

'The Conglomerate?' Roy started and then controlled himself. 'What information? And why will you help us? Aren't you in cahoots with the Qa'haQ?'

'I just want you to know that not all of us are alike. I was trained as a scientist, Mr Roy. I live to experiment, to strive, to seek, to find, and to run a for-profit organisation. Lust for money and power is all right by me as long as it doesn't destroy one's home. Toppling governments, creating global financial scams and sometimes part-time pogroms are okay, but extermination of the entire human race is not. Who would you rule over then, eh?'

'Why are you calling me?'

'To *help* you, Bipolab; why else?' Roy could sense Blue's tone was genuine. 'It was I who told Basheer the truth about his genetic abnormality and told him to go help you. As far as I can see, he's doing a good job!'

'What do you know?' Roy could feel his head swimming. 'The Genetic Transmutor is...'

'Stop worrying about the Genetic Transmutor. Yes, it is almost impossible to destroy when it has a Sinium crystal powering it. However—luckily for you—the ISI agent who stumbled upon the Genetic Transmutor also somehow chanced upon how Qa'haQ technology operates—through telepathy—and was able to stop it.'

'Huh? ISI?'

'There is much you don't know.'

This was the license Roy needed. 'Are you saying some Pakistani stole *our* Sinium? Using telepathy? What nonsense!' Roy was livid.

'Indeed. All your bombs would not have dented the force field Sinium erects around the Genetic Transmutor. The Sinium crystal is quite a special power source—it defends itself. With the ISI agent somehow—even I don't know how, I admit—stumbling upon the fact that only a psychic connection can stop Sinium from integrating itself with the Genetic Transmutor, the machine was left defenceless. No Sinium, no shielding...'

'Are they...'

'Yes, Mr PM, your team has successfully destroyed the Genetic Transmutor.'

'What should I do now? There is also a secondary source.' Roy was begging to tire of this cat-and-mouse game.

'Then you *must* destroy that, too. And focus on locating the Sinium crystal. If the Qa'haQ find it, then they will create another Genetic Transmutor and the radiation amplification process will begin anew. It is the Sinium you need. You do that, and the Qa'haQ will no longer be able to focus EM radiation to change humankind's DNA. The mutagenic radiation will dissipate automatically—EM radiation levels will go back to the way they were, and life will return to normal. The Qa'haQ will return home, licking their wounds. Moreover, a cure lies in the Sinium crystal...'

'A cure?' Roy couldn't believe his ears. 'In the crystal?'

'Affirmative.'

Basheer heard murmurs around the room at that.

'But how do we find it?' Roy pressed home. 'If the ISI have it they will *never* give it to us!'

'They don't have it. *She* does. And soon the Conglomerate will have it, if you don't act fast.' Roy heard Blue laugh. 'Check your inbox—it has an address. Go for it!'

Blue hung up before PM Roy could ask him any more questions. Roy looked at the officer from NTRO, who merely shook his head, his shoulders drooping. The call was untraceable.

A PS sneaked in carrying a tablet: Roy had received a new email.

He scanned the message, jotted something down, and gave the piece of paper to Mishra. 'That's an address in New Delhi. Get our teams there. Now!'

'Yes, sir.' Mishra nodded.

'Well,' Roy looked at Basheer, 'you'd better hope this...Blue... gave us the right information.'

'I think I can vouch for the truth of...' Basheer barely had time to finish: a stream of a brownish liquid started oozing out of his nose, and he slumped forward. His face hit the table with dull thud, and a bloody tooth rolled out, but that hadn't hurt Basheer. He was unconscious before he saw the glass on table crack by the force of the impact.

Basheer had moved to the next stage of the mutation—a stage different from what was happening to other humans.

Roy shouted for a doctor as the people in the room, who had been quietly sitting in the background processing all this new information, instinctively rushed towards Basheer, unsure of how to handle a human who would soon cease to be one.

Munirka, New Delhi, India
48 hours into the invasion

'*Andar nahi jaounga*, ji.'

The three-wheeled vehicle swerved in the heavy traffic of South Delhi, blared its horn a few times, and defiantly parked itself at the curb next to Anupam Restaurant, right under the flyover. The auto driver had a prominent beer belly and even more prominent male-pattern baldness. He leered at Sonya's white top and her blue, flowing skirt through his rear-view mirror, and then proceeded to shake his head as if to cement his earlier decision.

Suddenly fully awake, Sonya adjusted her hair, devastated by the auto ride, and stared at the middle-aged driver, who just sat there. Sonya saw gods—and Katrina Kaif—stare back at her from the insides of the auto, gathered some courage, and smiled weakly. She squirmed, leaned forward, and placed her left hand above the (obviously) non-functional meter. 'Please, *bhaiyya*, drop me inside, *na*,' she begged.

The man didn't respond, and reached for another packet of *khaini*.

Sonya decided to change tactics. She puffed her face up and smirked. 'Should I lodge a complaint with the traffic police? You don't want to mess with me. Do you know who my chacha is?'

The driver's neck snapped back—and his eyes widened with newfound respect. He pleaded about the cramped by-lanes of the locality. 'Please madam, it's too crowded inside. The auto will get stuck. Moreover, one dent on the cars inside and the residents will eat me alive.'

Sonya smiled inwardly. If you can't make them do things your way, at least make them feel bad about it.

She muttered something under her breath, thrust a fresh 100-rupee note in the driver's direction, and climbed out, careful to avoid a puddle.

Her destination was quite near. With a deep breath, she jumped headlong into the vibrant colony.

If there was something called pure chaos, this was surely it, she thought. Personal space was a concept unheard of in this location. She could barely walk a foot without bumping into someone. The constantly moving, shape-shifting crowd reminded her of the rave parties she frequented as a Berlin teen, except this featured copious amounts of dirt, grime and puddles, and was sans the associated drugs, booze and music. It was overwhelming in more ways than one. However, what really pissed her off was when people who bumped into her or jostled for space merely kept walking without so much as an apology. Everyone seemed to be headed in a different direction—and for a different purpose, making Munirka seem a living specimen of Brownian motion.

People were the particles; she was the bombarding atom.

She smiled despite herself. Sonya had been jokingly called just that by Imran. 'Hello, Bombardment,' he used to call her teasingly.

Sonya tried to force him out of his head, focused on the shops around her, and took another turn. The heady smells, mooing cows, crowded shops, and gridlocked traffic were beginning to make her head spin and eyes water. She increased her pace, consciously ignoring the stares around her, and made a few right turns in the narrow by-lanes. Sonya was now in a cramped alley, though thankfully, it was not that crowded. She gritted her teeth as a couple passed by. The girl stared at Sonya's maroon KLM flight bag, one whose yellow stripes had made her fall in love with it, and the boy ogled at her legs.

She thanked God when, after a brisk walk of a few minutes, she finally reached her destination deep within the bowels of this modern-day village. It was a four-storey house, freshly painted and literally comprising four small rooms stacked on top of each other. A disused, rusting Bajaj Chetak that had once been green was parked at the entrance and a white cat lay stretched on its footboard.

Sonya swung the creaking door open, adjusted her bag and walked in. She reached a spindly staircase that winded all the way to the top, jogged up to her room on the fourth floor, and stepped inside the hovel.

She flicked on a light switch and scanned the room—it was empty. She turned back to close the plywood door that smelt of varnish, double-checked the bolt, and walked to a small cot.

Her head felt heavy, and it hurt. She plopped down on a folding bed, reached for a bottle of packaged water from a rickety side table and gulped it down. She then staggered to a washbasin, looked at her haggard reflection in the dirty mirror, and rinsed her face, eager to get the grime off.

She cursed the man who had sent her there. The room was devoid of ventilation and smelt funny, maybe because the sunlight never reached there, thanks to the haphazard construction all around it. The strange noises, shortage of water, frequent power cuts and barking dogs had kept Sonya on her toes since the moment she had arrived. She still couldn't fathom why she was told to stay here instead of a good hotel or a residence in a posh colony. When she had voiced her concerns, her source had gently chided her and told her to do as directed. She could sense there was something she wasn't being told.

At that moment, a sudden outpouring of a Rammstein song startled her. She hastily snaked a hand inside her purse, and fished out her cell phone. *'Hallo?'*

'Sonya...Sonya? Where are you? I am so worried about you!'

The voice at the other end was unmistakable. It was Imran.

Sonya had not expected Imran to call her after what she had done before she left. She had told him he was just a professional acquaintance and that he should stay away from her. She was beginning to get uncomfortable with his advances, and his attempts to get close to her constituted nothing short of harassment, which she might report to her friends in law enforcement if he persisted.

'What do you care?' Sonya's cold, neutral voice was as distant as it could be. 'Please leave me alone.'

Imran hurriedly responded. 'I wanted to confess something, Sonya, please listen to me.'

'I'm hanging...'

'Please don't. You should know something about me. I woke up in the hospital with you gone and I realised I wanted to tell you something,' Imran said without stopping. 'It might appal you.'

'Oh good,' Sonya cut him off icily. 'What do you think you might say, *Major* Imran Bhatt, that will shock me?'

There was a stunned silence at the other end for some time. A shocked Imran digested the information that his cover had been blown. Though he realised a small part of him was more concerned at having lost a woman who he had developed feelings for.

'How did you...' Imran croaked.

'Oh please.' Sonya's voice was mocking. When she spoke up next, she was almost taunting. 'You really don't think I fell for your looks, did you?'

Imran didn't know whether to be offended or surprised. He wasn't *that* bad-looking, was he? Instinctively, at an ISI safe house far away, where Imran currently was, he turned to his reflection in the mirror attached to the dressing table. 'But...why did you leave so suddenly after admitting me to the hospital? And my leg is better now; thanks for asking,' Imran said.

'Does it matter? You betrayed me.'

Ironically, it was Imran who felt betrayed. 'Since when have you known about me?' he asked, sullen.

'I was informed by a friend,' Sonya replied, knowing fully well it was her source that had informed her about Imran's duplicity.

'Why did you play along, then?'

Sonya smiled. 'Because I wanted something only you could have led me to. I was given the task of staying close to you and seeking out some juicy stories. Little did I know I would hit the jackpot!'

'What...You...?' Imran panted and tried to form words that just refused to come out.

'Indeed!'

'You used me!' Imran shouted, fury seeping in his voice.

'Look who's talking,' Sonya shot back.

'But why?' Imran moaned. 'Why do you want the crystal?'

'Why do *you*?'

'I was following orders!'

'Well, so was I,' Sonya retorted.

'Listen to me. This is far bigger than what it seems to you. You need to give the crystal to me.'

'Dream on, Imran. The crystal stays where it is.'

Imran could take it no longer. 'But...'

'Too late, Imran. You had a chance and you blew it. And I think it's time for me to cut off all contact,' Sonya whispered. 'Don't reach out ever again. Goodbye.'

Sonya hung up, stung. She sat rooted for what seemed like hours, her mind totally blank. Her reverie was broken by footfall and a gentle knock at her door. Sonya quickly blew her nose, washed her face again, and tiptoed to the door.

She peeked through the eyehole.

A dusky girl of around twenty-five years and medium height stood outside. She was dressed in a white salwar kameez and a saffron dupatta. The man with her, who wore a green khadi kurta, frayed black jeans and dusty sandals, completed the *tiranga* image that sprang in Sonya's mind. His untrimmed beard and unkempt appearance was the exact opposite of his companion.

'Who's there?' Sonya asked.

'Namaste, ji,' the girl replied. 'It is us only—your neighbours.'

Under ordinary circumstances, Sonya would have never opened the door. But she was still seething inside. She could feel the crystal playing tricks with her head. She knew she had to focus elsewhere; the radiation was beginning to make her act without thinking. Without worrying too much about the future, she opened the door and let them in, hoping this would not turn out to be another colossal mistake.

It did.

The woman slowly walked in, and the man followed as if unsure of himself.

'Hello, ji. Myself Ritu,' the woman smiled again and waved her hand. Then she pointed at the man, 'And this is Pankaj. We have rented the room next door. Just thought we'd come say hi.'

Pankaj, trying hard to look a tad mysterious, merely bowed slightly, and gazed around the room serenely as if lost in his own thoughts.

'Hey. I'm Sonya...Sonya Loewe. Please sit.' Sonya pointed at the two reed chairs kept in the corner of the dingy room.

'How are you, ji?' Ritu asked.

'I am good,' Sonya answered, '...and you?'

'Not as pretty as you. You are so pretty. Are you a foreigner?'

Sonya nodded. 'Indian dad, German mother. I am a reporter. What do you guys do?'

Ritu started chattering. 'I'm studying in JNU, whereas Pankaj is doing his masters from IIT. We plan to get married soon.' She glanced at the guy sitting alongside her; he looked as if he didn't want to be there. 'After all, what good is education without a family?'

Sonya merely listened to her innocent—if slightly politically incorrect—musings and smiled to herself.

'Where did you buy this bag? So retro this is. Pretty!' Ritu wasn't one to stop so soon.

Sonya smiled. 'Thank you. Sarojini.'

'Oh. I always shop at Sarojini. Good market. I like shopping there, but shopkeepers are very *kameena* with their gaze, if you know what I mean...' Ritu declared

They chatted for a couple of minutes before Sonya got up. 'Let me get you some tea.'

She walked to the attached kitchenette and put the kettle on.

These people may have been slightly weird, she thought, but at least they had helped her forget about recent events, even if momentarily. She smiled and turned back to enquire about sugar. Before she could speak, she felt a vice grip hold her hands as a damp cloth was pressed to her mouth. A pungent odour forced its way down to her stomach, making her gag. Oh God, she said inwardly as tears sprung to her eyes, I should never have opened the door.

Within a couple of seconds, Sonya was out cold in Pankaj's arms. He gently placed her on the floor and briskly walked to Ritu.

'Search the room. Retrieve the crystal,' Ritu ordered, and rushed to the door to bolt it from the inside lest they be disturbed in the middle of the activity.

'Yes, ma'am,' Pankaj nodded and sprung to action.

He busied himself with a few cartons kept in a corner and Ritu dug into Sonya's purse—both were wearing gloves by now. They reached for every object in sight, studied it carefully and then put it back from where they had taken it.

Ritu looked around the dusty apartment, and Pankaj rummaged through Sonya's bags. The two kept searching for a few minutes. Thankfully, the room was too small to hide all its secrets from persevering, prying eyes.

Ritu was the one who saw it first. She was going through the contents of a wooden box under the rusting folding bed—and there it was, between layers of clothing. She stared at this crystal, her mouth hanging wide open. The crystal was the size of her palm and as light as a feather. Weirdly, it began to gently glow with a light of its own when touched. Ritu didn't realise she had hit the jackpot. Someone was to collect the crystal that very evening, and the duo had reached Sonya's place just in the nick of time.

'Found it, Pankaj. Come here. What do you think this is?' Ritu asked curiously.

Pankaj shrugged. 'I just hope it's not another "Made in China" trinket! They're still coming, despite the unofficial ban.'

Ritu nodded as Pankaj gently hid the crystal in his pocket.

Pankaj suggested, 'Let's bail out, ma'am.'

Ritu was the senior officer and he knew he had to follow her lead. Still, he went and snooped around the room for more clues.

Ritu looked around for one last time, hoping she hadn't missed anything. 'Fine,' she said when satisfied, 'let's go!'

They looked through the eyehole, ensured no one was around, and stepped out confidently. They locked the door from the outside with the key they had found in Sonya's purse and climbed down. Thankfully, the actual occupants of the room next door, aspiring civil servants, were visiting their ancestral village in Bihar.

Ritu and Pankaj climbed down and headed towards the main road. They jumped over piles of steaming cow dung, darted behind carts selling fruits, passed bicycles laden with goods, and avoided teenage groups huddled together in the streets. No one even glanced at the duo more than once—they blended well with the crowd. Within moments, the two had disappeared into the back alleys of the locality. Both had been briefed on an escape route and they came across no complications. They reached Baba Gang Nath Marg and leisurely boarded a waiting Tata Sumo, and the car started moving towards Lodhi Road.

Ritu dialled 100 on her burner cell, told the operator about an attempted robbery and directed them to the house she had just exited. She knew the call would not be traced and the first Delhi Police team in would, wittingly or unwittingly, erase all traces of Ritu and Pankaj ever having been there.

What Sonya had not known was that the two 'neighbours' she had let in were actually Deputy Field Officers with RAW.

What Pankaj did not know was that once they were clear, Ritu had whipped out her cell phone and sent a cryptic message to her boss, a Senior Field Officer, who had been directed to forward the message straight to his top boss, the Secretary (R)—a rare honour.

What Ritu did not know was that Pankaj, an officer of the technical cadre, had been specially assigned to this case for another reason. He had already cloned Sonya's SIM Card and downloaded vital data from her phone. Once he was done, he mailed the information he had unearthed from Sonya's phone to an email ID. The email was redirected to another ID, and then another—a process which was repeated at least 10 times, bouncing off servers across the globe, until the information from Sonya's phone reached someone known only as Blue.

DRDO Laboratories, Metcalfe House, New Delhi, India
50 hours into the invasion

The gathered, motley group of physicists, biotechnologists, telecommunications experts, government scientists and corporate engineers murmured amongst themselves as they prepared to burn the midnight oil. Drawn from both the public and private sectors, these men and women represented the best technical minds India had to offer. The government of India had called in a few favours to ensure that all private consultants worth their salt were invited for this joint endeavour.

The operation was headed by Dr Amrit Pal Dhillon, the DG of DRDO. Personal histories were sifted through, technical acumen quantified, research areas combed, and clearance levels designated, before 10 teams were created. Each team was briefed about the problem, provided a state-of-the-art laboratory and equipment, and tasked to come up with a solution.

After what seemed like eternity, it was the fourth team that stumbled across a viable answer.

The victorious group trooped into the office of Prof. Kavita Aggarwal, who was supervising the experiments since the DG had been called to the PMO for an urgent briefing. Prof. Aggarwal, a veteran from the Department of Atomic Energy, had recently been deputed to DRDO.

Triumphant smiles played on their lips, but Prof Aggarwal was more sceptical than convinced—as her job demanded. It was her duty to be the devil's advocate, most of all in such situations.

'So, how did you do it?' She motioned at the team to sit down. They did not need to be told twice. They shuffled in a line and made themselves comfortable on the leather couches kept in Aggarwal's temporary office.

The team leader, a good-natured senior scientist from the Indian Space Research Organisation, beamed and replied, 'Ma'am, since the mutation is caused by cell phone radiation, we approached the problem with an understanding that telecommunications might be where the answer lies. Tests have shown that if we pass an electric current through Sinium at sub zero temperatures, the crystal emits a specific anti-radiation that, when filtered and processed through mercury, counters the mutagen. Thus, we can cure the ones already infected by administering a preset burst of radiation from the Sinium crystal under controlled conditions.'

'So this para-radiation makes the rDNA revert to its earlier double-helix form? Interesting. And how does one check the infection from spreading?' Aggarwal queried.

'Mutation is triggered by a unique waveform operating at a specific frequency. Let's call this mutation-causing entity "Dark Wave". It actually rides the cell phone carrier signal we use.'

'We cannot just shut down all wireless communication. I hope that's not your solution,' Aggarwal shot back.

'No, madam, of course not!' The ISRO man sounded hurt. He recovered quickly and continued, 'But we can block the Dark Wave. We have been successful in isolating its specifics, and now we intend to counter it.'

'And how would you do that without hampering telecommunications?' asked Prof. Aggarwal.

'We will let the carrier signal be. By doing this, our telecommunications will not be affected. But we can place suppressors that negate the frequency of the Dark Wave. All we need is sine-wave modulators inbuilt in each of the suppressors.'

'Hmm,' Prof. Aggarwal nodded in agreement, 'so if we can somehow filter the carrier signal and remove the Dark Wave, then the cell phone signal would become clean and cause no mutation?'

'Yes, ma'am.'

'And these suppressors that you mention? They sound like devices that can transmit certain signals whose waveforms can cancel out the erring frequency on the Dark Wave.'

'Yes, indeed! These devices would be relatively easy to construct, install and operate.'

'But where do we install them?'

'Wherever the levels of Omtronic radiation are the highest. The nearer to the source these suppressors can get, the better they'll be able to block and filter out the harmful mutation causing the frequency of the Dark Wave.'

'I believe we do have a way of detecting the Omtronic radiation. This plan might actually work—theoretically, at least.'

The ISRO man and his team merely nodded.

'You've done well. Start working on the suppressors. I will talk to the DG right away and brief him on how we can put an end to this madness. Thank you, gentlemen.' Aggarwal finished speaking and was about to wave them away when she realised something. She looked at two particular members of team, and corrected her last statement. 'Thank you, too, *ladies*. This is great work. You may go.'

The team smiled, sprang up, and streamed out. Through the corner of her eyes, Kavita Aggarwal saw one of the young team members give another a zealous high five.

Aggarwal smiled—at least they still had hope.

Prime Minister's Office, South Block, Raisina Hill, New Delhi, India

52 hours into the invasion

The prime ministerial cavalcade stopped a few feet short of South Block. An impressive SPG staffer held open the door as Bipolab Roy absent-mindedly stepped out of his black BMW 7 Series. He was still engrossed in conversation with Cabinet Secretary Ajay Mishra, who had been travelling with him in the same car.

The two were greeted by the ISRO chairperson, who had been patiently waiting for the duo to arrive. Bharathi Amanda Joseph, the poised, sari-clad woman, had a regal bearing that was hard to miss. Having arrived just moments ago, she stood at the entrance, leafing through a file on her tablet. The only words she heard being exchanged between the PM Roy and Cabinet Secretary Mishra were 'Secondary…source…neutralised…China…PCM' before the two, realising Bharathi was in earshot, stopped. She knew better than to ask. If it concerned her, the information would reach her—*through proper channel*. Everything else was hearsay.

At an acknowledging nod from Roy, Bharathi walked towards him, smiled softly, and reported, 'Sir, I have received confirmation.'

Roy nodded happily.

The trio started walking towards the privacy of four walls.

'Are you sure about the radio link?' Roy asked.

Bharathi affirmed. 'Yes, sir. We have located the presence of an emergency beacon within the Qa'haQ Genetic Transmutor—the one we disabled in Uri—which is now sending out a distress signal directed towards an orbiting entity.'

'Can it be communicating with one of our satellites in orbit?'

'Impossible, sir. The frequencies are all wrong.'

The group started walking through the buzzing corridors of South Block, and people parted way to give the three their space.

'Some other country's satellite?' Roy was hoping this might have been the case. 'Could it be an American or Chinese signal?'

'Negative, sir. No other country uses these frequencies—and I have never seen such a signal in my entire career.'

Mishra joined the conversation by asking what was on everyone's mind. 'The source of this beacon is extraterrestrial in origin. Is it safe to conclude the receiver is, too?'

Bharathi closed her eyes for a moment and faltered. Before she could reply, they reached the office; Roy was ushered inside by his private secretary, who then closed the doors from the outside, giving the three policy makers some much needed privacy.

The NSA, Manish Ranjan, was already seated there, waiting for the PM to arrive. He sprang up to greet the PM and then huddled near the group. The Situation Room #2 of the PMO was a small chamber with a long table and comfortable chairs that inspired dread because of the times they were used in.

Roy's coming to South Block was a pit stop between his official residence at 7 LKM, which he had left minutes ago, and his next destination, Rashtrapati Bhawan. As his office at South Block and the Presidential Estate were a stone's throw away from each other, he had decided to make a quick stop for some paperwork—and to retrieve something he kept in his safe.

'Yes,' replied Bharathi the moment doors closed, 'I believe the Genetic Transmutor was communicating with an alien mother ship, which, in all probability, is presently in geostationary orbit.'

'Which implies that…' Mishra's voice trailed into silence.

Roy understood his dilemma. 'Speak freely.'

Mishra nodded. '...The craft we shot at was just a smaller craft—part of a landing party; call it a Surface Impactor, if you must. The actual threat still circles above us.'

'Hmm...' Roy turned pensive.

Ranjan spoke for the first time—and brought the topic to brass tacks. 'So? How does that help us? How do we use this information to our strategic advantage?'

'Options?' Roy too jumped in the fray. 'We need to destroy that thing.'

The ISRO chairperson thought for a moment and then gently cleared her throat. 'We can track the distress beacon by modifying some of our equipment aboard RISAT...once that is done, we can triangulate the position of the alien ship...It might be a rough estimate, but I believe it is possible.'

'Let's not sit idly as Rome burns down!' Roy saw a glimmer of hope and decided to grab at it.

'But...but...' Now it was Bharathi's turn to play the devil's advocate. 'Even if we manage to track the alien mother ship, or calculate its approximate trajectory in our orbit, how do we take it out? It is probably going to have some sort of sophisticated energy shielding!'

Mishra put her doubts to rest. 'From the little I could learn from the aliens' tactical operations, they are still in stealth mode. They have not yet entered into an all-out war or gone batshit crazy. The craft we shot down was cloaked—not shielded. And as far as we know, the alien ships can either be shielded or cloaked, not both together.'

Ranjan was confused. 'Why not?'

'Hang on. We need another pair of eyes before we go further.' Roy lifted the receiver and asked his PS to send in the man who was waiting outside.

There was a knock at the door. It was General Rohit Malhotra—he had been summoned by the PM for his inputs. Not only was

Malhotra the serving chief of the Integrated Defence Staff, he was also the former head of India's Strategic Forces Command.

Malhotra walked in and crisply saluted; the PM nodded, pointed at a chair, and gestured for him to settle down.

'Okay, so you were telling us why the alien ship could either be cloaked or shielded, and not both together,' Roy continued.

'Simple,' Mishra supplied, 'if you're trying to cloak your ship, I reckon, you use camouflage. All power is rerouted to specialised circuits that imitate the external environment and make the ship invisible to the naked eye, maybe even to radars. This is how I would do it. However, if you raise energy shields at the moment, all attempts at stealth are wasted as the ship starts glowing like a light bulb!'

Ranjan almost rubbed his hands in glee. 'So you're saying that it is possible that we *can* get through the hull of their mother ship?'

'Yes, in theory,' Mishra answered.

Bharathi was at a loss here. 'But with *what*?'

Ranjan turned to Malhotra, reminding him of why he was there in the first place. The NSA had invited Malhotra for a reason—he knew something that the PM did not.

'General, can we deploy the IAF?'

Malhotra thought for a moment—having listened to this conversation, a nascent idea was beginning to form in his mind. 'Our fighter aircrafts, no matter how high their service ceiling is, cannot attack the orbiting Qa'haQ ship. There is no air up there and the jet engines need an atmosphere to operate.'

'Missiles?'

'As for our inter-continental ballistic missiles, the aliens will see them coming from a distance and either change course or raise shields. I assume that our projectile weapons are useless against their energy shielding,' Malhotra countered.

'A logical assumption,' Mishra nodded.

'What do we do?' the PM asked the gathering.

Ranjan spoke up. 'I believe we need something whose presence in our orbit is seen as normal...'

There was a brief silence as minds raced to arrive at solutions.

'We need a satellite!' Roy supplied.

Mishra smiled inwardly. A satellite made perfect sense.

'But what do we *do* with a satellite? Ram it into the alien ship?' Bharathi asked, seriously considering the flaws in this approach. 'Even without shielding, I believe the hull of the alien ship can take this impact—no matter how fast the satellite is travelling; unless, of course, it is somewhere near the speed of light, which is impossible. Let us not forget that the alien ship is an inter-stellar craft. Its hull is bound to be durable!'

'Durable enough to withstand a nuke?' Malhotra asked slyly.

This sent Bharathi into a tizzy as Roy watched, not sure of what was unfolding before him.

Bharathi stood up. 'This is preposterous, Manish ji! You expect me to blast off a functional nuclear warhead aboard a PSLV? Do you know how many complications can arise with such a foolhardy scheme? If the warhead detonates during the process of launch then...I'd rather let the aliens kill us than murder our own people.'

Ranjan started shaking with laughter. It was soft and slow at first, but then he burst out, and looked at Malhotra, who tried to suppress a grimace and looked away.

'What's so funny, Ranjan?'

In response, the NSA stopped laughing, straightened up, and looked straight at PM Roy with a gaze that sent shivers down Roy's spine.

'So, Mr Prime Minister, sir,' Ranjan queried softly, 'what *exactly* do you know about Chandrayan II?'

Beijing, China
54 hours into the invasion

PCM had hardly landed back at Palam Airport when he was whisked away to the Lodhi Road HQ for an emergency briefing: a new mission awaited him.

He swore to himself as the white Maruti Suzuki Ciaz picked him up at the airport, an orderly ready with his luggage. 'Am I the only RAW officer in the country?' he asked himself. However, PCM knew it was his former boss, the current NSA Manish Ranjan, who must have been pushing for his inclusion in such missions by specifically asking that PCM be deployed for these covert operations. He didn't know whether to feel honoured at the confidence placed in him, or get angry at being driven like this. If you are good at what you do, you live a great life. If you are really, *really* good, then people don't let you live at all.

PCM did what he did best in these moments: he stopped feeling the fatigue, and focused on the job.

A couple of hours later, he rushed to Terminal 3 of the Delhi airport again; this time to catch another flight—one bound for Beijing. Luckily, he already had a Chinese visa stamped in one of his passports.

PCM transformed again. This time he became Peter Charles Moreno, a Goan academic with a fondness for physics, philosophy, and *feni*.

The Air China flight to Beijing had been uneventful except for a slight incident. A newly-married Haryanvi couple sitting next to him had gotten drunk and started singing corny *ragnis* to each other. PCM, sitting at the aisle seat, had covered his face with his pillow and tried hard to rest. The singing didn't stop; nor did the drinking. Pissed off, he had turned to the couple and muttered something unintelligible in Arabic, taking care to mention the words 'jihad' and 'aircraft' in English. The stung couple had immediately stopped their antics. They had stared at PCM throughout the flight and flinched every time he moved.

He had chuckled to himself and fallen asleep to their fearful stares.

Hours later, the Airbus A330 landed at Beijing Capital International Airport. It was not his first visit to the country. He had to ensure it wasn't his last.

Once in Beijing, he had completed all the pre-immigration documentation, disembarked, and followed the yellow line till he reached Border Control. The terminal was sparkling, sprawling and efficient; passengers queued up for immigration, and security personnel maintained a careful vigil.

His turn came in a few moments. PCM walked up to the nearest empty counter and thrust his papers through the little slot in the glass window.

'Welcome to the People's Republic of China,' a bored-looking immigration officer, a youth no older than 25, mechanically spoke up as he sized up PCM from head to toe. 'What is the purpose of your visit?'

'Hey.' PCM smiled nervously, adjusted his (newly bought) spectacles, and began speaking in a nasal, arrogant tone that many Indians thought made them sound cooler. 'I'm here to attend a conference at Peking University'. He pointed at the letter from the university, slipped it past the glass window, and prayed it worked. The Indian Embassy in Beijing had had to pull quite a few strings to arrange for it.

The man typed something in his computer and looked up at PCM. 'Okay. Mr Moreno, what is the duration of your stay?'

'Three days maximum.'

'Which cities do you intend to visit?'

'I guess I won't have time to explore anything other than Beijing.'

'Do you have ample funds to sponsor your plans?'

PCM pretended to fumble as he reached inside his jacket, careful to only pick a couple of traveller's cheques he was carrying.

'Yes, sir. Here,' PCM showed it to the officer.

The officer glanced at those only briefly. He yawned, stamped his passport, and remarked, 'Thank you. Have a good day.'

PCM was through.

He smiled inwardly. International travel was a tad easier with an Indian passport.

PCM followed the signs and reached baggage retrieval. He picked up his luggage and slowly walked towards the exit. Within a few minutes, PCM had emerged from the airport terminal, hailed a cab and was headed towards downtown Beijing.

He checked into a hotel, freshened up and ordered room service. As the food trolley glided in moments later, PCM realised he could never get used to authentic Chinese food, having grown up on its spicier Indian-Chinese counterpart. He somehow shoved the bland squid fried rice in his mouth, washed it down with beer, and thanked the gods there was time for a quick catnap.

***

PCM was ready for action in a couple of hours. Sleep had managed to counter his earlier gruffness and his limbs no longer felt heavy. He allowed himself the luxury of a smile, happy to operating within normal parameters again. His mission was daunting. PCM was to locate and neutralise the secondary source of radiation, which was complicated by the simple fact that it was located in an extremely high-security area.

He took out his cell phone and fed in the address he had been made to memorise. Once that was done, PCM just walked through the city and followed the map to his final destination. The grey skies were ominous, and a cold breeze had started to blow. Undeterred, there were hordes of people out on the streets as far as eyes could see—a mixture of locals, tourists and government officials.

A few minutes later, PCM gazed at the screen of his cell phone and double checked the area. He was where he was supposed to be.

The Great Hall of the People was located at the western edge of the infamous Tiananmen Square—a building that constituted the heart of the People's Republic. Thankfully, there were no state functions planned that day and the building was open to the public.

PCM sauntered to the ticket booth just outside the building, purchased an entry pass, and went in. He counted seven alert sentries of the Central Security Bureau eyeing him, their QCW-05 suppressed submachine guns gleaming in the sun. He avoided their suspicious gazes and whipped out his Nikon D5300 DSLR. The message was clear—he was an inquisitive tourist, nothing else.

He climbed the stairs of the Great Hall and made his way to the main auditorium. The sheer size of the structure dazzled him; its craftsmanship made him awestruck. With the capacity to seat 10,000 people, this was one of the most beautifully and artfully decorated auditoriums he had ever seen.

PCM walked around the structure at a casual pace, taking his time and clicking pictures, careful not to be seen in a hurry. When a quick sweep failed to get any results, he reached bang in the middle of the auditorium, and took another look around. Only a few staffers stood on duty, and a couple of tourists wandered around. PCM checked his watch. The source of the radiation was right there, but where exactly? He had already checked every nook and cranny. He cursed under his breath, and his brain tried to find the missing link.

He looked into the distance when it suddenly hit him—the Omtronic radiation was coming from *above* him.

PCM instinctively directed his gaze at the ceiling and whistled. He saw an exquisite red star studded in the ceiling and gently throbbing. There was a strange power source at the centre of this red star that made it glow luminously, filling the hall with a soft, soothing light.

He marvelled at the craftsmanship and was about to look away when he saw some movement near the star.

It seemed to be nothing at first. Out of curiosity, he pointed his camera at the ceiling and zoomed in the red star. What PCM saw was a house-lizard scurrying on the ceiling, happily darting around. But then something told PCM all was not as normal as it looked. He kept monitoring the situation through his camera, though he was mindful not to arouse suspicion.

PCM spied the lizard positioning itself right next to the red star, pressing itself to it and glow pure white for a brief moment. The lizard shuddered, changed colours like a chameleon and then completely *disappeared*.

He almost jumped, and inhaled deeply; was he hallucinating? PCM rechecked: his camera, and the pictures in it, clearly weren't lying. The facts were clear as day: there was a source of mutagenic radiation present inside the hall. A strange object here made lizards vanish. He now had proof—there was something funny about this red star. In all likelihood, this was the source of the Omtronic radiation being emitted from the Great Hall.

His mind started working furiously. PCM now knew he had to destroy the red star but he didn't know how. Any show of a weapon or hostile intent, and the security would take him down. He had no intention of finding out what a Chinese prison looked like from the inside. Moreover, he was not carrying a weapon.

A plan began taking shape in his mind. It was slightly unconventional, but he had to try it.

Without waiting for another second, PCM dropped the camera and started screaming.

'Hellllllp!'

The world stopped around him.

He winced as the lens shattered as it hit the floor.

Necks craned, feet shuffled and faces turned in his direction.

'Terrorist! Gun!'

PCM did not stop his fit. He pointed at the ceiling, right where the red star was, and continued braying at the top of his lungs.

Within moments, two sentries had made his way to his location. Their faces were contorted—whether with rage or fear, PCM could not tell. He hoped for the latter.

'Why you scream, mister?' a sentry blurted out.

In response, PCM just looked up at the ceiling, and pointed at the red star. 'Terrorist! I saw a terrorist!'

'Where?' the guard, Yin, barked and unlocked the safety on his weapon. He swerved around to spot the invisible foe and motioned his buddy to go take a sniping position.

The auditorium had been emptied by now. PCM knew he had only minutes before the much more experienced Snow Leopards Commando Unit reached the auditorium. If they did, his plan would fail. They would see right through his act.

PCM was counting on the inexperience of the guard, hoping the two youngsters assigned to guard duty would be more trigger-happy and eager to prove a point.

'There!' PCM wailed. 'I saw him there!'

'What?' Yin asked disbelievingly. 'Where? The ceiling?'

'Yes...in the red star! *Inside* it!' PCM cried out in panic. 'A face, a hand. A weapon!'

PCM could feel the sentry observing him carefully, trying to decide whether it was a ruse or not.

'What sort of a face?'

'I don't know!' PCM moaned. 'He looked Central Asian to me. He... He was wearing a skullcap and carrying a gun. I saw his lips moving. Almost as if he was reciting something. I swear it.'

'But how could he be inside the red star?' Yin muttered.

'I don't know! It looks like a false ceiling.'

The main doors, which had clanged shut once all the civilians were evacuated, creaked open.

PCM could hear security vans grinding to a halt outside. It had only been a few minutes but backup was here already. He had to hand it to the quick response teams of the Chinese anti-terror units.

He decided to up the ante, giving this one last shot before what was bound to be a long, hard and possibly bloody interrogation by the Chinese Ministry of State Security.

'There! He is there again!' PCM yipped in false terror. 'Look up; see, he is reaching for his gun! He is going to fire.'

The guard was breathing fast by now. Via two statements, PCM had implicitly conveyed misinformation that could lead Yin to a conclusion PCM wanted him to arrive at. The invisible assailant might have been a separatist from the Xinjiang Uyghur Autonomous Region. The Turkistan Islamic Party, an Islamist terrorist and separatist organisation founded by Uyghur militants in western China, had long been trying to attack China's state apparatus. Secondly, PCM had taken care to weave this lie with a fact. Though it was not officially acknowledged, it was common knowledge—at least among the Chinese uniformed personnel—that the Ministry of State Security always had agents recording and listening to every public gathering, especially in a sensitive area such as Beijing, using well-concealed rooms in the buildings themselves. The red star on the ceiling, with its glass area, might have been part of one such structure, for all the guard knew.

At that moment, PCM heard boots rushing towards him. The commandos had reached the location. He judged they would reach his—and Yin's—exact location in under 10 seconds.

PCM, huddling on the floor, pointed a shaking finger at the red star embedded in the ceiling and moaned, 'He's firing! Oh my God, he's firing!' He turned towards Yin. 'He's going to kill us all, right in the middle of this hall!'

Yin's eyes hardened. If, by some chance, this crazy tourist was right, he thought, if there was a Uyghur separatist getting ready to destroy this monument, he needed to stop him.

Yin's sub-machine gun pointed towards the sky and spat fire in a single-burst mode. His aim was true.

With a sound like the crack of a whip, the bullet went straight up and lodged itself in the red star.

For a moment, nothing happened. By then, a platoon of commandoes reached PCM and cordoned him off. Angry and suspicious faces looked at PCM, then at Yin, and a medic rushed in to extract PCM from the situation.

Before PCM could be loaded onto a stretcher, the red star stopped glowing. A part of it shattered and fell to the floor with a sonic pop that confounded him. A blue-green light started to emanate from the star, but it disappeared almost as soon as it had appeared. The red star flickered and actually imploded, taking a part of the ceiling with it. Those present in the hall below instinctively raised their hands to shield their eyes from this sudden but harmless mini-supernova.

As PCM was carried out, he looked at his watch and stopped his twitching lips from breaking into a smile. The Omtronic radiation was no longer present in the room.

Before he lost sight of the gathering, he caught a glimpse of Yin's face—it was scarred by confusion and guilt. PCM felt sorry for him; he wanted to pat Yin as the commandoes took him into custody for discharging his weapon inside the Great Hall, and to tell him that his bullet might have had ended his career but might also have saved this planet.

DRDO Laboratories, Metcalfe House, New Delhi, India

56 hours into the invasion

In another sterilised lab within the same complex, Dr Revathi Balakrishnan was busy working with Prof. Kavita Aggarwal. The team was closely monitored by Yasser Basheer from a control chamber located right outside the Primary Lab #1.

'Room sealed,' Aggarwal announced curtly. 'Commence operation on my mark.'

Revathi smiled nervously and looked at her colleague as if to say, 'So it begins!' but Aggarwal's face was hidden by a glass visor. Both the occupants of the lab were dressed in yellow anti-contamination suits; the object they were studying was still emitting low levels of radiation. Right in the middle of the empty lab was a four-by-four-foot, vacuum-sealed chamber that housed the Qa'haQ Sinium crystal.

It just sat there, Revathi thought, like any harmless trinket, but she knew better.

'Begin stage I. Get a sample.'

Revathi nodded, and slowly pressed a lever.

There was a faint sputter as a slab popped open and an orifice formed in the glass chamber.

'Activate arm,' Prof. Aggarwal commanded. 'Extract a sample from the crystal.'

Revathi pressed a button and a mechanical arm slowly moved towards the Sinium crystal and chipped away a small piece. A strange blue-green energy rippled around the crystal, as if anticipating and resisting their assault.

'Full power to the arm!' Revathi turned the 'power' dial to full.

There was a shriek of metal as the arm went even deeper.

A loud bang resounded and the chamber was plunged into sudden darkness. All the equipment around them seemed to fizzle out. Revathi could feel time slow down as she saw blue-green light leaping out of the crystal, and disappear into thin air.

She cried out as the floor suddenly started shuddering. A steady stream of vibrating, colourful particles emerged from the crystal, rose in the air and then dissipated before her eyes. Within seconds that felt like minutes, she heard another explosion and the lights retuned.

The crystal imploded in a puff of greenish smoke. Thanks to the bullet-proof glass that harboured it, no damage was inflicted to the room, but Revathi was temporarily blinded by the flash.

'Done!' Revathi muttered excitedly as the arm parted with a piece of crystal. 'Stage I complete!' Revathi shouted in happiness over her suit's intercom. 'Sampling has been successful. Scanning the sample and transferring it to the BioTech Lab 3 now!'

She turned around to look at Aggarwal, who gave her thumbs up, and instructed for stage II.

'Simulations already underway.'

'Specify parameters?'

'How exposure to this crystal's particles could change our DNA. We are hoping it will counteract the earlier mutagenic radiation. At least that's what we have been told.' Revathi turned in the direction of the control booth to look at Yasser Basheer, who merely smiled at her.

'Good!' Aggarwal broke in with enthusiasm. 'Let's find a cure for this goddamn mutation!'

Revathi nodded and returned to her simulations. She knew it was going to be a long road ahead, but they were prepared for it.

Prime Minister's Office, South Block, Raisina Hill, New Delhi, India

56 hours into the invasion

It was not a good day to be a member of the secretarial staff at the PMO, taking minutes of the meetings. Shaking hands, jittery nerves and good stenographers weren't the best of friends.

The group turned to Bharathi Joseph as NSA Manish Ranjan repeated his question.

Bharathi slowly shook her head, unsure of the direction in which this conversation was headed. 'What exactly do you want to know?' Her eyes narrowed.

Ranjan realised this was going to be tricky. He coughed politely, turned to Roy, and said, 'Could the PM be kind enough to ask the lady about the payload of Chandrayan II? The specifics?'

The prime minister, a note of amusement creeping in his voice, duly obliged.

'Chandrayan II carried a lunar orbiter, a lander, a lunar rover and...and...'

'Yes...?' Ranjan leaned forward.

'A classified Military Emergency Rescue Vehicle—MERV—that was given to us by the DRDO,' Bharathi said quietly, her throat suddenly dry.

'There you are,' Ranjan softly thumped the table once with his left hand.

'MERV?' PM Roy was curious.

'It was an object we blasted off for the DRDO in the same mission as Chandrayan II—based on the request of a previous administration. I had almost forgotten about it till now. There were conspiracy theories but we had our orders—and, honestly, the rumours did not make *any* sense. It was just an experimental prototype…' Bharathi trailed off.

'Of what? And its function?' Roy asked.

'One. To repair or disable satellites that could no longer be maintained by ISRO. Two. To ensure Chandrayaan I or II, or any other Indian space hardware for that matter, never fell in someone else's hands.'

'Disable?' the PM queried.

'Yes, sir,' replied Bharathi.

'How? And why?'

'Thanks to the Chinese messing with satellites in orbit, the DRDO came up with a motor that could change the trajectory of satellites—give them a little push, either towards the sun, or away from the solar system, so that these satellites do not somehow reach hostile foreign powers,' concluded Bharathi.

The PM gazed questioningly at Ranjan. 'What is this about?' he thought.

Ranjan understood it was time to hit the nail squarely on the head. 'Where is this MERV now, Bharathi?'

'Orbiting somewhere between the earth and the moon, I guess, waiting for instructions. I still do not see how this is connected to the problem at hand,' came the slightly caustic reply.

Ranjan grimaced, and his eyes bore into those present in the gathering. 'What I am about to tell you is highly classified and must never leave this room. Mr PM, forgive me for not telling you this earlier, but this had happened during the times of your predecessor, and I had no idea we would ever need to use or even talk about the MERV.'

Roy nodded unsurely. 'Go on.'

'The DRDO "Motor" aboard the MERV is not a motor at all...'

Roy's interest was piqued by this. 'Then what is it?'

'It is an experimental 50 kiloton thermo-nuclear device.'

The gathering was speechless.

The first reaction came from Bharathi. '*What? How?* Why was the ISRO not told? We launched it into space!'

'I assure you that senior scientists from the DRDO had vetted it for safety hazards and deemed it fit for launch,' Ranjan countered.

'But we should have been told we were placing a nuke in orbit!'

'Would you have allowed it?' Ranjan's tone cut like a knife.

A sullen silence ensued.

'But why a nuke in space, for God's sake?'

'Two words—power projection. The new century is ours. No one screws with us again,' Ranjan spat out.

This is when the PM jumped in. 'We can discuss the ethical and political dimensions of this act later. I may have issues with this, but we need to use all means at our disposal. If the previous government thought of this—even if they meant it as a tool for international posturing—well, good for us! I am surprised Mishra did not tell me about this...'

Mishra shrugged, used to this restriction of information by now. 'Sir, I may be the cabinet secretary, but there is some information even I am not privy to. This seems to be a joint operation between RAW and Military's Strategic Forces Command. I had no inkling. Only Ranjan, Malhotra and handful of other key personnel knew about this...'

Roy was still unsure. 'But why did the DG of the DRDO not tell me this?'

Ranjan explained, 'Sir, even the DRDO scientists did not know that the device they created would be sent into space. Moreover, the feasibility studies they were asked to conduct were part of simulations and mock drills. They thought we were dealing in hypotheticals!'

Roy didn't know whether to be happy that they had a fighting chance at defending the country or awfully angry at not being informed earlier.

'So what do we do now, sir?' Bharathi asked Roy.

'If I give the order to detonate the warhead, how would we go about it?'

'We will have to first activate the MERV. Prime the warhead aboard it...and...' Ranjan answered.

'I will talk to the MCF located at Hassan about the MERV,' Bharathi said.

'MCF?'

'The Master Control Facility—it handles in-orbit operations.'

'Hmm.'

'Now that I have your approval, we can change MERV's trajectory right away. We can bring it near the probable location of the Qa'haQ mother ship once we have triangulated the signal, and then detonate the warhead at an appropriate, critical distance.'

The PM nodded. 'Can we operationalise this plan?'

The group muttered amongst themselves for a few seconds before announcing that it was possible.

Malhotra said, 'The Qa'haQ will never suspect it to be a nuke... they will think it's another decommissioned satellite, another piece of floating space junk, and will never raise their shields in time. Let us see if their hull can take a 50 kiloton nuclear blast from up close!'

'But what about the debris crashing back on the planet?' Roy was still not fully convinced. 'Won't this lead to radioactive fallout?'

Ranjan already had an answer. 'The nuke has been designed keeping this factor in mind. A special Explosion Vector Control Device (EVCD) has been added to MERV's warhead. The bomb will atomise any matter within its blast radius. Moreover, the

EVCD directional sensors will ensure that the broken fragments of the alien ship will be redirected away from the earth, and not towards our atmosphere. We are safe on that front.'

Roy sighed, looked into the distance, and rolled his fists into balls.

'Sir?'

A short command escaped Roy's lips: 'Mow them down!'

***

A few minutes later, the MERV—revolving hundreds of kilometres from Earth—received a signal from its mission control that made it change its trajectory. It coyly rolled over, realigned itself, and sped towards a geostationary Earth orbit, right where the Qa'haQ mother ship was.

The onboard computer had begun its countdown. The DRDO-built 50 kiloton thermo-nuclear warhead was primed and ready to thunder.

DRDO Laboratories, Metcalfe House, New Delhi, India

58 hours into the invasion

A few hours earlier, Basheer had been caught off guard by the vibrating phone in his pocket. He had reached into the depths of his white lab coat, taken out his phone and read the message. His eyes had widened.

The message was simple: 'Hyatt. 4 hours. B.'

So Blue wanted to meet him at a hotel in 4 hours, he thought, but why? Basheer chose not to think about the whys of it. Second-guessing Blue was impossible. He had called his driver to tell him they would be departing soon, and returned to work.

Presently, he was peering out of the glass cubicle, and monitoring the progress of the experiment; fatigue and drowsiness were written on his sallow face. He remembered every single second of the last three hours, despite having been semi-conscious. Basheer, after passing out at the PM's residence, had been rushed to the medical centre within the compound. It was a temporary loss of consciousness, however. He had stirred soon enough and was discharged within minutes—his recovery was astoundingly swift. Mindful of his promise, he had forced himself towards a lab where he, along with a team of driven professionals, was expected to crack open the sinister secrets of Sinium.

As if driven by a divine force, the scientists around him had succeeded in drawing up a procedure to extract pure Sinium from the lone crystal, and had perfected the idea that the crystal could emit anti-mutagenic radiation under controlled conditions—all in record time. He had provided them with a sample of his own blood so that they could comprehend the workings of Sinium better. Prof. Kavita Aggarwal and her team then started to replicate the essence, so that an effective antidote could be synthesised and administered, and the mutation could be stopped. All they had to do was map the chemical structure of the element, stabilise it, and then artificially create the same structure within a lab.

Basheer thanked his stars he was among professionals who knew what they were doing. He was working with the crème de la crème of the country, personnel hand-picked from the Council of Scientific and Industrial Research (CSIR), Defence Research and Development Organization (DRDO), and Indian Space Research Organisation (ISRO)—who had slogged hard to execute his schematics with a calm dexterity only trained hands could have mustered. There was zero room for error. If even one calculation was botched, then all would be in vain. Thankfully, everything had gone smoothly till now.

The woman heading this task force, a usually calm Prof. Kavita Aggarwal, was quite fired up to pay the aliens back in their own coin. Moreover, almost every person in the lab felt personally wronged by the attack on Mishra—a fellow technocrat and a man of peace. This gave them drive, which was good for results.

Basheer stepped out of the cubicle, hoping things would go as well in real life as they did in the computer simulations. He walked to a squirming, balding man and cast a questioning glance towards Prof. Aggarwal, who was supervising the entire procedure. Basheer's uneasy stare was met with a nervous smile—yet there were no indications of failure in those eyes.

Any moment now they'd see the test results coming.

Basheer shut his eyes in anticipation and a few seconds later, upon hearing a delighted whoop, snapped them open. He knew it could mean only thing. The antidote, which was being tested on a rather severe case of the mutation, had succeeded. He stared into the test cage, praying to a god he knew did not really exist.

Instead of a human-crocodile that was yellow-green in colour, he saw a pale boy, hardly 20, regaining consciousness. The test subject was not exactly fully human again, but he was slowly losing the scales and the leathery skin, thanks to the intravenous drip of Sinium. The young lad was emaciated from all the sudden physiological changes, and had lost all body hair. However, his face, though sweating, was beginning to beam with a new life of its own. Basheer saw relief in those eyes—coupled with bewilderment, pain and gratefulness.

They were no longer yellow, but brown.

Basheer squealed in delight—they had succeeded! He felt a small ball of exhilaration suddenly inflate in his beleaguered heart as he laughed and instinctively patted the scientist standing closest to him.

Then, after a brief round of zealous congratulations and studying some more test cases, he came out of the lab—he knew the Indians could take it from here. He was needed elsewhere at the moment.

He whirled around, exited the building and walked towards the secondary exit, where a car would be waiting to take him to the hotel where Blue wanted to meet.

Basheer cared little for the uncouth IB agents tailing him; they were too distraught to even change cars, he noticed. Moreover, there was nothing they could do to him as long as he had a carte blanche from the PMO itself. With his role in making the antidote a reality, he knew he had bought himself some more time.

What truly worried him at that moment was not how the Indians would react to his presence but what was happening to *him* from the inside, and to a slightly lesser degree, the implications of Blue's message.

He only hoped he was not too late.

Basheer reached his waiting car, climbed in, and did something that would earn him the absolute, unflinching loyalty of the man who drove it. He smiled and pushed a fresh, newly issued 2,000-rupee note into the eager hands of the waiting driver.

The car sped forward.

Earth Report 2: On board Qa'haQ Shuttle *D'bHin* Pitampura, New Delhi, India

Commander S'aulk was an unhappy Qa'haQ, despite finding a suitable power source to recharge his shuttle batteries.

S'aulk could not believe a human attack craft had seen through his cloaking shields and fired on him. The damage was not extensive, but was cause enough for him to lick his wounds. To make matters worse, the mother ship had been attacked by the humans. He had received an informal message that the crew aboard the mother ship believed his carelessness on Earth had somehow led the humans to find a chink in the Qa'haQian cloaking armour—though they did not dare speak it out loud since he was still in command of this expedition.

S'aulk's ego had been bruised—so had his career plans. How could he return with his honour hurt thus? Thankfully, the integrity of the mother ship's hull hadn't been compromised by the atomic blast, though multiple decks had depressurised and the ship was venting plasma. It needed immediate repair in a dry dock. He had to take a decision fast—tuck tail and run, or attempt one final push.

S'aulk cursed in indignation. He wanted to do neither.

The shuttle had re-cloaked and attached itself to the 235-metre tall Doordarshan TV Tower in Pitampura. The Qa'haQ used a Differential-Propulsion Drive and his craft, a *D'bHin* class vessel, was fitted with this system. This technology utilised the difference between pre-amplified and post-amplified waves to generate power.

S'aulk sat inside his gestation cubicle, which was specially fitted in this craft. The warmth inside the shell made him relax and allowed him to think. He closed his eyes, curled up his body into a ball, and retracted his claws. It was guilt-tripping time.

He could not believe that the Genetic Transmutor had been neutralised by the *Homo sapiens*. Worse, the Sinium crystal was missing. Word would already have reached his home planet Qa'haQam that S'aulk, second in line to the Mountain Hives, and commander of the Eleventh Order, had failed in a critical mission to a Class III Planet.

S'aulk could feel the repercussions already. Sub-Commander Dac'ish had reverted to her secondary mate the moment the mission had exhibited the first signs of trouble. She had made it clear she wanted nothing to do with a Qa'haQ who could lose the Holy Land so easily. 'Could things get any worse?' he thought bitterly.

His reverie was broken by a gentle chime. The bridge was trying to reach him. He came out of his rest-chamber and strutted towards the bridge. He was met by Dac'ish—who saluted him half-heartedly, almost contemptuously.

He dismissed her immediately. There was only one way to regain lost honour, he told himself—through a resounding victory.

Once he ensured he was alone on the bridge, S'aulk walked up to the communication console and inserted his right primary claw into the device. The computer authenticated his identity, and then conveyed that there was a transmission from Earth that merited his attention.

S'aulk listened to the broadcast very carefully. The words were not lost on him. He re-heard the message and closed his eyes for a full five keks as his brain whirred to make sense.

Finally, he got it. There was a time to fight, and a time to talk. Maybe the humans responded better to words, he thought. Yes, he was going to do something that no one had thought of doing in centuries.

He was going to talk to the natives.

Hyatt Regency, Bhikaji Cama Place, New Delhi, India
62 hours into the invasion

The three-bedroom Presidential Suite smelt of lavender and freshly brewed coffee. Red stood near the garden terrace but was unable to enjoy the panoramic view of Delhi from the Regency Club floor, thanks to the uncharacteristic, unseasonal smog. He muttered something under his breath, walked back inside, and plonked on a white couch kept in the living area. Dressed in a brown tee shirt and black jeans, he fired up an ultra-slim laptop kept on his unimpressive paunch.

Red was not alone in the room. He reached forward to pour a cup of coffee, and graciously handed it to the distressed woman beside him.

Sonya Loewe tucked a lock of hair behind her ear, accepted the cup gratefully, and started to sip.

'They forcibly took it from me.' She sounded shaken. 'I kept waiting for you, holed up in that tiny room in Munirka, but your contact never showed up.'

Red did not speak—he just stared into the distance.

Sonya continued, the silence eating into her. 'What do you want me to say? I stole the Sinium crystal for *you*...'

Red placed a reassuring hand on her wrist, 'Don't bother yourself with this now...'

He saw the colour drain from Sonya's face. 'Relax, nothing will change between us. I will still keep directing you to the greatest of stories, mostly even before they happen!'

A flicker of relief played on Sonya's tense countenance. 'That means you won't punish me?'

The man threw his head back and laughed in a grandfatherly manner. 'Of course not!' He spoke with twinkling eyes. 'You did all that was asked of you.'

'Thank you, Red, thank you!' Sonya stopped and whimpered. 'What about...' She fell silent.

'Yes?' Red encouraged her to continue.

Sonya kept quiet for a few seconds. The sky had darkened by now and fat droplets of rain had started to pitter-patter against the huge glass windows.

'What about Imran? Will he live?'

Red, head of the Conglomerate High Council, stared at her for a long, long time.

'Ah. *That* boy.'

The man went silent and tapped his fingers on the armrest of the sofa. 'Life is already complicated enough, Sonya. You should be with someone who can help you, rather than being with someone who needs *your* help instead. Why do you want...'

Sonya did not let him finish. 'Could you let him go? Please?'

Red grinned from ear to ear. 'Had I not known better, I'd have thought that you have developed a soft spot for him. You'd still be with him if I hadn't told you about his true identity. He is an enemy spy!'

Sonya chose to remain quiet. She knew she could never see Imran again, but a part of her wanted to, for one last time. She spoke after a few uncomfortable moments. '...Can I meet him?'

Red, his contempt for these teenage emotions evident in his unblinking eyes, looked away. Sonya was a trusted reporter who often helped him get good publicity, but now she was just proving to be a liability. He could no longer have Sonya running around asking questions about an ISI agent who would soon cease to exist, he realised. People like him encouraged the world to arrive at the wrong answers, not ask the right questions.

Red turned to look at her, a cold smile spreading on his face. 'I have nothing against that boy. If anything, I am impressed that he managed to crack Qa'haQ security codes and get to the Sinium. Thank God you stole the crystal from him—but what was the point, tell me? You lost the most powerful energy source known to mankind.'

Sonya's relief suddenly vanished. She felt Red would not let her off the hook so easily, and it angered her how she had to beg this slimy creature to repay his debt. 'Okay, I am out of this. It is done. No more! I refuse to be your pawn anymore—you and your tips can go to hell!'

'Do you think it's wise to antagonise a powerful man?'

'You underestimate me, Red. I don't make threats—I execute them,' she said.

Red started laughing in response, his belly shaking. He knew what she was hinting at. She'd be dead before she even thought about leaking information about him to the press, he thought. Red always had a mental checklist of targets he needed out of the way. Currently, Sonya topped that list; Basheer and Miller followed. They knew too much. Politicians he could easily manipulate, but these intelligence officers were paranoid by design. As for Imran, Red knew no human could connect to a Qa'haQ telekinetic source and retain his sanity.

He turned to face Sonya. 'Just try it.'

'What do you mean?' she whispered.

'Never mind what I say. Just mind what I *do*.' Red bared his crooked teeth in a repulsive grin, rose, and started walking towards a drawer.

'And how will you kill him?' Sonya resigned herself to her fate. 'I thought you were a trusted colleague.'

'Correction. I was your source. You are but one of the many, many reporters I utilise to spread information that benefits me—come now, don't give me that look; these leads benefitted you too in the process, did they not?'

Sonya backed away slowly. 'What will happen to me now? A tragic accident?'

The man raised his eyebrows and scoffed at the idea. 'Am I a barbarian?'

Sonya didn't know what to say. 'Then how?' Her eyes flitted towards the door and she wondered if she should make a dash for it.

Red simply stared at the cup from which Sonya had been sipping the hot beverage.

Sonya's mouth dropped open in absolute horror and she recoiled. 'What?'

Red pressed an inhaler to his mouth, and spoke again. 'It is considered customary in my profession to possess certain substances that can be administered on the go. Incidentally, you just sipped something with your coffee. Had you not persisted with your line of inquiry, I'd have made you have another cup, this one with the antidote.

At that moment, the effects of the drug became more visible. Sonya's eyes widened for a brief instant before she crumpled to the floor, senseless. Acting as if nothing had happened, Red went to his wardrobe and started to pack a few things into his bag. He knew his men would appear soon and take care of the body. Red wanted to leave no clues for that nosey Miller—he had start sniffing around already, something that needed to be remedied soon.

Lost in thought, Red was preparing to stuff a jacket inside the red duffel bag when he heard a faint thump. He froze.

With agility far past his age, Red whirled around and reached for a firearm hidden inside his bag. However, before he could lay his hands on the pistol, the door to his suite flew open, and he saw a gun emerge out of the shadows.

'Not so fast, Red,' the newcomer sneered through clenched teeth. His eyes spat fire.

A strange tension gripped Red's body. He cursed out loud as he saw the assailant. '*You?* What are you doing here?'

'I just dropped by. Hope it's not a bad time for you,' the man mocked and continued. 'It has been a long time since we met, Father.'

Red's ruddy face lost all colour, for there, pointing a gleaming SIG P226 pistol at him, stood the man who Red feared—and admired—the most.

His own blood.

His sole surviving child.

Yasser Basheer.

Oltar Cornfields, Iowa, USA
64 hours into the invasion

A vast, desolate cornfield in the middle of nowhere was the last place one would imagine to harbour a classified military presence. Perhaps for that very reason, during the peak of the Cold War, the Department of Defense had convinced some patriotic landowners in the Midwestern United States to lease a few hundred hectares of their farms for the purpose of constructing life-support bunkers under their homes. The attempt was part of a federal project aimed at creating multiple 'safe' locations around the US that could withstand a Soviet nuclear assault and then act as a nucleus for life to re-emanate in case the unthinkable happened.

Years down the line, with the Cold War over, the structures were largely forgotten. Later, a mega-corporation had approached the farmers with an offer to buy their hollow lands for a handsome price. Due to a decrease in the prices of corn and increase in the prices of seeds, the deal had been instantly clinched.

Once the land was acquired, the Oltar Corporation had started working towards refurbishing and expanding the subterranean facility located under the cornfields. Management at the corporation had recently realised that it was time to diversify and join the most profitable of current business endeavours—the War on Terror. Oltar Corporation had just won an important bid; its idea to convert a disused nuclear shelter into a state-of-the-art maximum security detention facility had been granted federal approval. The entire complex was now fully operational—but held only one prisoner, along with hundreds of soldiers belonging to the United States Marine Corps.

Private Daniel McPherson was one such guard.

He had recently joined this assignment and was still fuming over the task he had received. McPherson had not refused, of course. He was sworn to follow orders—and one of those orders was to keep the man he was guarding quite alive, even if he hated that job, or that man, for that matter.

Private McPherson signed the logbook as he made his way towards the main cell; the tunnel walls around him were solid concrete and lit by a dim bulb every 20 metres. The tunnel led to the main holding area, which was a windowless 200-square-foot bare hall, in the middle of which was a metal cage. Inside this was a cell, a third layer of security.

Out of sheer habit, Private McPherson glanced at the solitary resident of the cell. The man sat on the floor, muttering something to himself, as he often did. McPherson felt a bolt of rage strike his heart. This man was within his grasp yet he was ordered not to harm him. What senseless political game was this? Before he could think any further, he was startled by an incoming mess worker. It must be feeding time again. McPherson sighed, picked up the standard meal tray from a trolley, and inspected it dutifully. He briefly glanced at the mess attendant. He hadn't seen him before, but it did not strike him as odd. The mess often rotated staff from other departments.

McPherson nodded at the man, received the tray, and asked him to leave. The prisoner deserved comeuppance—but not on his watch.

He pressed a few buttons and the outer doors to the metal cage opened. He rolled the tray inside, left it there, and came out. With another push of buttons, the outer doors of the cage closed and the doors of the cell opened—a basic security procedure.

The inner doors of the cell could only open when the outer doors were closed.

McPherson saw the man inside the cell get up, walk to the tray and bend down to retrieve it. Slowly, he brought the tray inside his cell, and the inner doors swung shut with a metallic clang.

Osama bin Laden smelt the food, spat on the floor, and grimaced in disgust.

He got only one meal every 24 hours and, having nothing else to do, he couldn't help but look forward to the tasteless gruel he was usually served. However, this meal smelt positively rancid. He reached for the soup first. The piece of mouldy bread looked much less appealing—though, ironically, that was the only food he could have eaten in his past without having any doubts. Now, he was past the point of caring whether the food being served to him was halal or not, for he was no longer bound by human morality and gods. The rDNA inside him had made him realise that dietary restrictions were unnatural: mankind had fought its way to the top of the food chain for a reason.

Bin Laden knew that the Qa'haQ treatment had made him invincible; he could not be killed, he could face any torture and no amounts of pain made him uncomfortable. He could alter his biochemistry, move little objects with his mind, and was becoming even more powerful with each passing day. He just wished these foolish Americans kept him in confinement for a few more days. Soon, he would be fully transformed, and would then break out of this pathetic prison and rule the world. No one could stop him then.

No one could stop him *now*, he thought and grinned.

Without thinking, he put the spoon in his mouth and gulped down the tasteless liquid. He chuckled to himself, serving this food was true terrorism. Bin Laden reached for the unbranded salt pouch, hoping that the condiment would help him eat at least.

He tore open the sachet, sprinkled some salt on the soup, and hoped it would infuse some taste into his meal.

Bin Laden was lost in thought as he finished stirring the soup; he blew into it out of habit, and then took another mouthful. The soup burnt his throat with a marked unfamiliarity.

Suddenly, his world went out of focus. Bin Laden's hands started to shake—it became difficult to breathe, and his head felt dizzy. It felt as if molten lead was being poured down his windpipe.

He coughed and desperately tried to clutch at anything around him to retain his balance but he was unsuccessful. The bowl clattered to the floor, spilling its contents on the grimy concrete, and he went into a fit.

As McPherson watched this via the camera mounted inside the cell—his face a peculiar mixture of horror and happiness—bin Laden's eyes grew wide, turned bloodshot, and started to water. Bin Laden looked in horror at the salt sachet, and took it in his wildly shaking hands. He opened his mouth to scream an Arabic obscenity but before he could, he slumped forward. His heart had stopped beating within microseconds, and his lungs had started to decompose.

Little known to bin Laden, the salt contained particles of synthesised Sinium.

Sinium, as Yasser Basheer had told Blue, might have been harmless to humans when ingested, but to the rDNA bin Laden had inside him, it was utterly, fatally poisonous.

The last thing that struck Osama bin Laden before he stopped breathing was the presence of a coloured dot on the salt sachet, as if sketched by a doodling child: it was an unmistakable blue.

Rashtrapati Bhawan, New Delhi, India

66 hours into the invasion

Ajay Mishra walked to the yellow Delhi Police sentry booth, flashed his credentials, and saw the barricade lift. Even his vehicle could go no further—he had to walk from there.

He looked up at the young, energetic sub-inspector in charge of the post, compressed his lips in a curt smile which lasted a little over a second (that passed as a formal gesture of acknowledgement for people below his station), and started towards the full bloom of the Mughal Gardens.

Things had moved so fast, Mishra pinched himself in disbelief. A couple of days ago, he had been lobbying for a plush post-retirement position, and here he was now, trying to save the earth from total annihilation.

Mishra kept mouthing the word 'extraterrestrial' again and again, as if to convince himself of the actuality of the danger. A couple of days ago, he would have burst out laughing had he been informed of the Qa'haQ. Today, however, was a different story.

Within moments, Mishra reached the second tier of security. He stopped at the CISF barricade, repeated the prove-your-identity drill, and thrust his iPhone into a hastily assembled lead container. He signed a form and was immediately issued a receipt.

His heart no longer skipped beats as he went deeper into the belly of the Indian state. Mishra had had 30 years to get accustomed to the lifestyle.

He crossed the iconic fountain of Rashtrapati Bhawan and jogged towards his destination. PM Roy had invited the Qa'haQ ambassador to discuss the terms of ceasefire. A message had been broadcast on all frequencies and Mishra was sure it had reached the Qa'haQ shuttle and mother ship, which were bound to be monitoring the airwaves.

The third security tier came into view. Mishra showed his I-card to the National Security Guard (NSG) sentry on duty, signed in another entry register, and then increased his pace to reach the next checkpoint in time. The safari-suited men of the NSG checked his name in the 'allow entry' list they were issued for the day, nodded uninterestedly, and let him through.

Mishra mustered a soft smile as he recalled the contents of his latest phone call. Lady Luck was finally beginning to smile on them. They had managed to trace the Sinium crystal to a locality in Delhi. It had ended there via a German journalist named Sonya Loewe. With the help of Basheer and his newfound knowledge on the wonder element called Sinium, the process of extraction, synthesis and replication of the vaccine had gone smoothly. Computer simulations on the dosage of the vaccine had been successful. Fortunately, the National Centre for Disease Control had realised during the vaccine trials that if administered intravenously, Sinium not only provided robustness to the human genetic structure, but also reversed the Qa'haQ stratagem—and the tissue reverted to its original specifications. The DRDO was already working with the ISRO and the NCDC to come up with an airborne delivery mechanism for the vaccine. America, Japan, and Russia had volunteered to deploy cloud-burst technology so that the vaccine could reach the maximum number of people in the shortest possible time. To top it all off, the Air Force had located and damaged the alien ship and the Qa'haQ had been called to discuss peace. The apocalypse had just been averted.

Or so he hoped.

As he felt the red sand crunching under his boots, a sweet smell wafted to Mishra's nostrils and made him beam in pleasure. The orchids, roses, tulips, marigolds, sunflowers, jacarandas, and other flowers, were a psychedelic riot of colours. He realised he had reached his destination. Mishra went through the last checkpoint, this one of the SPG, and emerged in the middle of the Mughal Gardens, which by now also harboured a temporary shamiana set up for VVVIPs wriggling in eager anticipation of the great event.

'First Contact' was a phrase on all lips, apart from cups of strong filter coffee, and spicy paneer *pakoda*s the catering staff had magically conjured up for this august gathering. Eating never went out of fashion this side of the globe. Indians ate not only to celebrate, but also to mourn, and to prevent their insides from spilling out in sheer fear. There was nothing a milky, sugar-laden chai and an oily, piping-hot samosa couldn't have cured—though their gastronomic magic somehow seemed to be utterly wasted on protocol officers from the Ministry of External Affairs and Rashtrapati Bhawan.

The upper echelon of the bureaucracy was still arguing about *who* would receive the alien ambassador. Should it be the president, the vice president, the PM, or the minister for External Affairs? What rank would the alien ambassador be? Would Indians look soft if they let their president—the head of state—greet an alien ambassador? Or would Indians emerge as arrogant if the alien ambassador turned out to be a head of state and was not greeted by the Indian president but by the head of government, the PM instead? The camp was rife with speculations; it was the worst diplomatic nightmare India had faced since Pokhran. The babus had argued, debated, and conferred till an irritated Prime Minister Bipolab Roy had declared that he would do this himself. No one had argued—not even His Excellency the President.

Mishra walked towards the tent, picked up a cup of steaming chai served in a porcelain mug with the presidential crest from a table kept at the entrance, and went in. The more things got excited, the calmer he had to act. He could see the top brass whispering to each other amidst the backdrop of the majestic dome of Rashtrapati Bhawan.

He saw PM Roy standing at a distance, hurried to him, and said something in his ear. The PM nodded—visibly relieved.

The Qa'haQ came out of nowhere.

They made an appearance at the precise second they were asked to. A ruddy, moustachioed additional secretary was in the middle of biting into another *pakoda* when he dropped the plate he was holding and screamed.

The air right above the water fountain had started to shimmer with an unnatural, dazzling light. Then, within the blink of an eye, an unidentifiable object 50 metres in diameter materialised right in front of the shamiana.

The crowd gawked and parted.

The object was perfectly spherical in shape and constructed out of a smooth, black metal that seemed to absorb light, though Roy could see burn marks on the outer hull. He smiled inwardly and decided on the spur of the moment to confer the Vayusena Medal to the squadron leader who had engaged the alien craft.

The first thing that hit the people gathered around was not the shape or the size of the alien craft—it was the eerie silence that had descended on the Mughal Gardens. People had stopped talking the moment it had appeared. No one even dared to whisper. The breeze suddenly died down, insects stopped chattering, and birds stopped chirping. A mini black hole seemed to have materialised right in front of them, sucking everything in.

The craft hovered for a few more seconds and then, soundlessly, started to glide towards the white shamiana.

Bipolab Roy tensed—and attributed this flight to some sort of anti-gravity device. Moreover, it wasn't just the presence of extraterrestrials that bothered him; it was the *absence* of an America-centric threat. Indians were ready for an alien invasion somewhere in the future, but they thought the war would most likely be fought in and by the US, not them.

The Qa'haQ sphere came to rest a few inches above the ground, without actually touching the green, well-manicured lawn. After another few seconds, a 10-by-10-foot spherical hole opened in the middle of the alien ship. A shiny ramp slowly slid down and touched the ground. Roy stood up from his chair and dragged his feet towards the craft.

SPG commandoes, who had earlier sanitised and cordoned off the area and then withdrawn to a safe distance—lest the aliens saw their weapons as a sign of hostility—rushed in with lines of worry clearly etched on their sweating faces. Roy told them to back off with a curt shake of his head. He heard random phrases being murmured—words that made no sense in this context. He caught some of them: *tik-tiki*, *dino* and *chhipkali*.

His heart skipping a beat, Roy realised he now truly knew what the aliens looked like. He coughed and stared aghast as three 'lizard creatures'—all standing on their hind legs—made their way down the ramp.

The two lead aliens were dressed in sparkling black cloaks that shimmered as if they were alive, and a third alien—shorter than the other two—deferentially followed them, wearing a body-hugging, maroon fabric that resembled spandex. The reptiloid creatures were around eight feet in height and were covered with smooth, hairless scales that were somewhere between yellow and green in colour. Each Qa'haQ had two small forelegs and two robust, well-toned, hind legs on which it stood. To balance their body mass, they had thick, sinister tails that they kept swaying slowly.

The Qa'haQ faces, Roy could tell, were a cross between smiling velociraptors and grimacing humans. Their lidless eyes sucked in the gathering. As if to taste the air, forked tongues flickered out of their mouths—which were full of razor-sharp teeth. Their noses were but slits on their scaled faces and their manners were clearly menacing. The lead Qa'haQ turned to face Roy with a reptilian coldness in its eyes, and Roy instinctively put a hand on his mouth to prevent himself from gasping.

A chill ran down the spines of all those present. There was something so intrinsically dangerous in the bearing of these newcomers that it instantly gave Roy goosebumps. Before Roy could say anything, the bigger being amongst the first two stepped forward, strapped a device to its throat and opened its mouth.

A diabolical hiss seemed to permeate through the air. Roy could feel the neurons firing in his brain at such a rate that he wanted to grab his head and sink to the ground.

Before Roy could do anything, the alien stepped on the ground, and brought both its three-fingered hands together in front of its chest and pressed its palms together.

The being bowed, and opened its mouth. The hiss in the air was replaced by a metallic voice that Roy speculated came from some form of a translation device.

'This commander unit is called S'aulk,' the lizard creature greeted Roy and then pointed to the other Qa'haQ with him. 'My first officer, Dac'ish. We salute you on behalf of the Qa'haQ Republic. *Nomoshkaar*.'

Hyatt Regency, Bhikaji Cama Place, New Delhi, India
66 hours into the invasion

An appalled Red stared at the gun—and the resentful man holding it.

'You know?' Red licked his lips nervously and croaked, 'How on Earth...?'

Basheer replied so softly that Red had to lean forward to listen. '...And all this while I thought you worked for a government agency...an employer that sucked all life, no, humanity, out of you.'

Red winced, his cover now blown, and muttered something to himself, unsure of how to react—for Red was better known as Jason E. Cartman, Director General of the CIC.

'*Why* did you inject that Qa'haQ serum into me? Look what it has done!' Basheer pointed at his face—which was positively greenish by then.

Cartman's mouth opened and closed in quick succession—no words came out. He managed to rub his eyes and moaned, 'I... I never thought the experiment would reach that stage where you would be used as a live test subject.'

'But I was!'

'I just wanted to save your life, that's it! I couldn't watch you die.'

'And look what your efforts have turned me into!' Basheer screamed as his eyes turned yellow.

'I...am so sorry. I just wanted to look out for you. I left you before you were born but in all fairness, I did keep tabs on you. I followed your career, helped you rise, and looked after you...*son*.'

'Don't call me that. You died with my mother—a long time ago in Afghanistan. You couldn't even muster the courage to come and meet me. Thank God Blue told me about you.' Basheer shot a murderous glance at Cartman and hissed through clenched teeth, *'Look at me!'*

Cartman stared blankly, the colour draining from his face. Vignettes of his life as a young CIA officer in Afghanistan at the height of Operation Cyclone—which aimed at creating mujahideen to counter the invading Soviets—flashed through his mind. Cartman felt conflicting emotions rise within him: his meeting Basheer's mother, their brief courtship, the birth of Basheer, and Cartman's decision to leave his pregnant Afghan paramour as his tour came to an end.

A man outside coughed and Cartman tried to clutch at the last straws of the dignity he had left—he immediately turned professional and barked, 'How did you find out my identity?'

'I had help,' Basheer replied caustically.

'From whom?'

At that instant, another man sauntered in with such arrogance in his stride that it sent klaxons blaring in Red's subconscious. Red immediately recognised this man, and when he spoke next, the tone shocked him.

It was him.

'Hello, Red. Jason E. Cartman. Whatever you'd want to call yourself now. Good to meet the real you finally. Though I must admit, you look much less menacing without your mask!'

'Blue?' Red stammered.

Blue waved his hand, mockingly bowed low, and continued without missing a heartbeat, 'At your service, sir.'

'What are you doing here?' Cartman was livid by now. 'How did you find me?'

Blue snorted. 'It was simple.'

Cartman glared at him. 'Humour me!'

'We seven—as members of the High Council—could easily have deduced each other's alter egos, but we did not. Because we needed to be unaware of each other's true identities lest someone turned traitor and took the entire organisation down with them. Since the emails which called High Council gatherings were untraceable, I tried other methods. Mind you, I could have done this a long time ago, but I didn't. Not just to honour the oath that you made us take—the oath in which you promised we'd never reveal our identities to each other—but also because I knew I would meet my untimely demise if I tried to cross you. But now shit's hit the fan. I *had* to find out who you were, since I realised you might still be working for the Qa'haQ despite the fate they've planned for this planet. And once I decided to find the real you, it wasn't that difficult, surprisingly.'

'How...' Cartman said coldly, and grasped for words.

Blue smiled as Basheer sat down on an inviting couch while staring at Cartman over the barrel of his gun. Blue replied serenely, 'I knew that Red had moved Sonya to Delhi. She was no longer needed in Kashmir after she secured the crystal from that ISI agent, Imran. I know Red regularly fed her little scraps of information to satisfy the journalist in her and then used her to further his own propaganda campaigns. So, I pulled a few strings with Indian intelligence agencies, and got a hold of Sonya's cell phone. You have no idea what a gold mine of information that was. Sonya was just a reporter, nothing more. She lacked the paranoid mindset our trade members have to possess in order to survive. The poor girl had saved one of Red's numbers with your name on it. It was a burner, yes, but it wasn't that difficult to guess who was at the other end. When I cross-referenced it, I realised that the information you were supplying to her was known to only two people: me...and *you*. Since it sure as hell wasn't me, it had to be *you*.'

Cartman was sweating by now.

As if sensing his discomfort, Basheer joined in. 'What a great game you've played, Father. Who would imagine that the all-powerful Red would simultaneously be one of his spineless, helpless minions? Who would have thought you *were* Red when you projected yourself as Red's *victim*, another of those countless Conglomerate members who were conscripted against their will. Oppressor and oppressed can't be the same, can they? Except in your case, they were. It was the perfect alibi.'

Cartman tried to bluff his way out. 'My security will soon be here.'

Blue laughed. 'No, they won't. They have been taken care of.'

Betrayed, Cartman seethed inside, and decided to change tack. 'But why are you doing this?'

'Making money is fine, Cartman, but selling out Earth itself isn't such a great idea,' Blue countered.

'Stop him, Basheer. Blue is on the losing side. Help me escape. We have to aid the Qa'haQ. Sooner or later they *will* win. Join me, and we still have a chance to survive! For that's what we are—survivors, no matter what the cost. The Qa'haQ might even make me a planetary governor. I will need someone at my side, someone to further my legacy.'

Basheer snorted in resentment. 'No, thank you.'

Cartman realised there was no swaying Basheer. He spat on the floor, and burst forth, 'You tiny, insignificant people can only think about small matters. Power will always exist—and those who do not realise that power *must* keep changing hands to remain power can never have it. I just chose to be on the winning side.'

'*You*, not me. I will...' Blue countered vehemently, but a noise from behind the couch made him stop.

Sonya moaned groggily and stirred. Basheer, who had assumed that Sonya had been knocked out, went in for a closer look. He found her frothing—her maroon lipstick was covered with specks of white foam oozing out of her mouth. Her face was flushing, and she was having trouble breathing. Basheer instantly understood what had happened before he had arrived. He wrapped his fingers around the trigger, itching to do it.

'Where's the antidote, Cartman?'

A cloud of uncertainty passed over Cartman's face. For someone who always knew what was going to happen, uncertainty was horrifying—and linked to failure, which, in turn, meant death.

'Tell us or you die,' Blue joined in.

'You dare threaten me? Blue, you know how little emotional bonds mean to me. Let me out and you just might live. Remember Basheer...'

He was interrupted by a sudden bang.

Cartman stopped speaking. He looked down to see a small, blood-red hole appear in his chest, right where his heart was, and sank to the floor without uttering another word. Basheer, his face white as a sheet, had pressed the trigger.

Jason E. Cartman, the DG of CIC, and the head of Conglomerate as Red, was dead.

'Damn!' Blue groaned, dismayed. 'We needed him alive!'

Basheer merely grunted in response.

Blue immediately swung into action. He bent down, reached inside the inner pockets of Cartman's duffel bag and produced a small vial. He uncorked it and emptied the colourless contents into Sonya's mouth.

A barely conscious Sonya, whose tongue had swollen by now, felt immediate relief wash over her as the warm liquid made its way down her throat. She felt as if someone had thrown chilled water on a fire that was burning her stomach.

'Relax.' Blue patted her shoulders, gently placed her head on a pillow that Basheer picked up from an unmade bed, and muttered, 'You will be fine.'

Basheer was still staring at Cartman's body. 'How did you know?'

'What? How did I know where to find the antidote?'

Basheer nodded.

'Red always carried a broad-spectrum, anti-poisoning medication on his person lest he ever be poisoned. He was paranoid, I know, but that's what kept him alive for so long.'

Sonya stirred again and struggled for air. 'Is...am...where.' She tried sitting up and mustered enough strength to speak.

'Shhh...You're safe,' Blue consoled her.

Sonya clutched at Blue's fingers, nodded in thanks and closed her eyes again.

Basheer whispered urgently, 'All clear, Blue. We gotta bail out. Let's take the girl to safety and get rid of Cartman's body.'

Blue shook his head and sadistically remarked, 'I say, let his body stay here. It'll be nice to watch the reaction of Indian authorities when Cartman is found assassinated in Delhi, especially when there's no record of him ever entering the country. I think I love embarrassing governments as much I love saving Earth from alien attacks!'

Basheer grinned. Blue wasn't the second-in-command of the Conglomerate for nothing.

'So should we just let Cartman stay here?'

Blue nodded. He wanted to desperately see the aftermath of such a happening.

'And oh,' Blue chuckled, 'did I tell you? I've taken care of OBL, too—just the way you told me.'

Basheer asked, trying to hide a sinister spark evident in his intentionally downcast eyes, 'How did you do it?'

Blue laughed merrily. 'Many would prefer death to having no salt in their lunch, right?'

Basheer smiled inwardly, nodded in relief, and scanned the room one last time. He saw Blue stagger out, holding a semi-conscious Sonya in his arms.

Basheer's mind was whirring. Cartman was dead. A part of Basheer that he thought did not exist suddenly sprang to life. He realised he had to do one last thing before he left the building. He threw his phone into a jug of water. From now on, Basheer would be untraceable, and that suited him just fine. His eyes suddenly cold, he reloaded his pistol and sneaked after Blue.

Someone walking down the crowded Ring Road below would have noticed a surprising muzzle flash eat into the darkness of a particular room high up on the VIP floor—if only he or she looked up to appreciate the perfectly crafted, well-lit building of the Hyatt Hotel.

Thankfully, no one did.

Rashtrapati Bhawan, New Delhi, India
68 hours into the invasion

Prime Minister Bipolab Roy spied a venerable cabinet minister, who was standing right behind him, sink to the ground muttering something that sounded very much like the *Hanuman Chaleesa*.

When the Qa'haQ spoke next, its voice was instantly replaced by that of a human male, at least inside Roy's head.

'I apologise,' the voice said in a calm baritone that made Roy uncomfortable, 'I forgot that you're not used to the translation matrix.'

Roy—utterly bewildered—managed to whimper, '...How do you know our language?' A part of him instantly regretted asking the question. He knew he shouldn't have been surprised by such technology.

'I don't,' the answer came in the same manner as it had earlier, inside his head.

'Then how did you...?' Roy spluttered.

The alien continued, 'I greeted you in my tongue—but my vocal chords have been linked to a translator-communicator device. It studies your brain waves, analyses your linguistic programming, isolates a language you are most comfortable in, and then conveys the message to you in that particular language. It does the same when you speak, thus allowing us to communicate properly.'

By then, the upper echelons of the Indian establishment had started inching towards the alien—their morbid awe was replaced by a curiosity only a giant, talking lizard could have fostered.

PM Roy nodded slowly. 'I am Bipolab Roy, prime minister of India. Your greeting…'

The being seemed to notice Roy's voice trailing off uncertainly and cocked its head to one side.

Its eyelids fluttered in quick succession. 'Did that greeting not suit you?' the alien hissed again. 'I thought it would have helped us have an amicable First Contact.'

'Amicable First Contact *after* you attacked us?' Roy had trouble coming to terms with the entire situation—and this conversation.

The Qa'haQ hissed again—its body went rigid and it crossed one paw over another in what looked like a gesture of defiance.

The buzzing continued for a full 10 seconds, and when the translation reached Roy's ears, he could only make out two words: 'We protest!'

Roy did not say anything—he merely pointed a hand in the direction of a table. Things were rocky, but they had to start somewhere—and he knew nothing broke ice like formalities.

The reptiloid Qa'haQ seemed to understand.

They slowly, cautiously made their way to a mahogany table that had been put in the middle of the Mughal Gardens, a few feet away from the shamiana, right next to a row of red roses.

PM Roy occupied his pre-designated seat at the centre of the U-shaped table, whereas the two Qa'haQ lizard creatures sat at the opposite ends. The third Qa'haQ, the one wearing what looked like spandex, didn't sit down—it merely stood in corner with a transparent data-pad in its hands. The slight anatomical variations made Roy wonder whether it wasn't a third gender—he also had a feeling it might be a junior-ranking staffer present to document the meeting.

After the delegates were seated, Roy forced open his mouth and muttered a formal introduction to begin the proceedings. 'I will not mince words. As of this moment, I have tactical nuclear warheads stationed with a clear shot of your mother ship in orbit. Give me one good reason why I should not fire them right away.'

The tallest Qa'haQ, one who had introduced himself as S'aulk, looked like a ranking officer based on the number of stripes on his robe—and was the first to respond. The PM heard an excited chatter and an unnerving hiss burrow in his ears before he heard a soothing, comprehensible translation.

'...You must get it. We did what we did to *save* Earth!'

Roy was surprised. These aliens must think that humans are really, really stupid, he thought. 'Save us?' He was genuinely puzzled by now.

'Yes. We received orders from our home planet to activate the Genetic Transmutor.'

'So you do confess...you did activate a device that poisoned our cell phone radiation and made us...sick!' Roy had not foreseen this being handed to him on a platter.

'Yes, we did. But it was the only way...' S'aulk's voice trailed off into nothingness.

'The only way? For what?'

'To ensure that Earth lives on.'

Roy was getting a tad irritated by now. 'Huh? This tautological argument makes no sense! Please explain.'

S'aulk swirled his forked tongue—perhaps its equivalent of getting ready for a long speech. 'Our calculations unambiguously predict that humanity would wipe itself out in the next world war—which will be quite soon. Frankly, we would not mind that. But the nuclear devices that would be used in these wars will not only devastate Earth's flora and fauna, but also affect the core of the planet. Research shows this will lead to radical seismic activity across the globe since the inner core might liquefy. A loss of atmosphere will follow. Earth—a habitable Earth, as you and I know it—will end. It *must* be protected!'

Roy still could not understand the logic. 'How does that explain your venomous radiation?'

'It was done to prevent wars. By activating the Genetic Transmutor, humans would have become one with the Qa'haQ. We could have controlled you better and ensured you became less violent. It was the only way to save this planet from total destruction.'

Roy's mouth hung open in amazement. He was about to respond when a question struck him. 'But...why this love for Earth? Is this planet so important that you would go to war over it? The universe is so vast—you can always find another planet!'

There was silence for a few seconds. S'aulk and Dac'ish dropped their gazes, looked pensive, and turned reddish-brown. The smaller Qa'haQ stopped taking notes and looked up at the skies.

A small ripple seemed to cleave the air between the two parties. Dac'ish stared at S'aulk and seemed to nod.

'Are you prepared to know?' muttered S'aulk.

Red drops emerged out of the yellow, unblinking eyes.

Roy wondered what was going on. Were his guests seriously crying, he thought?

A grating, female voice filled Roy's head. 'You *Homo sapiens*,' it was Dac'ish who started talking this time, 'what are you made of?'

Roy was taken aback by the question. 'What do you mean?'

The second Qa'haQ repeated her question, this time slowly.

The staffers present inched closer, no longer able to contain themselves. Even members of the diplomatic corps leaned forward in their seats.

'We humans,' Roy spluttered, 'we are a carbon-based life form.'

Dac'ish kept silent for a few moments and then asked one more question. 'And where do you think *we* are from?'

Roy was quick to answer. 'I have been briefed that you're from the Horsehead Nebula.'

'Well done, Mr PM; that is correct.' Dac'ish swayed her tail. 'But that's not the whole truth.'

The recording team from Doordarshan peeped out from behind their cameras, their mouths open in amazement.

'Then what is?'

'Yes, we *are* from the place you just mentioned, but we didn't originate there.'

Roy was getting more puzzled with every passing moment. 'Then where did you?'

'The Qa'haQ originated from Earth.'

Roy was speechless. '*What?*' he managed at last. 'How is that possible? How...?'

'We cannot talk about this, but you need to know.' S'aulk joined in a heavy voice, as if it took a great effort to talk. 'Years into the future, a technological singularity will occur. Human scientific advancement will reach its zenith—humanity will develop at such an exponential rate that they would learn to control consciousness itself. All life forms on this planet will fuse with Earth's own consciousness—and not just human, mind you. This super-conscious matter will then attain plasma form...'

Roy almost shrieked in bewilderment. '*What* are you talking about? How does it have any bearing to this conversation?'

'Do you want to know why we did what we did?'

'I do, of course!' Roy fumed.

'Then you must hear me out.'

'Please continue,' Roy nodded resignedly.

S'aulk went on. 'This intelligent primal matter comprised silicon, iron and carbon—this conscious matter, though powerful, would be unstable. It will split and give rise to three different, super-sentient species—the reptiloid silicon-based Qa'haQ; the iron-based insectoid Soryaks, whom you are yet to encounter; and the carbon-based MetaUmans, *your* ancestors. So powerful will this Great Separation be that this conscious matter will be thrown back in time—to millions of years ago. Then we will begin charting our own future again. We as dinosaurs, you as apes and the Soryaks as insects—the great evolution would thus begin anew. Yes, Earthling, we have the same ancestors. This is why the Qa'haQ Omtronic radiation was able to mutate you into hybrids so easily. You have a similar genetic structure that lies dormant inside you.'

'Oh my God.' Roy couldn't process it any further. 'So Earth's evolutionary history is not a straight line but a circle.'

Roy kept mum for a full minute before something else hit him. 'You said this event will happen in the future. Then how come you are here? Are you really from the future?'

S'aulk bared his teeth in what could be termed as a wistful smile. 'I never said *we* were from the future. All I said was that the Great Separation happened, or will happen, in the future. But since the post-singularity conscious matter was thrown back in time and seeded life on Earth, we are from the *past*.'

Roy was getting more confused with each passing moment. 'But...why will you...I mean, *did* you travel from your age to now? I'm sorry, time travel and tenses make strange bedfellows.'

S'aulk carried on. 'Post the Great Separation, after we were thrown back in time, the Soryak and the Qa'haQ chose the path of peace, logic and exploration in the New World—which, teleologically, is really the old world, but your ancestors, the primates, decided to build an existence around faith. They fought for power, lands and material goods. Soon,' S'aulk said with a heavy heart, 'we were overpowered by the war-mongering primates who had augmented their physical bodies with yet more machinery. The singularity had changed them at a basic level.

They were no longer human, no longer bound by rational feelings and nature. They became so full of malice, greed and hatred that they refused to share the planet with us. Our civilisation aimed at gathering knowledge, but your ancestors coveted weapons of war. Soon, both the Soryak and Qa'haQ races were cast away—defeated, tired and nearing extinction. We somehow managed to build ships capable of interplanetary travel and found new homes in the stars.'

'My God! But you make the MetaUmans sound so evil!'

'Because they *were*,' S'aulk smirked. 'We rebuilt, yes, and this time we, too, created weapons of war, so we could defend ourselves the next time the primates attacked us.'

'But where are these MetaUmans? You said they won. Shouldn't they be around?'

S'aulk smiled. 'They are gone, heavens be praised.'

'Gone?'

'Before we were chased off this planet, we deployed the most powerful genetic weapon we had. A DNA Devolver. We detonated a device that destroyed the MetaUman civilisation by reverting the MetaUmans to their less refined ancestors...the survivors of our final assault began from scratch, their knowledge-structures forgotten, their genes compromised, their technical skills neutralised. You call them *Homo sapiens*.'

'But that is...us!' Roy's mind was desperately trying to assimilate this. But a part of him accepted what the aliens told him. Was imagining the MetaUmans as a species so blinded by power that they fought every other life form on the planet for total control that difficult for him? However, what made Roy really nervous was this whole business of reverting to the 'barbaric' *Homo sapiens*.

He was curious to know more. 'What happened when the MetaUmans fought you in the past?'

Dac'ish was the one to reply. 'Most of our ancestors perished in the orbital bombardment and electromagnetic weapons unleashed by the MetaUmans. Some of them, however, managed to escape, far from the persecution of the new all-powerful invader, but only a select few. It took us time to reach our past glory.'

'So you were the dinosaurs of our past? The war waged by the MetaUmans made you extinct?'

'Not exactly, though we are related to the dinosaurs the same way you're related to apes. And yes, an asteroid did make us extinct, but what you do not know is that it was propelled by your species, the MetaUmans, towards Earth...While they planned to wait out the crash period in their space stations, their intent was to kill us all, so the MetaUmans could have Earth all to themselves when the dust settled. They almost succeeded...but we left before the asteroid hit us, and as the MetaUmans hurled bombs at us from their safe orbit, we also had a trick up our sleeve. We targeted their space stations with energy weapons that made them crash back to Earth and then with a genetic weapon—our master stroke—that made them devolve into their less advanced ancestors...

'Us! But...this doesn't make sense. Where is the documentary proof? The historical records?'

S'aulk glanced at Dac'ish, and started talking. 'You don't find fossils of your ancestors before the dinosaurs since they lived in orbiting space cities, around us, almost like gods. Why, even ancient human cultures of your planet somehow retained the racial memories of the MetaUmans. Remember the Greeks? The Romans? Don't you find the anthropomorphic gods they worshipped quite similar to the MetaUmans, yet vastly dissimilar?'

Roy was speechless. 'So classical gods were MetaUmans? What happened to them?'

'Their genocidal oppression and soul-crushing tyranny could no longer be tolerated. We executed a counter-attack. The plan almost worked.'

'Almost?'

'*You* are still here. We cannot let the MetaUmans win again. So we travelled to your Earth from our current home, a task given to my people millennia ago, and came to you...knowing that, ironically, your time is the only temporal location when we can stop the singularity from happening in the first place. If we don't stop you, the cycle will begin anew: the *Homo sapien* wars, Singularity, the Great Separation, and the Time-Paradox. MetaUmans would again wage war against us.'

Roy was livid. 'By giving them cell phones and then a dose of mutagenic radiation? By turning us into Qa'haQ?'

'Yes, we have been waiting for centuries, hoping for a time when we could sneak cell phones into your technological evolution without raising suspicion. Once that was done, we would have turned you into Qa'haQ in a couple of months. This way, there would have been no Great Separation—the organic singularity would not occur. The MetaUmans would never have been born. We would, thus, not have been thrown back in time. The MetaUmans would not have come into existence—and we could have ruled this planet as Qa'haQ.'

'But won't this erase you from the time, too? The timelines would...'

'They would not be compromised, if that's what you mean.'

'But why are you here? I mean, now?'

'Isn't that clear?'

'What?'

'For generations we were given one sacred task. Reclaim the planet. We can no longer run away.'

There was something in the way S'aulk said it that scared Roy.

'How?'

'We will snatch Earth from the MetaUmans' less-evolved descendants. We want our planet back—from you. It is ours!'

Roy realised he had had enough. 'You wanted your planet back? You intended to do it by transforming humanity into Qa'haQ hybrids...?'

'Yes. It is better than allowing you humans to lay waste to this planet. Surely, even you must see the logic. Species come and go, but Earth *must* stay habitable!'

'I'm afraid I don't see things from your perspective. You tried to invade, and you *failed* spectacularly,' Roy spat out with such latent anger that he surprised himself, too.

The Qa'haQ's demeanour suddenly went cold—colder than anything Roy had ever experienced before. 'This was but one attempt...that too marred by the fact that we somehow underestimated you. We never thought a human could operate the Genetic Transmutor and steal its Sinium crystal...or we would have guarded it more preciously. However, that is now irrelevant. What is done is done. The future is ours alone.'

Roy shook his head slowly. His blood was slowly beginning to freeze at the tone in which S'aulk spoke. 'What do you mean?'

'We are coming back. Prepare for our return.'

Roy laughed incredulously. 'Return? You want to return? After what you tried doing to us?'

'We come back with your consent, or without it. What you decide here will decide how we treat humanity once we are back.'

'Treat humanity? You will never succeed in making us acquiesce to a plan that makes us second-class citizens inside our own homes!'

Dac'ish looked deep into Roy's eyes, and softly whispered, 'Then you have chosen poorly, human.'

'Excuse me?'

'We will end you!' she spat with a ferocity that shook Roy's core.

'Only if you get away!' Roy snapped, aghast and exasperated at this insolence. 'In fact, you will not leave this compound. I do hereby charge you with crimes against humanity and place you under arrest!' He looked in the direction of Mishra, who in turn nodded to a couple of black-clad NSG commandos who emerged out of nowhere and pointed their MP5 guns at the three Qa'haQ. There was a sudden thudding noise in the distance—within moments, they were joined by an IAF gunship providing air cover.

Barua's Mi-35 had reached the spot, and was poised for the kill.

Roy felt his heart soar. He whirled around to stare back at the alien visitors, who remained unfazed by these weapons.

The Qa'haQ stood their ground and spoke together, as if mentally linked, 'You will regret this!'

'Famous last words,' Roy jeered.

Dac'ish slapped her forearm and spoke, 'We will be back.'

Before Roy or the NSG could react, S'aulk and his Qa'haQ team disappeared in a beam of rapidly swirling colours.

Their ship—which was under crosshairs of the IAF—vanished at exactly the same moment.

Roy grunted in frustration. The NSG commandos wheeled around, trying to see if they could still spot and engage their quarry. The security forces rushed around to sanitise the area but the aliens were nowhere to be found.

The cabinet secretary knew better—Mishra realised he had been a fool not to take into account that the Qa'haQ must have come prepared with an exfiltration plan in case things went south—which they just exercised.

As far as he could tell, the aliens had used some sort of teleportation technology. By now, their craft could be headed back home, from where they could get fresh reinforcements. Mishra grimaced. This was not a good start. The battle for Delhi was over.

The war for the planet had begun.

Qutub Minar, New Delhi, India

70 hours into the invasion

He was on top of the world.

Yasser Basheer leaned forward to retch—he could still smell Blue's blood on his sinewy hands. With considerable effort, he spat out a thick, brownish liquid that gurgled noisily out of his swollen mouth.

He could not forget the expression of horrified disgust on Blue's face when Basheer had shot him in the hotel. Basheer had let Sonya go, though. He had no quarrel with that girl, but he also knew that allowing Sonya to live was somehow not enough to assuage his guilt.

Basheer tried to steady himself by putting his bruised hands on the railing at the top of Qutub Minar; the last thing he wanted was to fall down to his gory death. He knew that it might have taken him only a few moments to climb to the top of this ancient minaret, but the fall down would have been even shorter. Before he could turn around, Basheer doubled over in pain. He whimpered, swore, and tried to control the spasms raging through his body.

A few moments later, he stood up straight—the fit had passed; so had the pain.

Basheer ran a hand over his face to see if he had changed externally. He hadn't, much to his relief, but his eyesight had suddenly improved, his stamina had increased, and he had this fleeting feeling that he could move small objects with his mere thoughts if he concentrated hard enough.

Something screeched in the distance, making him whirl around with a swiftness that was certainly not human. It was a speeding car. The moon had risen by now, throwing a silvery sheet over the entire landscape. Like an eagle poised for the kill, he waited with bated breath to locate any movement down below.

Basheer was alone—he had chosen well. The night, coupled with this altitude, ensured that the chances of being caught by random hikers were pretty slim. Absent-mindedly, Basheer dabbed his mouth with a wet tissue and tried to breathe deeply.

Warily, he poured a few drops of water from a canteen into his waiting mouth. Reflexively, he coughed and spat them out the moment the drops touched his chapped lips, thus beginning the process of retching all over again. His throat was parched, he was thirsty, his belly was bloated, yet surprisingly, he was unable to ingest any water in his present condition. Without another word, he passed out at the edge of the railing.

When Basheer woke up hours later, he was drenched in a slick layer of moist, foul-smelling sweat. The moon had changed position as evident from the lighting around him, and a gentle, soothing breeze had started to blow. He tried sitting up, expecting it to take considerable effort, but it surprised him how quickly he sat up—he seemed to have forgotten what gravity felt like. Better still—the pain that had wracked every single cell of his body for the past few days was inexplicably gone. Basheer smiled and felt stronger.

He understood why.

Basheer's body harboured a hybrid human-alien consciousness that was acclimatising to this new planet. Millennia of slow evolution were colliding with days of explosive genetic re-engineering. Curiously, he no longer felt the same adoration for the Qa'haQ that he earlier did. The human, nay, MetaUman in him was finally beginning to stir.

Basheer no longer felt guilty about what was inside him. He had realised by now that the only viable option he had was to ensure that he facilitated the process as well as he could. If he failed, he would end up extinct—which no longer scared him as much as it should have.

His family flashed by in his mind, but only for a split second. Basheer missed his wife, of course, but he had realised human emotions only made him weaker. What was the use of such human pining? The only constant about humanity was its suffering—eternal, unforgiving, and ubiquitous. Basheer suddenly became all the more determined to leave this ephemeral *Homo sapien* shell behind. He thanked the creators for the alien serum that now coursed through his throbbing veins—a drug that rearranged his cellular structure at a micro-level, and made him inch closer to true perfection.

Those he loved were gone but *he* would conquer death.

Basheer whistled to calm himself, and glanced around.

The area down below was utterly deserted at this hour, though he could see a nightclub in the distance, spewing a steady stream of humans out into the street. The sky stretched before him—numerous residential colonies around the medieval structure were shining softly in the moonlight.

He suddenly realised that Earth had been a planetary battlefield a long, long time ago. The Qa'haQ and the MetaUmans had fought for the supremacy of the planet. It was Mutually Assured Destruction.

They had both lost.

The losers—the Qa'haQ—were cast away into the depths of space, ashamed and battered. The victors—the imperious MetaUmans—had to pay an even more terrible price. The Qa'haQ genetic weapons had made them devolve into barbaric

Homo sapiens, and destroyed their superior technology and genetic structure.

Until now.

Basheer smirked at the scenes of war which started flashing through his mind, and bared teeth which were neither human nor fully Qa'haQ. At a deep level, war had begun to arouse him, physically. He was still human—at least externally—but something inside him was no longer the same. His threw his head up and shamelessly stared at a distant pinprick in the sky.

It was Qa'haQam, the tranquil oasis that was the Qa'haQ home planet. He could see it if he focused hard enough. Telepathy, combined with powerful, re-engineered eyes, gave him that ability.

Basheer could feel that the Qa'haQ were coming for Earth—again. This time with more firepower to finally succeed—and he could not let that happen. He could not allow his home to fall to such inferior monstrosities emerging out of the stars. Only the strong and pure would rule Earth—and the humans and the Qa'haQ were *both* weak, frail and unfit.

It was time for the MetaUmans to return.

Basheer's eyes glossed over as he felt a wave of animosity and hatred arouse him. Let the Qa'haQ come, he vowed to himself; they would find that Earth would be protected this time. No longer would the third planet of the Solar system be a cherry ripe for plucking by any passing sentient extraterrestrial intelligence. This time, he would lead the forces of this planet to eternal glory.

Basheer threw his head back and shrieked at the stars.

It was time to become a god.

Epilogue

The heavens call to you, and circle about you, displaying to you their eternal splendours, and your eye gazes only to earth.

Dante

Earth, Sol, Milky Way
72+ hours into the invasion

Pandara Road, New Delhi

PCM somehow dragged the heavy suitcase up the chipped stairs. Out of habit, he looked around when he reached his door, and inserted a key into the rusty lock. No one was around to welcome him. Before he had been sent across the border, PCM had been chummy with the family of the Indian Revenue Service officer whose D-II flat was right next to his. But he seemed to have moved, perhaps transferred to a different part of the country. The new family that occupied his pal's flat did not really know who he was—they had only seen his empty flat for the past few months.

He had been away for way too long, PCM reminded himself with uncharacteristic bitterness. He knew no one would ever know what he had achieved. For friends, relatives and acquaintances, he would always be another babu at the Cabinet Secretariat with weird working hours and an even stranger mental setup. It was good he had not married—his wife would have left him a long time ago, he rationalised.

He unlocked the main door, went in, and jumped on the creaking bed without removing his shoes or clothes. Thankfully, a junior had told someone to clean up his flat and prepare it for his arrival. PCM sneaked into the covers, but not before grabbing a bottle of Glenfiddich kept on the bedside table, courtesy his office. He uncorked the bottle, sipped directly out of it and blankly stared at the ceiling for what seemed like eternity, until his cell phone started ringing.

PCM was jolted back to reality: someone knew he was back in Delhi, someone who had access to his Delhi number. He reached for it and answered it cautiously.

It was his younger brother, welcoming PCM back from his deputation at the Indian embassy in Qatar (as he had been informed). PCM, glad at hearing a voice he could trust, laughed and promised his brother that he would come dine at his C.R. Park residence later that evening. He hung up smiling.

PCM was finally home.

***

The aftermath

Islamabad, Pakistan

Imran Bhatt disappeared from the hospital after talking to Sonya over the phone. The CIC speculates that direct contact with the Qa'haQ technology drove him insane. Imran was last seen wandering through the snowy mountains somewhere between India and Pakistan, muttering about the eerie things he had seen and the strange nightmares that haunted him. There have been unconfirmed reports of Imran mouthing three distinct words over and over again—'Qa'haQ,' 'Sinium' and 'Sonya'—before he finally vanished.

Sources at the Inter-Services Public Relations (ISPR) categorically deny having any Major Imran Bhatt on the payroll of the ISI.

***

Bonn, Germany

Sonya Loewe was found unconscious in the elevator of a prominent South Delhi hotel. When she woke up, she pressed charges against unknown assailants who drugged and kidnapped her. The German embassy had to step in, and after a rushed investigation, she was put on a Lufthansa flight back to where she came from. Sonya has now returned to Deutsche-Welle and refuses to cover politics or even business. She currently handles the local fashion desk, and vows to cover *only* fashion.

***

London, England

With the mutilated, rotting bodies of Red and Blue surfacing in India, the Conglomerate realised someone was coming for them. The Conglomerate High Council was temporarily disbanded and went into hiding. Little did they know that this time the threat was from within. Only time would tell if Yasser Basheer's defection had any impact on the global operations of the IMIC.

Maybe not.

***

Paris, France

Jean-Pierre Bazin is now the deputy manager of Le Jules Verne. When not busy catering to high-profile clients in the hospitality industry, he freelances for the DGSE (*Direction Générale de la Sécurité Extérieure*)—the military external intelligence agency of France—and the CIA. Even Bazin prefers to keep the CIC at an arm's length.

***

Jamshedpur, India

Pooja Srivastava was exonerated of all criminal charges after a much-hyped trial—her lawyers cited 'temporary insanity brought about by extraneous, extraterrestrial factors'. She recovered from her mutation—and humiliation—thanks to a robust constitution and aggressive medical intervention, though it took time, money and spirit. She left the television industry post this incident, fell back on her academic major, and now works for a small microfinance institution that focuses on the tribals living in India's unstable Red Corridor.

***

New Delhi, India

Dr Revathi Balakrishnan left GIBRI and is now an associate professor of biotechnology at Jawaharlal Nehru University. She insists she has had enough of giant lizards for one lifetime and now works towards increasing the per-hectare yield of GM rust-resistant, pest-proof wheat.

***

Bihar, India

Ajay P. Mishra took up a consulting job with the United Nations after his superannuation from the government of India. He is currently visiting his native village situated somewhere between Samastipur and Khagaria. Mishra will soon be leaving for New York, where he is to head a UN subcommittee on expanding the Security Council.

India is a strong probable.

***

Delhi Cantonment, India

Bishwanath Barua has been promoted to the rank of wing commander. He is now the second-in-command of an integrated, tri-service 'Alien Combat Unit' (ACU) constituted by executive action in order to safeguard human interests. Operating as an independent institution directly under the PMO, the ACU draws personnel from Indian defence forces, CSIR, DRDO, ISRO, Paramilitary and Civil Services, etc. ACU is tasked with Research and Development using recovered Qa'haQ technologies, and is the premier institute for evolving tactics, weapons and protocols to better respond to alien attacks in the future.

Barua is hopeful that India will be better prepared when *they* appear next.

And they will.

The skies will soon weep.

Author's Note

What you hold in your hands began as a thought experiment, and the first draft was completed in December 2012. It was written to addresses two distinct, yet related questions. One, do characters make a genre or do genres make characters? To answer that, I took a few major characters from *Red Jihad* and placed them within a wholly different genre (science fiction) to locate the said changes in their behavioural patterns, if any. Two, what happens when one fuses an established genre (thriller) with one not-so-well-established in India (SF—at least in Indian English)? The first novel I wrote might have had a certain political nucleus in an effort to foreground my belief that extremism/fundamentalism/violence of *any* sort is utterly detrimental to human progress. This novel, however, has no such desire for social betterment behind it, I confess: only a missionary zeal towards promoting a genre (SF) that I love so much, and yearn to read more of (especially from desi writers).

Aliens in Delhi begins as a political thriller and then mutates into SF. I hope this 'genetic mutation' of the narrative takes Indian SF in English back to the gutters. This is an anti-highbrow text with just one aim—to tell a *crazy* story, something that makes the reader see the old in a new light (cell phone radiation as a possible mutagen) and the new in an old light ('humanised' extraterrestrials). I had a great time writing this novel; I hope you enjoyed reading it.

I am grateful to many people for making this project a reality. The support of my mother, Shaheen Anjum, my father, Barkat

Zaman Khan, my younger brother, Mohd. Salman Khan, and the entire Khan family, was pivotal.

I am indebted to my teachers and the academic institutions that shaped me: Bal Bharati Public School, Rajdhani College and Hindu College (University of Delhi), Jawaharlal Nehru University (JNU), and the University of Iowa. Prof. G.J.V. Prasad and Prof. Saugata Bhaduri from JNU—you two are the most awesome guides any researcher could ever work with.

I owe this novel to my friends, students and colleagues, whether former or present, at the Indian Institute of Technology (IIT) Delhi, OP Jindal Global University and GGS Indraprastha University (GGSIPU).

Special thanks to Anil K. Tyagi, Anup Beniwal and Ashutosh Mohan from GGSIPU for providing me with the time, space and encouragement to pursue my writing.

Niyogi Books, for their support: Nirmal Kanti Bhattacharjee, Tultul Niyogi, and of course, my wonderful editor with Niyogi, Saachi Khurana.

The detailed editorial critique and feedback from the inimitable Jaya Bhattacharjee Rose, Indrapramit Das, Lakshmi Menon, and Mohd Salman made this novel what it finally is.

Ajay Prakash and Vivek Mishra, for reading the very first draft I wrote four years ago. You two do possess a certain (unsettling) Qa'haQ air about you.

Anil Menon—the awesome SF writer I turn to when in doubt.

My seniors at All India Radio and Doordarshan. Fayyaz Sheheryar, who saw in us what we couldn't ourselves see—and encouraged us. Basharat Ahmed, for the constant support. Obaid Niazi, Amlanjyoti Majumdar, Basudha Banerji, A.J. Mahanta, Naveen Gupta and Sanjiv Datta, for their chin-up advice.

Not to forget the Baba gang: Shahnawaz, Puneet, Apoorva, Dhiraj, Abhishek, Santosh, Ashish, Adesh et al.

The Mostly Harmless CES famiglia at JNU. This book is more yours than mine. Akash Raha, Sujay Thakur, Ujjwal Prasai, Jhinuk Sen, Farah Ishtiyaque, Ved Prakash & Co., for all your faith.

Abhinandan Dey, Manjula Padmanabhan, Mainak Dhar, Guneet Walia, Shovon Chowdhury, Kulpreet Yadav, Suraj C. Prasad, Amandeep Sandhu, Vandana Singh, Tiainla, Jugal Mody, Arvind Mishra (and ISFWA), M.H. Srinarahari (and IASFS), Mita Kapur (and the Siyahi team)—for all the help and support.

I'm thankful to Erich Von Daniken for his 1968 classic *Chariots of the Gods?*, from which I quote. By the way, all the information contained in this novel is freely available on the internet for all to see.

To all my friends, who somehow (against their better judgement) did not go, 'Cell phone as an alien device used to invade Punjabi Bagh? Sheesh, Sami! Have you completely lost it, finally?' Your support kept me afloat.

Zaara Haroon Ahmad, for being herself.

My ultimate acknowledgement is to those of you who lie awake at night, staring at the starry skies, hoping to find something that stirs...

Sami Ahmad Khan
New Delhi, India.
December 2016

'Aliens in Delhi *combines the best elements of classic Science Fiction and the political thriller. The result is a double serving of extra-crispy entertainment.'*

– Anil Menon, author of *Half of What I Say* and *The Beast with Nine Billion Feet*

*

'Sami mixes a potent cocktail—two parts thriller, one part Science Fiction, with a generous topping of aliens. Intoxicating stuff!'

– Mainak Dhar, bestselling author of *03:02* and the *Alice in Deadland* series

*

'A quirky, imaginative, fast-paced SF thriller that is full of twists and turns. A worthy and sparkling piece of Indian SF!'

– G.J.V. Prasad, writer and critic

*

'Do you yearn for classic Science Fiction, with reptilian space aliens and flying saucers that look like fried eggs? If so, fear not! Sami Ahmad Khan has turned his considerable skills as a scholar and researcher of the genre, to plunge in and write his own racy, uranium-enriched saga. Set in a city close to you: New Delhi.'

– Manjula Padmanabhan, author and artist

*

'Sami will be India's Gene Roddenberry! Read this gripping page-turner to know about alien-hybrids, extra-terrestrial machinations, and a cerebral-boggling alien-human conflict!'

– Suraj Clark Prasad, author of SF thriller *Baramulla Bomber*

Sami Ahmad Khan is a writer, academic, and documentary producer. He studied Literature at Delhi University, completed his master's in English at Jawaharlal Nehru University (JNU), and then went to the University of Iowa on a Fulbright grant. He holds a PhD degree in SF, and is a member of the Indian Science Fiction Writers' Association (ISFWA) and the Indian Association for Science Fiction Studies (IASFS). He has taught at IIT Delhi, JNU, the University of Iowa, and OP Jindal Global University.

Red Jihad, Sami's debut thriller, won NBT's National Debut Youth Fiction Award and was runner-up in the Muse India Young Writer Award. He also won third prize in the US-based Islamicate Science Fiction Short Story Contest for his time travel/alternate history piece 'Operation Mi'raj'. His short fiction, research papers and articles have appeared in leading magazines and journals across the globe.

Sami currently discusses life, language and literature at GGS Indraprastha University, Delhi.

He can be reached at www.facebook.com/KhanSamiAhmad and @SamiAhmadKhan (Twitter).